Wall

A tale of
Love, Sex, and Immortality

To see a world in a grain of sand
And heaven in a wild flower,
Hold infinity in the palm of your hand
And eternity in an hour.

William Blake

(1757 - 1827)

A few excerpts from 5 STAR reviews on Amazon
WALL—Love, Sex, and Immortality
Book One of the Aquarius Trilogy

WALL - Sex, Love and Immortality' ...is like a breathe of literary fresh air. ...The author has exceptional experience writing (some twenty books published) and obviously has a wide following, but for some reason he has not jumped onto the stage of famous contemporary authors with the other famous (and less talented) ones.

Reading Stan I.S. Law is an invitation to absorb not only a sensuous love story but to also expand your mind into fields that perhaps are a bit foreign until Law makes them so explicable. This is a wondrous work - wise, witty, enthralling.

Grady Harp
HALL OF FAME, TOP 100 REVIEWER, VINE VOICE

The thing that scares me most about reading books by Stan I. S. Law, is that I know he is brilliant and has written both fiction and nonfiction books in his fields of expertise--so that I don't know whether to think his fiction is fantasy or really reality!

I'd like to say that Stan creates a wonderful love story! Reading Wall as Romantic Fiction is bound to please any lovers out there!

GABixlerReviews

Stan I. S. Law does a fantastic job of merging reality and fantasy together to come up with this incredible read.

Monica G
"Monica G" TOP 1000 REVIEWER

The absolute brilliance of this novel is that it somehow manages to push through the WALLS of form just as effortless-seeming as its characters move through the walls around them in every way.

Alex Prosper, author, USA.

This is a book that will take you on a journey through emotions, locations, and dimensions. Fun, heartfelt, and thought-provoking, "WALL" is a must-read for anyone who likes witty fiction.

J. Linson, author, USA

I am in awe of this author's talent and seemingly endless ability to write books which, over and over again, leave me breathless from satisfying intellectual exertion.

Monica LaSarre, author, USA

By the same author

ALEC (Alexander Trilogy, Book I)
ALEXANDER (Alexander Trilogy, Book II)
SACHA—The Way Back (Alexander Trilogy, Book III)
YESHUA—Personal Memoir of the Missing Years of Jesus
PETER AND PAUL (An intuitive sequel to Yeshûa)
ONE JUST MAN (Winston Trilogy Book I)
ELOHIM (Winston Trilogy Book II)
WINSTON'S KINGDOM (Winston Trilogy Book III)
THE AVATAR SYNDROME (Prequel to Headless World)
HEADLESS WORLD—The Vatican Incident
(Sequel to *The Avatar Syndrome*)
MARVIN CLARK–In Search of Freedom
THE GATE—Things My Mother Told Me
NOW—Being and Becoming
GIFT OF GAMMAN
THE PRINCESS
ENIGMA of the Second Coming
WALL—Love, Sex, and Immortality (Aquarius Trilogy Book I)
PLUTO EFFECT [Aquarius Trilogy Book II]
OLYMPUS—Of Gods and Men [Aquarius Trilogy Book III]

Short stories

THE JEWEL & OTHER STORIES
CATS AND DOGS
Sci-Fi Series 1
Sci-Fi Series 2

Non-fiction Books by Stanislaw Kapuscinski

VISUALIZATION—Creating Your Own Universe
KEY TO IMMORTALITY
[Commentary on the Gospel of Thomas]
BEYOND RELIGION: Volumes I, II and III
[Collections of essays on perception of Reality]
DICTIONARY OF BIBLICAL SYMBOLISM
DELUSIONS—Pragmatic Realism

Poetry in Polish
[with illustrations by Bozena Happach]
KILKA SŁÓW I TROCHĘ GLINY
WIĘCEJ SŁÓW I WIĘCEJ GLINY

INHOUSEPRESS, MONTREAL, CANADA
http://inhousepress.ca

WALL

Love, Sex, and Immortality

Book One of the
Aquarius Trilogy

Prequel to
PLUTO EFFECT
and
OLYMPUS
Of Gods and Men

A novel by

Stan I.S. Law

BY INHOUSEPRESS, MONTREAL, CANADA

Paperback Edition 2015
Kindle Edition December 2013
Smashwords Edition December 2011
INHOUSEPRESS, MONTREAL, CANADA
Copyright © eBook 2011 by Stanislaw Kapuscinski

ISBN 978-1-987864-00-7

Cover design and layout
by Bozena Happach

CONTENTS

PART ONE   The Ankle

PART TWO   As good as it gets

PART THREE   The Escape

EPILOGUE

PART ONE

The Ankle

"You don't go to heaven. You grow to heaven".

Edgar Cayce

1 Chapter
The Ankle

In the Wild, Wild West men were men and women were what men wanted them to be. We all know that. What most of us don't know is that in English Jesuit Colleges there were no women. Men in order to become men had to fight other men. They did so by playing rugby. Rugby, or rugger, is a game wherein men try to kill each other. The game is not unlike the American or Canadian Professional Football, but it is played without the benefit or protection of pads, helmets, or the game stopping every few seconds to collect the wounded.

In a Jesuit College, everybody was forced to play rugby. There were dozens of teams, but only one team represented the College. That was the First Sixteen. The best. The elite.

I'd managed to get into the First Sixteen. And that is how the story began. Almost. Actually it began a few thousand years ago, but, well, hear me out.

My ankle has been bothering me longer than I can remember. Even at school, Mt. Saint Ignatius College, in the Old Country where, as already mentioned, by sheer accident I'd made it into the First Sixteen Rugby team, my ankle would seize up, on occasion, quite unpredictably, without any apparent reason. Just, now and again, for a few seconds at a time.

Imagine, First Sixteen! That was as good as one could get. Prefects' table in the Refectory, right-of-way down the long, cold, dank corridors; exemption from AROTC—the boy soldiers organization in the UK…

It made you something special.

Those were the days…

And then, within about three weeks, the stupid ankle went on the blink in earnest. Still only sporadically but, within a few months, the stiffness would last for minutes at a time. By the time it seized up for the third time in the middle of a game—that last time when I was about to score a try—my days of fame and glory were over. The SJs—that's the Jesuits as in Society of Jesus for the uninitiated—sent me to the hospital in Sheffield. I've been examined within an inch of my life. Nothing at all.

NOTHING!? I could scream. I very nearly did.

"It must have been just one of those things," said a frazzled looking intern. He'd sent for a resident.

"There is nothing wrong with your ankle, Mr. ah, Jones," repeated the intern's elder colleague, looking studiously at a series of X-rays. I was six-one, by then, weighing 220 pounds. In Canada, and just about everywhere in the world except for the States, that's about 185 centimeters, and almost 84 kilos. The attending resident physician called me Mister. Then he glanced at my First Sixteen blazer and called in the Chief of Staff.

We waited a while until the illustrious orthopedic surgeon rolled into the examination room. At least he could have rolled in—he was fat enough. I wished then, as I do now, that physicians would set an example.

Never mind.

The solon confirmed both previous diagnoses. I was, he announced pontifically: "perfectly healthy, with, possibly a mild predisposition towards attacks of hysteria."

I was big enough to slog the pompous jackass. I didn't. To this day I wonder why.

Some years later, there have been times, months at a time, when I would walk normally and then, when crossing the street, or raising my foot to the break pedal on my old Chevy, my ankle would seize up. It wouldn't bend. Solid as a rock. Minute of two later, little cold ants would crawl down from just below my knee... they would descend, lethargically, effortlessly, to restore the flexibility in my lower joint.

I was glad when finally, on arrival in Canada, I could drive an automatic, thus treating my left foot as an appendage dedicated to walking only. Even if, occasionally, with a limp. Sometimes. However, no break pedal (or had it been the clutch, I don't remember), and certainly, no rugby exacerbated my condition.

Year after year I'd visited orthopedic surgeons, later physiotherapists. They x-rayed my foot more often than any man in the history of the Montreal General Hospital.

"Sorry, Mr. Jones, ah, Professor, but as I told you before, there is nothing, absolutely nothing wrong with your foot. Nothing at all, Mr. Jones."

Yes. Professor. I think that did it—my becoming a professor, I mean. Specifically, professor associated with comparative religion, hence Associate Professor. Just kidding. Since three years ago, I have been appointed Associate Professor at the Department of Religious Studies. The day after my appointment, my ankle seized up for a week. Yes, I had to walk with a cane. There was little pain, but the discomfort made up for it. Try walking without bending your ankle.

I suppose I have the SJs to thank for that. Not for the stiff ankle only for the professorship. I matriculated with distinction in religion. No other distinctions—just religion. The other distinguished marks were mostly passes, some with credits. To this day I have no idea why I found religion so... absorbing?

Actually, I do. It must have been to avoid the strap. In those days, the Jesuits were strong advocates of corporal punishment, a method of persuasion I was never enamoured with. By being a scholar of religious subjects, I must have been assumed to be a practitioner of them. By excelling in religion they, the SJs, practically left me alone.

Actually, I only got down to religion, in earnest, after I got kicked out of the First 16. The ankle, remember? Before then, the 'colours', as they were called, gave me sufficient protection.

They must have hammered the history of the Church, Apologetics, and all the peripheral religious subjects, well into my youthful head. Daily Mass—attendance compulsory—with occasional Vespers, Confirmations, a funeral or two, took care of the liturgy. The moment I left college, I checked out other religions to see if any of the stuff I'd learned made any sense to other people. The pagan lot. The unbelievers. To the sheep from other stables.

Other folds?

After a little while, I found it quite fascinating to learn that people will believe anything if you repeat it to them a sufficient number of times. When civil authorities do so, it's called brainwashing. Solzhenitsyn explained that. When a Church, any church, does it… well, you know the answer. Obey or you're on a one-way ticket to hell.

My reasons notwithstanding, I now had a good base for Comparative Religion. After only three years of post-grad, that is Canada already, I became accredited at the McGill University of Montreal.

That only left me with my hysterical ankle. I wondered if I should test myself for excessive female hormones. No offence, but hysteria is supposed to be a woman's prerogative. Men should have *prostraria*, or something like that. Really.

Still as a student, I decided to take my ankle into my own hands. No pun intended. I tried massages, salt baths, soaks, compresses, eastern teas, effusions and other concoctions, powdered Chinese extracts, and a dozen of more esoteric cures. I got pretty serious.

They all worked—until the next time. Until the next time I raised my leg to step down from anything and landed flat on my face. And that wasn't the half of it.

I've also lost a lot of weight since my Rugby days. Once a solid 215-220 lbs., now a slim 185—mostly to take the weight off my ankle. It didn't help. The fair sex must have preferred my previous macho contours, or... it could have been my ankle, but my social life was somewhere between dismal and none. My dating was limited to one dinner per month or two, no dancing, no romantic walks in the park, and a lot of prayer that I might make it to my car without tripping over my own legs. Actually it never happened, yet, but I developed an acute case of cold feet. Ankles. One ankle.

The very thought of what might happen if the stupid joint would seize up was enough to keep me glued to my TV set when others, my colleagues, were scoring with the chicks. I must have been the most frustrated senior student in the history of McGill.

I remember, on one occasion, I got as far as the girl's bedroom. Actually my bedroom, but with a girl in it. She in her late teens, cute, slim, well equipped, looking experienced (probably was)—I desperately trying to lose my virginity.

It was a case of now or never.

I was doing all right. We finished our drinks, together. I offered another, she declined. I slipped next to her, on the sofa, my hand finding its way along her slim leg, upwards, slowly, very slowly, insinuating itself where it oughtn't. She responded by leaning back, tilting her head backwards, her lips parted, inviting.

This was in the days when I still lived in a bed-sitter. I still had muscles from my Rugby days. I lifted her in my arms to deposit her on the bed. I didn't quite make it. At least, my ankle didn't. We both landed on the sideboard.

Don't laugh. She twisted her... ankle!

A message from the gods?

If there were any justice in the world, she would have twisted something else. On top of it all, by the time I picked her off the floor, my ankle was perfectly all right. My ankle, not hers. That was the last time I'd invited a girl, a woman, to my digs.

For the next three weeks my ankle behaved itself. I almost forgot I had a problem. Then, must have been a month or so later, I repeated my performance in a different girl's bedroom. Yes, this time I actually got to her digs. It was great fun until I tried my macho lifting trick. At least his time it was her elbow, not her ankle. Things got quiet after that. Quiet for quite a while. In fact, more or less, until I finished my post-grads.

Two years later, after I got, what I'd hoped would have become, my tenure, I met Ambrosia. Yes, I know what it means: nectar of the Gods. I only caught a glimpse of her, but right there and then, I'd be willing to drink anything she'd deign to offer me, a mere mortal. Anything.

Well, all right.

I hadn't actually met her. I'd fallen down the stairs at her feet. She hadn't said anything. At least, I don't think she had. I wasn't quite myself.

As an associate professor, I now rent a one-bedroom apartment, on the 26th floor, overlooking Mount Royal. A beautiful view. A view specifically designed for seduction. For making love without having to draw curtains.

High up, among the gods...

Only the gods I've studied all my life weren't on my side. Perhaps they didn't like anyone peeking into their private business. The SJs hadn't told me that. The apartment is still waiting to lose its virginity.

For weeks after the Ambrosia incident, I'd lie staring at

the ceiling, trying to recall the goddess I'd fallen into. Onto? She was tiny, a Dresden Figurine, dark long hair, dark complexion, as though she'd just descended from Olympus where she was basking in close proximity of the sun. Icarus, eat your heart out.

Some months later I ventured into hypnosis. Self-hypnosis was the last hope for my ankle. If that didn't work, I'd be destined to remain a virgin for life. I'm sure no goddess would tolerate such grievous *prostrarical* imperfections in mortals. *Prostraria*, remember? Masculine hysteria.

I bought a book in a second-hand shop on St-Catherine. Judging by its cover, it's been used by a number of men. People? I suppose women may well have had psychosomatic problems as well as men. Although no physician, other than the rotund surgeon, ever said so, I now firmly believed that my ankle's misbehaviour had been in some form psychosomatic. I looked it up in the dictionary:

1. of or pertaining to a physical disorder that is caused by, or notably influenced by, emotional factors.
2. pertaining to, or involving, both the mind and the body.

As by now it was obvious, even to me, that my ankle problem did not have physiological origins, I was either mad or there was some kind of psychosomatic base to my problems.

I once read about a case of man who walked with a limp. Like in the case of my ankle, he had been examined a number of times by professionals, and nothing could be uncovered that could in any way cause him to limp.

Finally he went to a hypnotist.

After a few sessions under expert hypnotic regression, the doctor discovered that once, during an operation—while under anesthetic—which his patient had some 12 years ago, one of the residents assisting in the operation mentioned that the patient might have to "learn to live with a limp". The poor fellow had learned to limp in order to stay alive. He continued limping until a skilled hypnotist cleaned up his memory of the event. After that, he never limped again.

It appeared that while his body, and presumably his conscious mind, were subject of anesthetic, his subconscious remained receptive. Perhaps it never slept. Perhaps at some level we have inner bodies that do not need sleep. I wondered if Dr. Steiger knew about that. He could put the subconscious body on his divan and pretend that it's asleep.

It seemed that the self-hypnosis I've been practicing was intended to teach me how to program my subconscious to act in accordance with its dictates even when fully awake. Like the man with the limp had.

The problem was that I never had an operation on any of my extremities. Yet my ankle liked to act up. On occasion. When I least expected it.

Ah, yes. Dr. Steiger was the resident psychiatrist at the McGill. You haven't met him yet? Perhaps you're lucky.

***

2 Chapter
The Lecture

The amphitheater was filled to the brim. Usually religion was not a subject to fill all the seats, but, for some reason, I appeared to have been recognized as a lecturer of repute, and in the opinion of my colleagues, endowed with a good sense of humour. Others gave me other reasons.

"C'mon, Sy, anyone with your looks could fill anything to the brim. I bet your bed is never empty."

Little did they know?

Nevertheless, for reasons I couldn't quite understand, I was referred to as a 'looker'. Whether it was my six-one, my shoulders, which must have developed during my Rugby days, or generally my sporty appearance, I have no idea. I didn't dress in any natty clothes, didn't even attempt to make eye contact with the fair sex, nor did I even remember to comb my hair properly. I was dabbed a 'looker', and that was that. Some 80% of the amphitheatre attendees were women. Young, many beautiful, blonds, brunettes, redheads, (is there any other?); fresh looking women. I wondered how many would remain if they knew that I was a, you know… a virgin. Well, they were not about to find out from yours truly. The few men who expressed interest in my lectures have relegated themselves to the back row. They seemed as shy as I was. Or appeared to be.

The subject of today's lecture was the four-fold nature of man. Man being, of course, a generic term, though in this company it made me vaguely uncomfortable.

Did you ever try to deliver a lecture when some hundred and fifty young, attractive women are staring at you? Once, still at St. Ignatius, when I had to play my violin in front of an audience of parents at the annual concert, my professor told me to imagine the whole public being naked. It was funny, at the time. Now, the idea filled me with panic. One hundred and fifty naked women. In front of me. Staring.

HELP!

I drank three glasses of water before I could utter a word. For the rest of the lecture I desperately tried to keep my bladder under control.

For the umpteenth time, I cleared my throat.

Most of us are aware of the four aspects of the nature of man.

At last I said it, glancing judiciously at the carafe, which my assistant filled with fresh water. He must have thought I was seriously dehydrated. The very sight of more water made me a bit uncomfortable.

The silence stretched.

There are four Kalpas;
Four horses of the apocalypse;
Four man in the fiery pit of Nebuchadnezzar;
There are four aspects of the Egyptian Sphinx;
There are echoes elsewhere in the Old Testament, including the Genesis;

There are others.

This was too much for one lecture. I've spent years studying this. I wondered how many of my listeners would notice that two references concern the whole human race, and all others just the individuals. I also wondered if I remembered them all myself.

The Kalpas originate in Esoteric Buddhism. A Kalpa is a day, or a night, of Brahma. It also means an eon, or age. A thousand yuga *cycles of 4,320,000 year each is called a* Kalpa. *Thus a* Kalpa *is 4,320,000,000 years, which is pretty close to the 4.5 billion years stipulated by our scientists for the age of our planet.*

Puranas, however, had been completed between 400 to 1500 CE, ah... Era Vulgaris (I allowed myself a slight smirk, with SJs I had a grounding in Latin), ah... *Common Era, some little time before our present day cosmologists came to the same, or at least a very similar, conclusion.*

I looked around. I had their attention.

There are minor distinctions between Hindu, Jain and Buddhist cosmology. The Buddhists also divide their existence into four periods of time corresponding to the four stages; into the cycle of formation, continuance, decline, and disintegration.

The Hindus call those periods the golden age, which is followed by the silver, the bronze and the iron. As in the Bible, in the Torah or the Pentateuch, better known as the Old Testament, we start with the spiritual age, in Eden, and then, slowly descend to our present, materialistic level. That's right. We devolve. The age of Kali, the last and the most materialistic age, is followed by the dissolution of the universe.

Before I realized the dangers inherent in my action, I sipped—no drank—another glass of water. Well, half a glass. For some reason my throat was parched. Can the mere presence of 150 women parch your throat?

It bloody-well can, if you're a virgin.

This thesis is backed up in Jainism and, of course, the Christian religion accepts the concept of the end of the world. At least in Jainism there is also a concept of renewal, allowing for rotational progression of various stages. So don't worry. Both the Hindus and the Jains think of the creation and the dissolution of the universe as a cyclic process.

I glanced at my audience. They seemed spellbound. Almost scared. I couldn't help smiling. I was beginning to gain some confidence. Some. On the other hand, it's just possible that they haven't understood a single word. I was well aware that the info I was presenting sounded disjointed. For some reason, I just couldn't concentrate.

We might be well advised to think of the universe as a state of consciousness. From the material point of view, it is already essentially empty space. It's not there, really.

Not really.

A hand went up.

"Yes?" I might as well ask what bothered the listener, I mused.

And then I froze. The hand belonged to the young lady who acted as my cushion on my stair-fall. It belonged to Ambrosia. I swallowed hard. I suddenly realized that I didn't even know her surname. She had been addressed as Ambrosia by the man who'd helped her up. I remembered her name because of the drink. The drink of the Gods on Olympus? At the time, I had been too busy trying to extricate myself from an embarrassing situation and make a quick getaway.

"Yes?" I repeated. I was going to mention her name but thought better of it. The last thing I wanted was to make this personal.

"Professor Jones, Sir, are you referring to interstellar space as being empty?"

"Well, I, ah… why do you ask?" I was going to say innocently "and you are…?" but I didn't dare. She might have replied with a question "haven't we already met?"

"Because, Sir, I thought you might be referring to the void at the nuclear level where the atoms themselves are well in excess of 99% empty space."

"And you are…?" I couldn't resist it.

"My name is Milos. Ambrosia Milos. I am a post-grad at

the physics department. Just visiting…"

Her voice trailed off. Could it be that she didn't remember me? Not recognize me? Suddenly, solid or void, the universe was more inviting. My mind was working overtime. Ernest Rutherford Physics Building at McGill University on, ah… 3600 rue University… *Department* of *Physics*… McGill University… I walked past it every day on my way home.

"Of course, you are. I mean…" My mouth was dry again. "I was really referring to it in, ah, more metaphysical terms." I raised one eyebrow. I had no idea what I had been referring to.

"Thank you, Professor," the young lady replied.

"Thank *you*, Miss Milos," I offered, accenting the 'you'.

Actually, questions were always welcome. They made otherwise dry lectures more alive.

Milos. Wasn't there a Milosz? A Polish Nobel Prize recipient for literature? Or was he Czech? Or Russian? Was she Greek or Slav?

I dabbed my forehead with my handkerchief. People who only use paper tissues had never given a lecture. Not to one hundred and fifty women with a goddess named Ambrosia in the third row. If it hadn't been for my bladder, I would have downed another glass or two.

Why did I venture into this empty space business? It had nothing to do with the subject matter. Well, not much. I had to extricate myself from the hole I've dug for myself.

It is well to remember that most scriptures treat material reality as a temporal manifestation of various states of consciousness. This applies to us, humans, and to the environment in which we have our being. Becoming.

Becoming—I corrected myself. Being will be were we'll be, hopefully, after the dissolution. We? Some of us. Those of us who make the grade.

What the devil am I thinking about?

Thus, the golden age represents the time when we abide

in spiritual consciousness. This is followed by mental, emotional and finally, material or materialistic consciousness, as in the present Kali Yuga.

Was I making sense? The faces were all turned towards me. I didn't dare to look at the goddess in case our eyes met. The other eyes looked attentive.

The same may be extrapolated from the Old Testament, in the Hebrew Bible. We start at the spiritual level, enjoying the fullness of Eden, in a carefree existence, probably beyond time. Then... Well, the mental and the emotional states seem combined in the process of reaching out for knowledge. The tree of knowledge represents the mental state, the temptation the emotional one.

Somewhere in-between we were given skins. Those probably represent all three: the mental, emotional and the physical bodies. It is interesting to note that the emotional lifespan is represented by a number of ancient men, all exhibiting longevity well beyond that defined by our telomeres, ah, the sequences at the ends of our chromosomes.

My mind was wandering. It was her fault. She needn't have interrupted. By Jove, she was beautiful! Or should I have said by Zeus?

You'll find them listed in the Book of Genesis. The ancient sages, not the telomeres.

There was a short intake of air, followed by equally short giggle. I chose to ignore it.

While Abraham, the father of a multitude, had been, ah, rewarded with long life of some 175 years, his longevity pales when compared to biblical accounts of Adam, who is reputed to have lived 930 years, Seth 912 years, Enos 905 years, Cainan 910 years, Mahalaleel 895 years, Jared 962 years; and record is held by Methuselah, who was allotted 969 years.

If we were to take the Bible literally, wouldn't you say that God shortchanged Abraham rather than reward him?

I was rewarded with blank stares. No comments.

Probably not funny. Were those people all ardent believers?

We can reasonably safely assume that the longevity refers to life in bodies very different from those we are blessed with presently. I'd suggest that the Bible is talking about, what we nowadays refer to as astral, or emotional bodies.

The lecture went on for another hour. I mentioned, little more than peripherally, that the four horses of the Apocalypse represent the spiritual, mental, emotional and physical make up of man.

"Woman," I assured them, "I use the term 'man' generically." Every single one sitting out there, in front of me, I thought.

No, note that they were horses, but that we choose which horse to ride. Should I have told them that?

Then I told them that in the fiery pit of Nebuchadnezzar—the three men, Shadrach, Meshach and Abednego, also represent our emotional, physical and mental nature, which all had been thrown into the fiery pit, and only survived because their spiritual counterpart, the fourth man, appeared.

Although Noah neither burned nor drowned his sons, they, too, stood for the same three components. The Bible tends to repeat itself.

I saw some heads nodding.

"I'll tell you a story about Edgar Cayce," I changed tack. "He was known to have read his Bible round and round, never putting it down for long. When asked which was the best version of the Bible to read, he seemed lost. 'Which version, he asked? There is no version. The whole Bible says only one thing. Love thy God and thy neighbour as thyself. The rest of the Bible just tells us how.'"

For a while there was silence. I wondered how many of my listeners would accept that this was what all the great scriptures taught. Regardless of religions that sprang from them, of organizations that have been built on their misinterpretation, of the murders committed in the name of those very same scriptures.

"It seems to me that most of us only recognize the three aspects of our nature, omitting the white horse all together."

Did I go too far? Even to me it sounded like preaching.

Finally I told them that although in the Bible Egypt symbolizes limitation, and the Pharaoh our "lower-self", the Sphinx, nevertheless, indicated that Egyptians were in possession of deeper knowledge. The Sphinx has the body of an animal, the head of a man, with a little serpent on his forehead. While the animal stood for the physical body, the head and face were indicative of the emotional and mental nature, while the little adder represented spiritual power.

I could see by the blank stare of some of my listeners that it was time to call it a day.

"The next lecture in the series will take place next Thursday, same time. You are all welcome," I said with a forced smile. I wasn't pleased with myself. My thoughts weren't organized.

For the first time I dared to glance at Ambrosia. She seemed busy packing her stuff into an enormous bag. She was facing away from me, as though on purpose. Avoiding my eyes? What I saw was the luster of rich, cascading hair, flowing onto her shoulders. I've never seen hair that rich in texture. In spite of the raven colour, they also seemed to carry overtones of fresh chestnut, of deep brown, as though flames reflected in them.

I must have been dreaming.

I had little to pick up. I sat down and reached for the glass of water. In that instant I remembered my bladder, which, till this very moment, behaved itself. Now, the very sight of the liquid forced me to run for my life. Well, walk fast, while leaving all my stuff on the lectern. I made it to the men's room just in time. No one has any idea what pleasure is until they delivered an hourly lecture on three, large, glasses of water. Soon I felt as light as a feather. Almost light-hearted. I felt I could climb Mount Olympus.

I might have to, I realized, the moment I retuned. The theater was almost empty. Ambrosia was still packing her things. I wondered what things she brought to my lecture. No matter, I picked up my stuff, drank one glass just to be on the safe side, and made my way down the three steps. I didn't fall. My ankle was at its best behaviour. By now she was facing me.

"Ernest Rutherford Physics Building is on my way home," was my inspired opener.

"Hi," was her rejoinder. "Nice to see you standing up," she said without looking up.

So she did recognize me. Damn! I swallowed hard. It was easy after all that water.

"I'm sorry about that." What else was there to say?

"Are you?"

Only now she looked up. You should have seen those eyes from up close. They drew me in with the power of... I have no idea of what. They were dark, brown, and green, and hazel, hell... they had all the colours bottled up... I wished I had my glass with me. I would have drunk the whole Aegean Sea. Isn't that where goddesses come from? She must be Greek, I thought. Aren't all goddesses Greek? Except for the Roman and Scandinavian ones, of course. But not with those eyes.

"Wouldn't you rather have a spot to eat, Professor? Unless you eat late, I make it almost dinnertime," she said with those eyes still staring at me.

"Simon," I said, putting my hand on the edge of the bench for balance. I was playing safe with my ankle.

"Ambrosia," she said, offering me her hand.

It was small, like the rest of her, with an amazingly strong grip. She saw my surprise.

"Tennis," she said. "Twice a week."

I made a mental note to learn to play tennis.

We sat and talked till about eleven. Actually, she talked, I mostly listened. Except to answer her questions. I learned about the Greek Islands, about the way the sea changes colour during the day. I learned a little about the post-grad course she was taking, mostly quantum mechanics, she said.

"Quantum mechanics is more like religion than religion," she said, smiling. She did that a lot. Smiling. Her teeth were white, all equal, obviously placed in her mouth by an expert divine dentist. Nothing in nature could be that perfect. Except for her lips. And hair. And I told you about her eyes.

"I think we'd better leave the subject for the next time, don't you?" She glanced at her watch.

"Next time," I repeated. "Yes. Yes, the next time. Tomorrow?"

She treated me to those perfect teeth again.

"I have lectures till four."

Everything she said was quite natural. I felt as though we knew each other for years. Years and years.

"I'll pick you up at the Rutherford Building?"

She nodded.

"Shall I take you home?" I judiciously omitted to define which home. Hers or mine. Don't I wish!

The eyes said yes, but her mouth denied me. "I must spend about an hour at the lab." She glanced at her watch. "The results should be in about now. Something I started a week ago." She head-pointed behind her. "Just across the street."

I couldn't sleep that night. I kept tossing and turning, wondering what makes a beautiful woman go out to a dinner, without any apparent reason, furthermore with a man who had already proven himself to be not quite in command of either his senses or his ankle.

There was no doubt that she was beautiful. Although we stayed away from her particular expertise, quantum physics, she'd proven to be a delightful raconteur, a scintillating dinner companion with a well-developed sense of humour. Her stories about Milos, and the attendant multitude of gods kept me glued to her every word for more than two hours.

Her home was a volcanic Greek Island in the Aegean Sea. The island was famous, (alas not to me), for its statue of Aphrodite, known to us as Venus de Milo, now gracing the Louvre (this I knew). What is less known is that the island also famed for the statues of Poseidon, the Greek god Asclepius, now in the British Museum, and the archaic Apollo, presently in Athens.

The small island, of less then 5000 inhabitants, covers little more than 60 square miles of the Aegean Sea, just north of the Sea of Crete.

Until she turned sixteen, she lived exclusively on the island. She never saw any reason to leave it, let alone to live elsewhere.

"When you're in heaven, you are not inclined to descend to the lands of the mortals," she mentioned over the Balaklava, which see considered a must for topping off a dinner.

I listened, spellbound, watching the images she painted with well-chosen words. For all I knew, before she had taken up physics, she may have been a poet, or whatever goddesses did in their spare time.

When I finally succumbed to Morpheus, I spent my chimerical hours trying to restore the arms and legs to Venus de Milo. To Venus of Milos, my personal goddess's home. I was still doing it when I woke up next morning.

***

Chapter 3.
Autohypnosis

I **started with my right toe.** Then moved towards my heel and instep, towards my ankle, simultaneously. Slowly, all the time breathing easily, my mind visualized my calf, my shin, lingered at the knee (twisted it once, badly, playing rugger); then proceeded up along my right thigh towards my right buttock. I repeated the same mental examination of my left leg, this time lingering longer at my left ankle, the motivation and the purpose of my contemplation.

My legs relaxed, my mind swept over my torso, upwards, then draining all imaginary tension down, through my arms, hands and fingertips. By the time I reached up to relax my neck, I felt an overwhelming desire to forget the rest of my anatomy, and just take a nap.

With an effort of will I completed the instructions by relaxing my jaw, cheeks, eyes, and yes, even ears and the top of my head, all the time telling myself that I am slowly descending into a blissful, idyllic, state of hypnosis. Perfect. It really worked. Right?

Wrong.

I fell into deep sleep. The book I got warned me about it. Relaxed but alert, it repeated. Relaxed but alert.

"Easy for you to say, Mr. LeCron." He wrote the book I read. He was a clinical psychologist. It said so on the cover. The book was called *Self Hypnotism*. The subtitle said: "The Techniques and Its Use In Daily Living."

Just what I needed. To be in a hypnotic trance in my daily life. Frankly, that only happened when I looked at

Ambrosia. She had that effect on me.

This was my first attempt at relaxation after I read two other books on self-hypnosis that served mostly to confuse me. Finally I found something that seemed to work.

Next time I tried my exercises I managed to maintain a reasonable balance between my body, sending it into a deep state of relaxation, and my mind, which became carefree but aware.

Having reached, what I thought was, a desired state of repose, I used the fingers of my left hand to measure the depth of my 'trance'.

I posed the questions and expected my fingers to answer them.

"On the scale of three feet, have I reached the first 12 inches?"

If my index finger moved, seemingly of its own accord, the answer was: YES. If the middle finger moved it meant: NO. I would repeat the question, this time examining the 12 to 24 inches range.

I don't know if I was clear in all this, but I was determined to reach a positive answer somewhere between 24 and 36 inches. 36 inches would indicate a deep, deep, blissful state of hypnosis. Around 30 wouldn't be bad either. According to the book I could stick needles into my chest and not feel a thing. Providing I told myself not to, of course.

It may sound easy. It wasn't. All too often neither of the two fingers moved. Instead my pinky would show signs of life. Unfortunately it meant: "DON'T KNOW". I never realized my body could be that ignorant.

I continued my practice, desperately trying not to fall asleep. As I said, it wasn't easy.

I don't know...

My body wasn't the only part of me that was pretty ignorant.

I began to wonder what to do with the rest of my life. An Associate Professor could spend the rest of his life drawing a half-decent salary, certainly better than my father had done, and keep teaching whatever I'd taught the previous year. The problem with teaching Comparative Religion was the same as with teaching history. You lived in the past. You could not go back in time to change things, so that you could teach something new. I often wondered how the teachers of history managed to stay mentally alert year after year. I've only spent three years teaching my stuff, and already I needed to breathe deeper.

It wasn't that the subject lost its interest for me. I filed it among my favourite items of information as an art collector would his favourite paintings. If only one could discover something new, really new, about the past. I felt sure that what we knew of history was, must have been, at least in places, distorted. The truth often is. When we find it inconvenient, we nudge bits and pieces, to make them fit our idea of what the picture of the past should have been.

"History According to Jones."

"Life According to Garp," as in John Irving's novel. In novels you could make up history as you went along. In real life it was harder. People might believe you.

I knew from my study of symbolism that most churches, indeed, it is safe to say all of them, played the nudging game. For obvious reasons, my knowledge of symbolic meaning hidden, or veiled, in the Old and the new Testaments, vastly exceeded that of other religions. But even ignoring the etymological roots of various words derived from some twenty ancient, mostly extinct languages that remained *not* translated in the Bible for over two thousand years, there was the problem of separating myths from reality. In the English version of the Apostles' Creed consisting of 108 words, for instance, only 14 words dealt with historical reality, the rest... well, the rest were myth. That didn't make them untrue, it just makes them well, mythology. As in Greek, and

Roman and Hindu and Egyptian mythology.

And I, Associate Professor of Comparative Religion, was destined not only to compare the various historical facts, but the validity and gravitas of various myths.

Shouldn't myths be questions of faith?

And then I had an idea.

What if our subconscious was a depository of all the facts that touched our lives from the time we emerged from primordial slime? If not, I'd settle for the period beginning when we became humanoids. Upright. Like apes, I mean, like early humans. What if all the knowledge that touched our lives were to have been stored, diligently, indelibly, in our neurons, our cells, our genes? Or whatever is the physical equivalent of our subconscious.

Then, I thought… then the only thing we would have to do is to gain access to our subconscious.

That's all, folks!

What if I were a genius capable of such a feat?

Hypnosis? Autohypnosis? Deep trance?

A very, very, very deep trance? I'd probably need help.

I leaned back on the pillows and started relaxing. I had a choice to keep my errant ankle as the principle motivation in my self-hypnotic studies, or…

Would it really be possible?

I decided to discuss the issue with Dr. Steiger, MD, Ph.D, FRCP, and God knows what other qualifications. He was the lecturer at the Department of Medicine at McGill, with a reputation of solid professionalism. He was also a psychologist and psychiatrist. That says it all, doesn't it? I haven't met him, except in passing, but I felt sure the he, as a certified psychiatrist, must have an opinion on the subject.

I made an appointment to see him the following day, at noon, just after his lecture. I found him in his office, shuffling some papers. Dr. Steiger MD. etc, etc, was a short, slightly plump man, with bald head, which seemed to shine wisdom at all who came into his presence. He held himself very straight, adding himself an extra inch or so to his height. He got up as I came in, and came round his desk to shake hands with me. Nice man, I thought. Polite. I noted that his heels were also of a slightly exaggerated height. Lifts, I think they're called. Poor guy, I thought.

"And what can I do for you, Dr. Jones?" he asked affably.

"Information, Dr. Steiger. I feel I'm in great need of information, I replied."

"And how long do you feel that way, Dr. Jones? May I call you Simon?

"Of course. About two days. I felt that you might be able to help me."

"Well, I don't usually do consultations in this office, but since you're a colleague and are already here... Perhaps you would like to make yourself comfortable on the divan?"

"Thank you Dr. Steiger, I'm quite comfortable right here."

"Of course you are. Nevertheless, I'd prefer you to lie down..."

"Dr. Steiger. I didn't come to consult you in your professional capacity. I mean not as a psychiatrist."

"You came to ask me about a problem your friend has, am I right?"

I gave up. The man was either crazy or thought that I was.

"Could you just answer me yes or no? How much of our past is stored in our subconscious? Do we know? Alternatively, is there a way of finding out?"

"And just what is it from your past, ah, Simon, that you wish to find out?"

"I was trying to remember why I bothered to come here," I replied and got up. "It's been nice meeting you, Dr. ahhh, Steiger. Very nice indeed. I shall recommend you to anyone wishing to learn something from their past."

With that I got up, bowed slightly on my way out, and closed the door quietly behind me. Do you blame me?

So much for expert opinions.

My alternative was the Internet. Unfortunately, I read somewhere, probably on the Internet, that there, on the public worldwide computer network system, I could or would only find liars, bad liars and experts. In that diminishing order. I was alone.

I dug deeper into my books. I was fairly sure that my subconscious was the repository of past experiences. Only two questions remained. One, how distant past was recorded, and two, would I be able to recall it without resorting to outside help. The last thing I needed was another session with a doctor Steiger, or some self-styled hypnotist, who was trying to make extra money in addition to his nightclub act.

While as far as my own, very private past was concerned I trusted few people to start with, it was a no-no for anyone who wouldn't swear on all that they held holy to remain secret. At moments like these, I missed not having my family with me. Dad, or Mom, or even my sister, would help me. They may not have been trained in my self-imposed disciplines, including self-hypnosis, but they were my people. People I could trust. Always. I promised myself to call them more often, perhaps fly over to visit them?

Just for fun. For family's sake.

There was, of course, Ambrosia. A girl, a woman, I knew virtually nothing about, yet towards whom I felt an affinity as I did to my own mother or sister. Only it felt much, much more personal. Oh, all right—and much more sexually potent.

Could I ask Ambrosia to become the confessor of my past? In the first instant I would have to regress myself sufficiently to find out what the devil made my ankle behave the way it did. If that worked, we would, or could, go on. The very idea that I could separate myths from reality in my own field gave me a thrill I could hardly contain. I needed to share this concept with someone. Anyone.

With Ambrosia?

Only she was busy with her own work, apparently much more busy than I, though she did say she'd see me tomorrow. And then I'd see her at my next lecture. She was bound to come, although I never asked her why she chose to attend my lectures to start with. From what little we talked, to date, she struck me as a free thinker, not tied down to any particular articles of faith. A bit like me.

Suddenly it stuck me that although we already shared a meal, I continued to know virtually nothing about her. I'd learned a little about Greece, about her island, but I knew next to nothing about her interests, nothing about her personal life, little about her likes and dislikes. What if a boyfriend was waiting for her on Milos? A fiancé? What if she was married, mother of five children?

Our first date, if one could call it that, was a whirlwind of first impressions, a galaxy of restrained emotions, which I, at least, had to hold on a tight leash. All I really remembered were her eyes, her lips, her… her presence. The rest was a euphoric blur.

***

Chapter 4
More Lectures

The Hindus start, as do the Jains, at the very top, in a glorious Golden Age, Satya Yuga, more accurately *The Age of Truth.*

There were as many people as last week, but my goddess, seemingly, disappeared. The day following our dinner we did share a glass of wine, but Ambrosia seemed rushed, unsettled, as though something was praying on her mind. I didn't feel empowered to ask her directly what was wrong. After all, it was only my feeling that registered her discomfort. For all I knew, she may well have been like that most of the time. For all of the three or four hours that we knew each other, we were still strangers.

Even as I began my lecture my eyes continued to search the amphitheatre. She was nowhere to be seen. I knew that she would be busy with her atoms and quarks for some time, she told me as much, but I never imagined she'd miss my seminar. Obviously, there was a great deal I had to learn about women. Or it could have been just my ego that suffered.

This age of bliss and beauty is by far the longest of the four ages of the Maha Yuga, and lasts 1,728,000 years. I would suggest it is equivalent to the period humanity had spent in Eden. Let us not forget, that Eden means delight or pleasantness. Dr. Carl Jung postulates that the "condition of delight" is a state of consciousness wholly dependent on instinct. One immersed in such a condition cannot "contemplate a desire that is not part of his or her nature, and thus is capable of neither good nor evil. Hence the condition of pleasantness."

My fingers were busy inscribing inverted comas in the air. A latecomer slipped into a vacant seat at the back of the hall. No, it wasn't her. Goddesses wouldn't sit at the back.

The Satya Yuga is followed by Treta Yuga, the Silver Age, during which we are still blessed with considerable virtue and beauty for the next 1,296,000 years. Then things begin to deteriorate more rapidly. We lose a lot of our spiritual values and seem to straddle the ethical fence. This Bronze Age, the Dwapara Yuga, lasts for 864,000 years.

Who cares how long it lasts? I really thought she'd enjoy this lecture. This time I came better prepared. I had a screen and a projector, with nice diagrams and other illustrations.

I was about to give up. I couldn't, of course. Frankly, a hundred and fifty women should be enough for any man. There must have been that many, although there seemed to be more men this time.

Mercifully, the last age, in which humanity sinks to the lowest level and is steeped in materiality and egotism, is shortened to 432,000 years only. It is appropriately called the Iron Age, the least noble of the four metals. The age is also known as Kali Yuga.

At last women take over...

Kali is a very complex character in Hindu mythology. While recognized as the goddess of eternal energy, and the consort of Shiva, she is also connected with death and destruction. Imagine... in a number of ancient illustrations, Kali straddles, often stands atop the body of Shiva, the major god of Hinduism. Some power...

Of course, Shiva is also known as the destroyer of our ego, and ultimately of our universe.

I wondered if the first female president of the United States of America, Laura Georgina Bush, would also stand on the corpse of Western Civilization. God knows we seemed to have been tottering close to extinction ever since the United Arab Republics, together, became the greatest nuclear power in the world. And, *entre nous*, they weren't really that united. It all began with Pakistan, and they never looked back. Now, their combined nuclear arsenal was scattered over such vast areas, that no western power could even estimate its cumulative potential. Although the religious element became much less volatile, its explosive elements were still there. After all, Islam must expand or die. So teaches history.

While, at least until recently, the USA and Russia were busy disarming, the oil money bought nuclear technology in hops and leaps. At least the Chinese maintained a modicum of restraint, maintaining their ability to erase the human equation from the surface of the earth by no more than a factor of three. Some said four, if you don't count their own race.

At least the Chinese kept men at the top of their heap. They and the Arabs remained as macho as can be. But that still didn't explain where was Ambrosia.

I gave my audience more info on Hindu Pantheon, but my heart wasn't in it. There was lots of it. Gods, goddesses, and all sort of ancillary divinities. Then I run through some other religions just to add weight to my thesis of eventual destruction. According to the ancients, we had no need for any weapons of mass destruction, no need for absurd nuclear arsenals. The world would dissolve anyway. On the other hand, since, apparently, we entered the age of Kali in 3103 BC, we still had more than 400,000 years to go. So who cares about their stupid atom bombs?

On the other hand, we all know how time flies when we're having fun?

As for myself, I was growing peeved.

Even if she were late, she ought to be here by now. Or she could have called. I wasn't having fun at all.

I wondered why did people, women, really come to my lectures. In the pamphlets scattered in various parts of McGill, announcing the seminars, there were hints of the dissolution of the world, but surely, they didn't flock to this temple of wisdom out of fear. The paperback market was already flooded with imaginative fables about the forthcoming cosmic destruction. Some unscrupulous pseudo-historians were making piles of money out of their scaremongering.

A hand went up. No, it wasn't Ambrosia. No such luck.

"Yes?" I was glad someone was not asleep.

"You told us a lot about the Far Eastern Cosmologies, Professor Jones. Isn't there a Christian equivalent for the forthcoming dissolution?"

"I'm glad you ask, Miss…"

"Dolton. History, second year."

"Ah, yes, Miss Dolton. History does follow us, wherever we go."

I moved some papers on my lectern. I brought nothing on the Christian slant on the end of the world. I'd have to rely on my memory. I resumed my diatribe with less vigour.

"Well, the Christian theology is less generous as far as time is concerned. According to some sources, ah, including the New York Times bestsellers, the dissolution will be taken care of by a gentleman called the Antichrist. Unfortunately, this does not concur with the other source we know as the Bible."

I had their attention. The word Bible had that effect on people.

Both, the Oxford and Webster dictionaries define the Antichrist as a great personal opponent, an antagonist, of Christ, a person who will lead the forces of evil.

There is a veritable avalanche of pseudo-exposés of all kinds, presumably precipitated by the recent millennium fever. Indeed, it is fashionable to talk about prophecy, to expect the worst, to scare people out of their wits. Look at the successes of all the science fiction, horror, and fantasy films, books, and cults. The more the merrier.

But what has any of this to do with the Bible?"

The silence stretched.

Nothing.

I said it hardly above a whisper. I heard the expected intake of air, a sort of protracted gasp; then my audience stirring in their seats. Ah, ignorance of bliss! If it weren't for ignorance I couldn't even deliver this lecture.

Nothing.

This time I spoke louder. I had to smile. Nothing at all! It's all to do with bank accounts of writers and publishers. Pure and simple. That and peoples' inertia, mental stagnation, inability, or unwillingness to make an effort on their own. They would rather someone did their thinking for them. No matter how badly.

What does the Bible say about the antichrist? The Torah—nothing. The four gospels—nothing. In the 1341 pages of my King James Version, the word antichrist is mentioned four times. John uses it three times in his first epistle and once in the second.

Sorry, b-b-b-but that's all, folks!

My Porky Pig impression didn't score any points. I found the whole question of antichrist funny. Funny-pathetic. On the other hand, this time my audience sat up. I heard whispers. It seemed that they'd miss the illusion of being scared with impunity. I decided to become a comedian some other time.

And how does John describe the antichrist? Why, strangely enough, as an opponent of the doctrine of Christ. As one who denies the Father and the Son; The Yahweh and the El. The God without and the God within.

No wonder they crucified him, I mused. Why must people need to live under the Sword of Damocles? A god without?

And by the way, John assures us that the antichrists have been walking the earth in great numbers, already, in his day. Look behind you...

I couldn't resist that last one. I really couldn't. At least a third of heads made as though to turn, before their neurons caught up with my words and returned their heads to face forward.

Ah, what would I do if it weren't for the N.Y. Times bestsellers?

The lecture was over. This time at least a dozen people, women, made for my desk. I hoped this wasn't a lynching mob. I wondered if the men were too shy, or simply were afraid of making fools of themselves. So much for machos.

"Where can we find what you said, Professor Jones, in the Bible? I meant it's a really thick book..."

"That would be the New Testament, right?"

"John? John who?

"How many Johns are there?"

"Is it long, I mean, the John story, is it long...?"

"Was he an apostle?"

"Did you read the whole Bible, Professor Jones, I mean back to back?"

"Really?"

"Wow!"

This was our *crème de la crème*, the pick of our youth, who preferred attending free lectures at McGill than watching Desperate Women, or was it Desperate Men, on TV. Yes, they were the pick of the crops. At least the women were here. The men were probably glued to their TVs in search of a baseball match.

Maybe the New York Times bestsellers were right. Maybe we were approaching the dissolution of our cosmos a lot faster than the Hindus would make us believe. What did the Buddhists know, anyway?

When I got home, way up among the clouds, I couldn't help wondering what questions, if any, Ambrosia would have asked. There were, there always are, questions that remained unanswered. It would help if I knew how her mind worked. And then I remembered that, after all, she was a physicist. Was there room for scientists in the realm of comparative religion? Could a scientist accept the invisible as real?

Of course, they could. All the subatomic particles were invisible. So where did line of demarcation lie?

There had to be logic present. If a thesis did not contradict man's god-given ability to think logically, then scientists could accept it. So, if the antichrist were to bring about the dissolution of the universe, what would be a scientist's definition of the antichrist?

I was getting closer.

Since antichrist was against the father and the son, the Yahweh and the El, then people who rejected the divinity, the creative force residing within us, would bring about the dissolution of the world. Of the reality as we know it. The dissolution of the world would be brought about by people who rejected the reality we live in.

So the question really was, what is reality? Is it that which we perceive with our senses? Is that reality? I found this answer particularly unsatisfying. What colour is love? Is it hard, wide, tall, did it move fast, weaken with time, grow stronger? And what if that which we call love were to be little more than a genetic impulse developed in us over millennia of evolution? And if so, then what motivated such a development?

I knew the answer to that: Preservation of the species.

They say that beauty is in the eyes of the beholder. Yet, I never met a man, or woman, young or old, who'd describe a rose as ugly. Were there no absolutes we could fall back on in our search?

I wondered, what would Ambrosia say?

***

Chapter 5
Ambrosia

I **was as sure as I ever was** of anything, that a single sip of love from Ambrosia's lips would confer immortality on me. It was not just the nectar, some say the food, of Greek gods, for the mortals to become immortal, but it was also linked to ancient India, where gods used the Sanskrit *amrita* to achieve their own immortality. It would be interesting to note that nectar itself derives from *nek* meaning death and *tar*—overcoming.

Overcoming death.

Whatever the etymology, I was sure that my goddess could confer on me anything she'd want, if only she returned to one of my lectures. I, ignorant as I was, have failed to procure her telephone, her private address, or even the precise quarters where she conducted her experiments. The members of the McGill staff, would hardly consider it appropriate, let alone desirable, for a Professor, albeit an Associate one, were he, that means I, to stand on the street in front of the Physics Building, in the hope that one day, at an unspecified time, my goddess would appear at the front door.

Post-docs, on specific research projects, did not work regular hours, indeed any hours, should they choose not to do so.

"Are you hiding from me, Professor?"

The voice came from behind me. Coy, tempting, more like a nymph's then belonging to a goddess. Forgetting my ankle, I spun on my heel.

She was walking towards me, some ten feet away, smiling.

"Where were you?" I asked. Not that it was any of my business. I hoped my disenchantment with her being away didn't show too much.

"Milos," she said. "I've only been away a week. Now I've been following you all the way from my lab. You seem to have accelerated since you passed my building."

"You've been to Milos? In Greece?"

She looked at me with a quizzical smile as though asking if there was any other Milos. As quickly her smile reverted that euphoric expression I'd already learned to recognize each time the word Greece was mentioned.

"Why, Simon, did you miss me?" There was that coy voice again. Then her voice returned to whatever a goddess uses as normal for communication. "Do you have a minute?"

I had a lifetime. Importantly, I glanced at my watch. Then I nodded to the coffee house we've visited the last time. "Will that do?"

We sat at the corner table, wedged between the window and the alcoves, which lined the East wall. At least, I think it was East, never mind... I was sitting facing Ambrosia, drinking in anything and everything her eyes had to offer. We ordered coffee and some *petits fours*. When coffee arrived and the waitress left us alone, Ambrosia's face turned serious. I waited for her to come out, in her own time, with what was bothering her. With her sitting opposite me, I had all the time in the world.

"I really have no one to talk to," she began, her lashes covering her eyes. She stirred her coffee although she took no sugar.

I waited.

"Just before I left for Milos, last week... I'm sorry I didn't tell you, by the way, but my father took suddenly ill. A mild stroke. It turned out my mother panicked. He'll be all right."

I continued to wait. Ambrosia got up and peeked over

the high back of the alcove next to our table. It was empty.
This was the middle of the afternoon, neither lunch nor
dinner time.

"Did you always study religions?" She changed the
subject.

"Ever since the Jesuits wouldn't leave me alone if I
didn't," I murmured. At least it was half-truth.

"I am looking for reasons I can trust you," she said
softly. Then she looked up and studied my eyes.

"Well?"

"I can't see any subterfuge in them," she said slowly.

"That too would be the Jesuits. The Church's been lying
to her people for thousands of years. I had plenty of
practice."

"Simon. I'm afraid."

I decided to cut the humour. "Ambrosia," I began.
"Whatever bothers you, you'd better share it. I, like you,
don't have anyone with whom to share whatever you want to
unburden yourself of. You..."

Her delicate hand reached across the table and covered
mine. "Thanks, Simon, I needed to hear that."

For a little while we sipped coffee in silence. I pushed
the place with *petits fours* towards her, and she declined. I
didn't. They were delicious. I had a sweet tooth before I lost
all that weight.

"Yesterday, just after I got back, I've been called to
dean's office. They asked me to sign a document."

She looked up, I waited.

"The document committed me to secrecy regarding my
work at McGill. They wouldn't even tell me why. I asked
dad about it, and he said that the only people who played
such games were the CIA, or equivalent. Would RCMP do
that?"

"In Canada? At McGill?"

"It does seem strange, doesn't it?"

I suddenly realized that I had absolutely no idea what

Ambrosia was working on. It seemed likely that now, I might never find out.

I read somewhere that Canada would forego the expense of arming its Northern border to protect the Northwest Passage, in exchange for all research deemed to be of military value being shared with our southern neighbour. The defense aspect was academic, but it did save some money. Should the USA really want to, they could wipe Canada off the map of North America. We might as well be friends.

"I think we might as well continue this discussion outdoors, or," I hesitated for a moment, "in my place?" I held my breath.

"I don't even know your address," she said.

I reached into my inner pocket and came out with my card. This was the very first time I had occasion to use one. I felt as proud as peacock. What an initiation for my 'business' cards! Actually it had both, my McGill and my home addresses. With the abundance of my social life, there was little danger that the business angle would suffer.

"Thank you," she said, taking my card, her eyes avoiding mine. "I think it would be wise if we weren't seen together in public. At least not until I find out what it's all about."

"Why?" I was flabbergasted.

"It might prove detrimental to your health," she said, waving me to remain sitting, and making for the door.

The next moment she was gone. I hoped this wasn't a presage of our future: she blowing in and out of my life like a breath of air. After not seeing her for a week, I met her, accidently, on the street hardly more than ten minutes ago. I was halfway through my coffee, with a plateful of *petits fours* smiling at me from a round plate in front of me. I wondered if I should ask for a doggie bag.

I tried to think rationally what would induce the Dean of the Physics Department to force, or even to just ask, a research scientist to sign a document of secrecy. Was she connected, somehow, with nuclear physics? Bombs? Guided missiles? God forbid new weapons of mass destruction?

Impossible! This just wasn't her style. Was it? No. Not my Ambrosia?

My? My Ambrosia?!

Wake up Simon. You're dreaming. You're stark raving mad. You, my dear fellow, are… in love. At thirty-eight, for the first time in your life. You're in love. Not as in passing holiday fling, not as a student eyeing a pigtailed pixy sitting in front of you, but as a man completely obsessed with a mature woman.

I went to the library to see if I could find out something about the present research in physics being carried out at McGill. I did. Everything. Or, at least, it looked like everything to me. They weren't shy about bragging about their work. At least not in physics. They called it the Theory of Everything. I suppose, to a physicist, this might mean something. Something other than everything?

I continued digging. Theory of Everything was also called the Final Theory. Sounded like my end of the world postulate. Final Theory of what?

There was also stuff about the 11-dimensional M-theory, described in some sectors as matrix string theory, elsewhere as perturbative string theory, which some claim is the Theory of Everything. However there is also a superstring theory that could, apparently, upset the applecart. There was lots of other stuff I didn't understand either.

The Theory of what?

Dr. Leon Lederman once wrote that if the universe is the answer, then what was the question?

You might well ask.

By the time I left I'd learned that the Theory of Everything did not answer all the questions man has always asked. Not even the fundamental question: "Who am I?"

Sorry Mr. Socrates. Foiled again. The Theory would merely unify the fundamental interactions of nature. And that meant gravitation, strong interaction, weak interaction and electromagnetism. That's it. Sorry God. Now we know everything. We don't need you anymore.

Bye…

But if we know, or are about to know everything, what was the secrecy about. Why were they pestering me, I mean, why were they pestering Ambrosia? I felt sure she would have been happier with Archimedes. Although he lived in Syracuse, and although Syracuse is located in Sicily, to this day the town is still best known for its Greek culture.

Anyway, wasn't he the first to postulate questions, some twenty-two centuries ago, which sounded like theoretical physics? At least he was Greek and, to my knowledge, he'd never sworn anyone to secrecy.

At this point, Scrooge would have said Bah humbug!

That's it! She must have been working on theoretical physics.

So? What's so secretive about it? Isn't it all… theoretical?

I went home to practice my self-hypnosis exercises. I was beginning to get some results—slowly but consistently. No deep trances, as yet, but I managed to get rid of a headache, regulate my upset stomach, and fall asleep within minutes. That's right. My gastric problems that seemed precipitated by Ambrosia's absence. I was now practicing to wake up at a specific hour by using a post-hypnotic suggestion.

I still wasn't sure what all this had to do with my itinerant ankle, but I hoped that would come. I'm also not sure 'itinerant' is the right word, but my left ankle seemed to wander at its own pace, at its own time, in its own direction. Though it has nothing to do with Aristotle that sounds pretty peripatetic to me.

It was getting dark. Just in case my hypnotic inducement didn't work I decided to set my alarm clock. Then I stretched out to start relaxing. I suspect that I'm an incurable optimist—my bed was of a beautiful king-size variety. You could never tell when you might get lucky, and my luck was long overdue. The next moment I jumped nearly out of my skin. I couldn't believe it was time to get up.

It wasn't. It was my telephone. I made a mental note to change the signal of one or the other; my alarm or my cell.

"Yes?"

"It's me. Can I come up?"

Where are you?"

"About ten minutes away."

In ten minutes my goddess, my Olympian Goddess, would grace my aerie. I felt the beginning of sweat beads forming on my forehead.

"Of course. Push 26 C."

She replaced her receiver, or her cell, or whatever goddesses use to communicate with mortals, while I was standing in the middle of my bedroom, unable to move. Then I took a deep breath, then another. Just like in the book on self-hypnosis. It worked instantly. Methodically I cleaned up some loose ends lying about, dusted the TV screen, and washed my hands and face in the bathroom. Even as I finished combing my hair, a rare occasion indeed, the door rang downstairs.

"Come right up."

She did.

"What happened to your hair?" was her opening salvo.

"My hair?" I suddenly realized that no one, in my recent history, has seen me with my hair combed.

"It's OK. I like it both ways," she assured me, before I could lose the rest of my composure. "It's the gold I like," she added, "especially in the sun."

I took a close look at her. "You all right?"

"Of course. Earlier on I felt tired from my flight and the,

you know, the Dean thing. I took a nap at home, a bath, and
voilá, I'm back to my old self."

Was she ever…

I was about to make some sort of inane comment when
she ran up to the window. "My God! I've never been so high.
Not without an airplane!"

And this spoken by an Olympian?

I opened a bottle of red, Merlot, I think, I don't drink
usually, half-filled two glasses, and put them on a low table
in front of my settee. If we sat side by side, we'd both face
the mountain. We would also be no more that a two feet
apart.

She continued to stand facing the window, completely
ignoring my presence. From this height and distance, you
could see little more than the tops of crowns being swayed
two and fro by a gentle breeze. There was peace in the world.
The last rays of the sun reached the trees at low angle, almost
horizontally.

"I saw his eyes," she said after a little while. "That's
why I was scared."

"A glass of wine?" I countered. I knew from our dinner
that Ambrosia liked to talk in shortcuts.

Slowly she turned around, walked up to me, stood on her
toes and planted a gentle kiss on my cheek.

"You're really very kind, to let me invade your privacy,
Professor. I do appreciate it."

"Shouldn't you start at the beginning? And I thought we
were on first names' terms?"

"Yes, Simon. Of course we are. With the friendship
you've offered me, it could hardly be otherwise."

She took a tiny sip of wine and closed her eyes. Closed
or open, she continued to look beautiful. I was glad she
lowered her lashes. It enabled me to stare at her with
impunity.

"It really all started with my mother."

Another shortcut. I waited.

"She's the only woman I know, I've ever met, who was seemingly born with the ability to soul travel."

I had no idea what she meant.

"It is often referred to as astral projection, or lucid dreaming. She can actually control what happens in her dreams. Conversely, she can look at a man and see his inner state of mind. It is that last ability which she seems to have imparted on her daughter. On me."

My next swig on the wine was much deeper.

"This was what enabled me to trust you, Simon. This is also what scared me when I looked into the eyes of the man who stood in front of me, when I was signing the papers in dean's office."

I suddenly thought I was in trouble.

"You mean you can read peoples' thoughts?"

She laughed that pearly cascade falling on crystal. "No, silly, I can't read peoples' thoughts. Though that would be nice." She gave me what I can only describe as a naughty look, which seemed to have contradicted her previous assertion. Then her face turned serious, again. "What I seem capable of doing is getting a first impression of people I meet which, so far, never let me down."

I took a deep breath. For now, I felt safe.

"What did you detect from that, ah, that man in dean's office?"

"It was no more than an impression, mind you, but I felt that he'd think nothing of killing anyone standing in his way."

"That's it. No other impressions? I mean you have no idea who he was or where he came from?"

"No, Simon. Other than that first impression he looked perfectly normal. Middle aged, graying temples, a dark suit, good posture, clean. Yes, very clean."

He and ten thousand others at McGill, I thought.

***

Chapter 6
End of a Season

So Ambrosia flew to Greece to see her father. Just for a week, a little less—a week including travel. I haven't seen my parents since I left England. That's... that's quite a while ago. My recent resolution to see them more often remained just that. A resolution.

Tomorrow, I'd say. Tomorrow is another day.

This summer, after the seminars are over.

My parents chose to remain in Britain. Why not? It's not easy to transplant old trees. Trees, where every root, in all directions, carries a different memory. My father, a lifelong teacher in a grammar school, that would be called secondary here, I think, would lose all the tenable contacts with his old students. And their parents, I suspect. Not to mention his own pals, other teachers, their families.

So many pupils over the years... a whole generation?

Pupils they called them in my day. Students study, pupils—you teach. You're responsible for them. The students must fend for themselves. Mostly.

I would have remained in the Old Country also, settled with a nice English girl, in North London, East Finchley or Barnet, maybe as far out as Potters Bar (still accessible by the tube), if it hadn't been for my mother. If she had her way, her ideal way, I'd visit her, regularly, from the nearest monastery. God knows I love her dearly, but her often vocalized hope that one day I'll change my mind and go back to the... Church. I don't mean just to practice my religion. She assumed that my interest in religious myths was

equivalent to my inner need to become a priest. Or a monk.
A Jesuit?

"You could teach, like your father, Sy," she'd coo.

"My father's name is not Sy," I would counter, trying to
take the sting out of her dreams.

They only called me Simon because, in both their
youths, they seemed to have been enamoured with Simon
Templar, the Saint. The James Bond of their days, only self-
employed. Had I been born some ten years later, my first
name would probably have been Indiana, as in... Indiana
Jones.

I wondered what Ambrosia's parents thought of her
choice of profession. A physicist? A woman physicist?
Theory of absolutely everything? Doesn't sound very
feminine. Or maybe I'm just an old-fashioned macho ex-
rugger player. On the other hand I truly believe that
Ambrosia can be whatever she wants to be. In this world, or
on top of the Olympus.

I haven't flown over to see them, yet, as she had, but I
call them on a regular basis. Once or twice a month. They're
doing all right. They seem happy together. Quiet. Restful.
They are also quite independent. Father, at 69, has a
government pension equivalent to a civil servant's, and their
little hybrid takes them on regular, if short, trips. They like to
visit Virginia Waters, pop down to Brighton, or revisit the
Kew Gardens. Mother always comes back with fresh ideas
for their own back garden, stretching about sixty feet behind
their house. The house in which I was born, upstairs, in the
master bedroom. We didn't go to hospitals in those days.
Well, not all of us. Mostly we used midwives. Hospitals for
childbirth came only with Medicare, The National Health
Service we called it, when the visits became free. Until then,
midwives seemed aptly qualified to assist in something as
natural as childbirth.

As for my parents, in case of need there was my sister.
Although she married and settled in Wimbledon, that's on

the other side of London, she visits them on a regular basis. At least she's no longer a virgin. They have two kids. Both girls. Haven't seen either of them, yet.

Must fly over.

Last week I finished the Summer Series on Comparative Religion. Next week we'd have an open forum. Open to the general public. Ambrosia left a note; said she'd come.

My place looked strangely empty. I lived in this apartment for more than six years, and I never felt alone. Frustrated, sex-starved, angry as hell, but not really alone. I had no expectations.

Now I did. I had them. What is it about a woman that lingers behind after she leaves? A whiff of her perfume? An echo of her laughter? Or just memories. Intense, all-consuming, breathtaking memories. Even for a man my age.

Fascinating!

The last time we met, in my place, just for a glass of wine, she made a strange statement. She said that she clicked on her computer and wrote, "walking through walls" on the Google.

"I know it sounds absurd, Simon, but I got 3,640,000 results. Three million, Simon! Doesn't it hurt?"

I still wasn't sure when Ambrosia was joking. This was not exactly my area of expertise, but there had been cases in my field where people walked through some solid objects. In the Bible, I mean. At least, I think they did?

"I presume you are referring to walls in a figurative sense, like walls of difficulties?"

"I don't think so, Simon. Not the three million six hundred and forty thousand of them."

"Why did you ask?"

"Did I?"

"Why did you ask the computer?"

For a while she studied my face, then looked as though

she'd made a decision.

"It's my mother," she said.

I waited for her to explain. Nothing came. This is the second time she brought her mother into the conversation. She continued to look at me as if it was my turn to say something. I had no choice.

"What about your mother?"

She smiled. "Promise you won't laugh?"

I nodded.

"I told you about her ability to soul travel? To do the out of body projection?"

I nodded again.

"Well, it took on another turn." She looked at me as if to make sure I was paying close attention. "Yesterday I dreamt about her."

I wished she'd get to the point. "So?"

I also dream sometimes about my mother. And my father. I dream about all sorts of things.

"This was different. We talked… and, well, I don't know how to put it, exactly, but, well… I was aware that I was dreaming. I mean while I slept."

"I heard about that. It's called a lucid dream," I said softly, if only to calm her down.

"Simon, I'm a physicist. A scientist. I deal with facts. No matter how small, how tiny, they still must be facts."

I didn't have such hung-ups. I dealt with metaphysics all day long. "You mean like tiny quarks? Like strings and superstrings?" I read about them only a few days ago.

It was her turn to nod.

"Ambrosia… but aren't they *theoretical* particles? Just theoretical…?"

She looked at me as though she was ready to burn me at the stake.

"Simon, they are scientific assumptions that are confirmed by equations…" Even as she talked her tone was losing its intensity.

I sat next to her and softly run my hand down her hair. As if waiting for just such a sign from me, she shuffled herself closer, lay her head on my shoulder, then, slowly, lowered it to my lap. I had no idea what one is supposed to do in such circumstances. I stopped thinking. After all, it never got me anywhere, so far. I lifted her head and kissed her lips. I knew this would happen, sooner or later, but, well, now she was in my arms. She was firm yet pliant; responsive, yet seemed devoid of a will of her own.

"Make love to me, Simon. Make love to me like you've never made love before..."

I was not going to disillusion her. That last request would be easy. No, I didn't carry her to my bedroom. I wouldn't give my ankle a second chance. We walked hand in hand, like two lovers on a stroll on Mount Royal. Then we stood and kissed again. Slowly, savouring every moment, every movement, every second, I removed her dress. She helped me with my jacket, then trousers. The rest followed in equally slow motion. They say that passion is fast, possessive. They are wrong. Or maybe it is. But love is slow, lingering; time seems to slow down by itself...

An hour later we were still naked. There seemed no need for any clothing. Surely, in Eden people had nothing to hide? We were in Paradise.

I made love to her as I never made love to any woman. Even in my dreams. It was different than anything I'd ever imagined. It wasn't a question of losing anything, like virginity. It was more like giving and receiving, all mixed into a single experience. As though we were one. Inseparable.

Another hour passed. Maybe two, or three?

I don't know how many times we united our bodies. It must have been also an exquisite union of our minds, our emotions, our souls. It was as though we both waited for this moment for years, perhaps lifetimes?

Finally she said she had to go to the bathroom. When she

got back she planted a playful kiss where I've never been kissed before.

"I hope mother isn't watching," she said.

Believe me. I shared her sentiment. Don't forget. About three hours ago, either that or three lifetimes, I was a virgin. So, who cares?

We made breakfast together. Soon after the second cup of coffee, Ambrosia rushed to her lab. I lingered, cleaned up, and clicked on my computer. I had to read up on that business of walking through walls. Perhaps not only Ambrosias' mother could do it. Even if only in her dreams. All the same, I felt grateful that she didn't visit us last night. Even if it were true that she could. Or that anyone could. I was no physicist, but I still tried to separate myths from reality. Physical, tactile, perceptible, concrete, reality. Fancy that. And I—professor of Comparative Religion. Just associate professor, but still...

Fancy that?

There was nothing I could find. In the Bible, that is—the source most of my listeners were interested in. There were miracles galore, but no direct data on walking through solid objects. What little I could find were explicitly symbolic. I almost wondered why they wouldn't put in a trick or two in there. In the scriptures. Surely they had lots of opportunities? Perhaps there were some miracles that people were more willing to accept than others.

It is true that in Luke 24, Jesus appeared to the apostles seemingly through closed doors, or it could have been through a wall, but that was after resurrection, in his sanctified body. It hardly meant that a physical body could achieve the same permeability. The same feat is described in John 20, but again after Jesus had already died. By the way, the word "sanctified" had not been explained. I wondered what it meant.

This raised an interesting question. If Jesus could perform such a feat in a body that the apostles could see and touch, does this mean that at some level of consciousness we're all equipped with such bodies, too? And if so, could we detach them from our physical envelopes to perform such things as walking through walls?

At that time I forgot why I'd ever want to do such a thing. After all, unless one was in jail, presumably unjustly so, the ability of walking through walls would be of little use to us. Perhaps that was why the Bible didn't illustrate such a trick. When Peter and John had been jailed, they left their confinement by miraculously having the doors opened for them. It seemed like an easier way out.

Somehow I doubted that this was what Ambrosia had in mind. I wish I could find something that would impress her. I'm sure that in science there must have been particles that were so small that they could pass through anything. I think they're called neutrinos. Only she'd know a great deal more about them. More than I could ever find out on the Internet, and it still wouldn't explain her mother.

Nevertheless, I pursued my research. He who knocks, unto him it is opened. Or something like that. As I keep saying, I studied and taught comparative Religion, not comparative tricks.

***

Chapter 7
Tunneling

Ambrosia still had little if any idea why the evil-eyed gentleman witnessed her signature in the dean's office. She actually asked Dr. McGinnis, the Dean of McGill, several times who might be the enigmatic stranger, and each time the doctor dismissed her concern as a matter of no consequence.

"We agreed to do it, 'tis all," he said the first two times.

The last time he took Ambrosia to one side of his office, switched on the TV, opened the window, and said in a conspiratorial voice.

"We're getting over ten million dollars in donations, why won't you sign the stupid piece of paper?"

"I did sign it," Ambrosia replied.

"Well, there you are, then."

And that was that.

Ambrosia decided to draw her own conclusions. They were not very complementary towards the Dean, nor towards the evil-eyed grey-suited gentleman. Assuming he was a man of gentle persuasion.

"So what was it?" I asked, after she recounted the above exchange to me.

For appearance's sake, Ambrosia still kept her own apartment, but she'd already moved in with me. Virtually. Her postal address was still the old one. I think she kept it for the sake of her parents. "Letters, and all that," she told me, when I asked.

"To hell with the CIA guy," I told her. "If we die, we die

together."

"Of course, we might get the baddies first, right? I'm not that keen on dying right now."

That deserved another kiss. A long, lingering one. Don't look surprised. I had 38 years to catch up on; a little fewer, or whatever the number of years are usually counted from the first signs of puberty.

When we came up for air, I asked, "Do you have any idea what it might be that they are after."

"Tunneling," she said without hesitation. "At least I can't think of anything else."

I waited for her to expand. She didn't. "Tunneling?" I repeated, probably sounding like a congenital moron.

"It's quantum mechanics," she replied. "Nobody understands it."

Now that made it perfectly clear. An evil-eyed gentleman would do us in if either of us spoke to anyone about things that nobody could understand.

Then she smiled. "Really, Sy, many claim to understand quantum mechanics, but Richard Feynman, who did more for the quantum theory than anyone else, once said that anyone who claims to understand it is a liar.

"I could say as much for most of the scriptures," I mentioned for no reason at all.

"Why would you say that?"

"Most people who claim to understand scriptures get to the first layer of understanding. Some Sufis claim that there are seven layers to the Koran. Compare Jalaludin Rumi to the suicide bombers."

"Is the same thing true of the Torah and the Gospels?"

"I don't know about seven, but anyone who treats them as anything other than spiritual knowledge is missing most of the substance."

"It sounds more and more like quantum theory. Everybody believes in it, but nobody can understand it."

"So what about this, ah… tunneling?"

"It could be something the powers that be might be interested in."

"It's suitable for killing?"

"Almost. Mostly for spying."

"That might very well facilitate killing."

"My point precisely," she said, looking none too happy.

"So… tunneling?"

"Well, I'd have to start at the beginning." She patted the settee next to her. "What do you know about particle physics?"

"Somewhere between zero and nothing," I said, looking as proud as I would dare.

"Funny." She didn't laugh. "You know that atoms are very small. Everybody knows that ever since Democritus of Abdera said so around 430 BC, using the original name for a-tom, meaning that they are the smallest indivisible particles. He also said that they are real, and everything else is an opinion. Well, he was almost right."

"Almost?" I felt I had to take part in this discussion.

"Almost. While atoms have changed meaning in our vernacular, they also turned out to be mostly empty space?"

"You mean they have their being mostly *in* empty space," I stressed the *in*.

"No, darling. Atoms themselves are mostly empty space."

She'd never called me darling before, although what we may have called each other on that first night will probably remain forever a mystery. Then my mind went back to her lecture.

"Care to explain?"

"Well, atoms consist of a nucleus and one or more electrons, usually referred to as a cloud, spinning around the nucleus. OK so far?"

"I presume that's not just an opinion?"

"Ha, ha." Again, no laugh.

"Sorry."

"Now, if you enlarge, in your mind, the nucleus, that is to say the proton and the neutron, to the size of an orange, and place it in the middle of a football field, the electrons would be spinning around the field's perimeter. The space between would be void. The whole space taken up by the nucleus and the electrons together would be about .0001% of the space occupied by the atom. 99.9999% of the space would be empty." She scribbled the two percentages on a napkin.

I continued to stare at her. The length of a rugby field is about 144 meters, including the Dead Ball line. The US football field is, I believe, much longer, some 360 yards. We used to compare it, once. That's a lot of empty space.

"I'm not saying it very well, am I?"

"What you are saying is that solid matter is mostly empty space."

"You got it in one. That's precisely what I am saying."

"Then how come we don't fall through to Australia?"

"What, empty space falling through empty space? Something else must be holding it, or us, together and in place."

"What?" was my instinctive question.

She smiled. "What indeed! There are many answers, as many as why we don't walk through solid walls. Except..."

She let it hung.

"Except with tunneling," she added, almost reluctantly.

"Aha, back to square one!"

This was just about as much fun as trying to decipher which was fact and which was myth, in some old religions. Only it was supposed to be science.

"Go on..." I was fairly ignorant in both fields. Except for the rugby field. The last time I played...

"In quantum mechanics we don't really have facts any more. At such a small level, such small scale, we rely on probability. And the particles are so small, that we prefer to deal with groups of them. We call them quanta. While large

objects are prevented by various factors from passing
through each other, at nuclear level, an electron would treat
solid as a quantum field, and thus, given enough kinetic
energy, it might find itself on the other side of the barrier."

I continued to stare at her eyes. God they were beautiful.
Full of sparkle—and they shone, really shone, probably full
of electrons or something.

"So very small objects, like electrons, if you push them
hard enough, they would get to the other side?" I offered.

"That is pretty close to what happens," she affirmed,
then she corrected herself. "That is pretty close to what *could*
happen. There would be a great probability of that
happening."

"And that is what the CIA guy doesn't want you to talk
about?"

"There is a probability that he was from the CIA," she
corrected. "I looked them up, last night. He could have been
from your Old Country, a CID fellow, or even the US
equivalent, the USACIDC man, which is usually also
abbreviated to CID. I think all those guys are playing cops
and robbers, and there is little probability that they'll leave
me alone."

"And there is a great probability that if I ever meet him
I'll punch his face in," I added. "On the other hand, I might
offer him a vote of thanks."

"You what?!"

"If it hadn't been for him, there was only a small
probability that you'd end up in my place."

"Oh, yes there was every probability. I've been eyeing
you for some time now."

"You what?"

"We, women, are devious and scandalous vixens. That is
why we usually get what we want."

"Aye, there's great probability of that," I said, but I still
found it a little hard to accept that she saw me first. On the
other hand, there were an average of 150 women attending

my lectures, and I was but one. Women take unfair advantage.

It was time to go to work. She to her lab, I to polish my final public offering. I could only speculate what questions would be thrown at me, but I'd better be ready. As usual, I did it all on my computer.

Computer. Ambrosia did most of her work on a computer. I wondered how good the CIA was at hacking. So, unless the dean was looking for an extra buck, someone had to have had access to her computer to know what she was working on. Was that someone the CIA?

Of course, I had no way of knowing. Perhaps Ambrosia suspected something, but wasn't ready to share it with me, as yet.

Again, my apartment looked strangely empty when she'd left. It was hard to believe that but a few weeks ago I was quite happy—well, reasonably happy—to spend the rest of my life in my aerie, looking at couples flirting on the winding paths of Mount Royal. I have been little more than a voyeur of the human equation. Now? All of a sudden I became submerged up to my neck in high math. Even now, already, I couldn't imagine life without Ambrosia. She must have cast a spell on me. A vicious, devious spell.

And I loved it.

Just in case, I went back to examine the Bible for any mind-over-matter stories that might be explainable logically. While I had no desire to upset peoples' faith in miracles, I belonged to the small minority of researchers who believed that miracles, like magic, were but the science of tomorrow. If they contradicted everything we knew, they were probably myths. There must also have been events that people of the evangelists' day would reject, for reasons of the state of consciousness they held at the time.

I had work to do.

The proposition of going through matter leaving the barrier unaffected was a different proposition. After all, I could put my hand through water, or air, or any gas, and the atoms of my hand seemed to travel between the molecules of the barrier with ease. So when did a solid become a solid? Was it only a question of density? But if so, how come neutrinos got right through our bodies, right through the planet Earth, without even slowing down? Is this, what Ambrosia would call tunneling?

I looked up neutrinos.

"Electron neutrino, a lepton, postulated by Wolfgang Pauli in 1930, has no charge and almost no mass."

Aha! So it does have *some* mass! It is still a physical or material 'substance'.

I was getting excited.

So... unless the eleven followers of Yeshûa that "gathered together" (as a friend of mine had once said, they could hardly have gathered apart?) in Luke 23 and John 10 suffered from mass hallucination, Yeshûa's body must have consisted of elements similar to neutrinos. That is to say, it could still be physical, material, have—albeit miniscule—mass. Hence, "Behold my hands and my feet, that it is I myself: handle me, and see for a spirit hath not flesh and bones, as ye see me have."

Quite a mouthful.

Conclusion? Physical body *can* go through solid objects, but it must adapt its constituents at subatomic level. I wasn't sure if I've made it easier or harder.

Ergo, the postulate that solids can go through liquids and gases only—is wrong. They can also go through solids providing they have no charge and very little mass.

Right Doctor Pauli?

I wondered what Ambrosia would say. I felt pleased as Punch. With myself, that is. That's what we used to say in England.

As I sat back to rest from my meteoric rise in the knowledge pertaining to the field of quantum mechanics, I was again amused at the thought, that a week or two ago, I would have been more than happy to go through life without hearing the words "quantum" or "mechanics". I would have dabbled in myths, pretending that some were real, or could be, and giving my professorial acquiescence to my listeners insisting on miracles.

Now, I entered a new stage in my, heretofore exemplary, or perhaps exemplarily mundane, life. I felt a sense of deep dissatisfaction with both, my Comparative Religion, and Quantum Mechanics.

All for the want of a woman.

Fancy that.

***

Chapter 8
Psychokinesis

Ambrosia's office was overlooking the inner court of a quadrangle, with no trees but a nice, round fountain, which worked part of the time, and four clamps of flowers, which cried out for more sun. She passed little time admiring the scant flora of the quadrangle, as she spent most of her time in the lab proper, where computerized machines did their thing, seemingly on their own.

Her office had no door, affording her little privacy, until the visit from the gentlemen who had supervised her signature. Supposedly, she as of now worked on the hush-hush stuff. Two days after his visit, a beautiful mahogany door had been installed in the metal partitions, which, also as of his visit, have miraculously extended all the way to the suspended ceiling. The door boasted a small but elegant copper tablet with name Ambrosia Milos, Ph.D., engraved in copperplate letters. Such distinction would go to most post-docs' heads. Ambrosia countered them by keeping the new door to her office conspicuously and permanently open. What she did do, however, was to change the passwords on all her computers, a battery of which graced her office.

"I work in the lab," she told her Chief, Dr. Leblanc who asked her about the door. "Not in a cage."

Dr. Leblanc, Ph.D., was a gentleman of the old date. Slight, slightly stooped, slightly forgetful. He was told about Ambrosia's signature, but apparently not precisely why it had been deemed necessary. They gave him a different story. For some   years,   now,   his   function   has   been   mostly administrative. It has been his responsibility to procure the materials and means necessary for the post-docs to do their research.

Ambrosia's work, though officially dealing with aspects of tunneling, which to me would continue to remain incomprehensible for some time, dedicated most of her time to the rarefied field of PK, usually known as psychokinesis.

The science was so new that, at least as science, it did not exist, as yet, in the Webster dictionary. They had psychokinesia, which they defined as "violent cerebral action due to defective inhibition," which, at least before I met Ambrosia was probably true of me, but had nothing to do with her work.

It bears mentioning that, by contrast, under the heading: "From Abracadabra to Zombies," The Skeptic's Dictionary classified psychokinesis with all other things and subjects they could not understand.

None of the above deterred Ambrosia from passionately pursuing her work. She had motivations that reached far beyond zombies and skeptics, and recently, apparently also beyond the understanding, but not interests, of the CIA.

According to Dr. Leblanc, whom I met at one of our recent staff meetings, what made her work particularly fascinating was that she introduced psychokinesis to tunneling.

"She isn't the first," the aging doctor said, his head shaking in additional affirmation. "But she had the most advanced results."

In the competitive field of science, this was a complement indeed. On the other hand, perhaps sensing that I had no idea what he was talking about, he added, "Bright girl, Miss Ambrosia. Bright girl," apparently nodding to himself.

I suppose she was just too beautiful to call her "doctor". As for me, "girl" was just fine.

The premise of her work was that, if there was such a

thing as psychokinesis, then it was some form of energy, and if such it was, then it had to affect matter. We know of headaches brought about by tension, which increases blood flow, of a number of strictly physiological disorders originating in emotional and/or mental stresses. All these pointed to psychokinetic power having its rightful place in scientific research.

The CIA interest must have originated when Ambrosia managed to tunnel a specific configuration of electrons to another location through an impervious barrier using, supposedly, psychokinetic energy. No. Not in real space or time, but in equations which, to a theoretical physicist, are more real than reality itself. The spy organizations knew, or thought they knew, that from theoretical stage to practical application there is only a factor of time. Presumably, they wanted to be ready.

Or even more so, to be the first to take advantage.

There was one slight hitch that the CIA appears to have forgotten. The usual span of time between the discovery, never mind a theoretical discovery, and production was, at the best of times, twenty-five years.

"What's up doc?" I asked, as she ran into the apartment. She seldom walked. A slight jog was her normal mode of propulsion.

"I've done it," she replied, throwing the groceries on the kitchen counter and herself on the settee.

"And what might that be?"

"I convinced Dr. McGinnis that we must publish."

"And what about, what's his name, the spy fellow? Aren't you both going to be shot on sight?"

"McGinnis agreed that, at least at present, there are no military applications. As such we are free to act like scientists."

"So... congratulations are in order?"

"Well, they still have to accept my article. They are quite

choosy, you know."

"They?"

"The scientific journals."

"So, Dr. McGinnis admitted that military application was at the base of your sworn affidavit?"

"I more or less tricked him into telling me."

"I bet, you devious vixen."

"I simply told him I'd go back to Greece to continue my research."

"That's it?"

"It seemed enough."

"Dr. Leblanc was right. You are a bright girl." Then I weighed her words. "Would you really have gone?"

"Of course not. Don't be silly."

By the end of the ten minutes that followed, on the settee, I was inclined to believe her. Whatever her scientific achievements, on the settee she was extremely persuasive.

"So now what?" I asked.

"I suppose we could move to bed," she replied, her tone serious as can be.

Though strictly against my better judgment, I decided to eat first.

"I love you," she said. "I really do, you know?"

Apparently the food was going to wait after all.

There are moments in one's life when all things one has ever done no longer seem to matter. For instance, when the past is but a shadow of what the future might bring. When what really counts is the present. My present began just a few days ago. And yet, in spite of it being intensely genuine, it seemed unreal, ephemeral, as though I'd experienced a dream. Yet a dream of which I could recall every single second in minutest detail.

All this was so new to me.

I've always been a loner. I never thought of sharing my

emotions. I shared my knowledge—my acquired skills as a lecturer. But my heart hasn't been in it. Not really. Now, since I met Ambrosia, the very same actions, the same interests, studies, research, even lectures, became saturated with life. Even the everyday events acquired new meaning.

What changed was my experience of life itself.

Suddenly, my food had more taste. My wine was more intoxicating. The sky was bluer, the mountain outside my window, more green. It was as if, after some thirty years of strolling along the path that tagged me along, I suddenly became alive.

Yes. Suddenly I became alive.

We decided to eat outside. The advantage of living downtown was being within walking distance of a dozen restaurants. We decided on the café in which we enjoyed our first meal together. After only a week or so, we already shared memories there; we had 'our' place.

We walked.

First I thought I imagined it. Then we stopped in front of a large display window and I became sure that I was right.

"Don't turn around, but isn't that the gentleman you met at your signing ceremony at dean's office?"

"If that's not him than it's his doppelganger," Ambrosia confirmed, her hand grasping my arm a little more firmly.

"Let's ignore him. Perhaps he'll go away."

We walked on without looking back. Frankly, it was of little interest to me what the CIA guy, if he was a guy from the CIA to start with, would do, as long as he kept himself at a reasonable distance. Having a bodyguard was not necessarily a bad thing. Not that downtown Montreal was in need of such security arrangements. The city was reasonably civilized.

Within minutes we arrived at our café. The place was half-empty, as it would be on a weekday, and we managed to get "our" table. Ambrosia lowered herself gracefully into "her" spot, then just sat there, looking at me with those wondrous eyes of hers, making me feel like a youngster on his first date. She had that effect on me.

I tried looking through the window. I said tried, because I wanted to do so surreptitiously. Then I felt sorry for the guy outside. He had a job to do, a job which was probably the most boring on Earth.

"I'll be back in a moment," I said, getting up and making for the door. I was going to find the guy and tell him to get some food, as this was what we were going to do, and that he could pick us up within about 90 minutes.

Ambrosia, quietly but with tacit determination, called me back. I hesitated and returned to our table to tell her of my intent. When I came back she said something that sent chills down my spine.

"Remember his eyes," she said, her voice cool and impersonal. "Just remember his eyes, Simon."

Well, I've never seen his eyes, but Ambrosia's tone stopped me in my tracks. Then I saw *her* eyes, and sat down.

For a while we just sat quietly, somehow unwilling to share our thoughts. Till this moment I have been more or less convinced that Ambrosia was making a mountain out of a molehill. Sure, there may have been some interest in her work but, let's face it, our friends at the Pentagon must have been ages more advanced on all matters pertaining to their bellicose trade. To imagine that the work of a Greek girl on a post-doc visa would be of value to them was a little hard to take.

But then, there were Ambrosia's eyes.

"Care to explain?"

She had already, once, but obviously I needed convincing.

She sighed, then leaned back.

"It's not easy," she began, this time her eyes wandering over to the far wall, seemingly counting the squares on the faded wallpaper pattern. Then she sighed again and held my eyes.

"As I told you, it all began with my mother. Almost three years ago, just before I came to Canada, when dad was sick—it seemed like nothing much—my mother looked at him, and called for an ambulance. It turned out he had a coronary artery aneurism that needed immediate attention. She didn't know that, of course. What she saw—what she told me she saw—was my father standing up next to the armchair on which he was sitting. He looked as real, she said, as his other self, sitting in the armchair. The standing part of him was pointing to his heart with a worried expression on his face. What would you have done?"

"Call an ambulance?" I offered.

"Precisely. She did. It most probably saved his life."

While we waited for our food to arrive we sipped Chardonnay. We've ordered *Assiettes de Crudités*, which were light enough for a late supper. Neither of us liked to eat much at night. A heavy meal would certainly not agree with my post-hypnotic suggestion exercises.

"Did such a thing ever happen again? Or before?"

"I asked my mother that very question. She said that when I was little she'd watch me play outdoors, while she remained inside. I don't mean she watched me through a window. She told me that, as far and my father and I were concerned, there had always been two of us. The physical and the other. She never named the other, but she said she could detect our presence through solid objects. Then, when she concentrated, she could actually see us. Later, she said, she did not see us through walls at all, but that she, herself, passed through the wall and observed us from the other side. Not physically, of course. But, well, somehow... We never worked it out what really happened."

"And this has something to do with the guy outside?"

"Something. The real question was," she went back to her story, "which is the real person. The one mother saw outside, or standing by dad's armchair? The one passing through the wall, or the one staying behind; or still sitting in the armchair? As I said, we haven't really worked it out."

"Are you suggesting that we, the physical we, are not real?"

"You remember the story I told you about atoms and empty space?"

I nodded. Then I smiled. "There are more things in heaven and earth, Horatio, that are dreamt of in your philosophy."

For a moment she looked blank. There was no reason why visiting Greeks should be conversant with Shakespeare. On the other hand her English was perfect.

Then it was her turn to smile.

"Hamlet to Horatio. Act I, Scene V," her expression dared me to contradict her.

"Love you," I said.

"I know," she replied.

And then our mouths were filled with the *Crudités*.

***

Chapter 9
Open Forum

Apparently, having to make up questions that would sound fairly intelligent was more than my public was prepared to subject themselves to. Listening, nodding, changing facial expressions at reasonably appropriate moments, with an occasional spontaneous query, was one thing. Formulating something that required deeper cogitation was another. At Ambrosia's suggestion, she and I, and eleven other people, three men and eight women, decided to leave the amphitheater reserved for more auspicious occasions, and move to an adjacent conference room. More intimate.

That was all that came. Eleven people.

I decided to steer the discussion to the subject that Ambrosia raised with me at our last night's dinner. I did so under a loose, all encompassing question, "What is reality."

"Are we sure that the reality we experience with our senses is the real McCoy?" I asked.

For a moment there was silence, then all spoke at once. I tried to sum up what has been said.

"The essence of what I hear you saying is that if you can touch it, or smell it, or detect it with any of your senses, then it can't be real."

Heads were nodding all around the table. Not one questioned my thesis. Not one suggested it should be "can't" rather than "can". I finally knew why this small group has chosen to attend my summer seminars. They were the searchers. The seekers. People, men and women, but mostly women, who were not satisfied with the interpretation of reality given by our priests, and preachers, but also by our scientists. Why mostly women?

"Men," one man suggested, "may have been too busy putting bread on the table."

Perhaps. I read, online, that one in five women earned more than their husbands. That still left the other four.

About then Ambrosia virtually took over. She gave us a well-accelerated run through the history of science, concluding with the latest research.

"We started with a flat Earth," she concluded. "Then we increased out view of the world to three dimensions. This served us well—for a while. Now? Now the theoretical physicists are trying to decide if eleven dimensions are enough. Of course today we don't really observe nature. We decide how we want nature to be, and then produce equations to prove that it is so. If nature doesn't conform, we don't change the equations. We change our view of nature."

I wish I had such attention of *my* listeners when I delivered *my* lectures.

"And, my friends, you heard this from a theoretical physicist. Guilty as charged."

I recall reading a book by a man specializing in making physics accessible to the masses. I was part of that mass he catered to. The only problem I found, in his book, was that each succeeding chapter, more or less, contradicted each previous one. I only just understood what he wrote in, say, chapter four, only to learn that it was too late. That it was superseded by new discoveries, or by a different theory in chapter five.

"Too late to agree with me, I've just changed my mind," I muttered under my breath.

Ambrosia reached over and patted my hand. "I know,

Simon, I felt the same way a number of times."

The others nodded. It seemed that we all read the same books. We all stayed for another two hours. It was fun, but, alas, we didn't reach any conclusions. I closed the forum with words of encouragement.

"Don't get discouraged," I said. "Keep knocking."

So where do we go from here?" I asked.

We walked back to my, to our, apartment. At last we would be alone, hopefully, for quite a time; with luck, for the rest of summer.

Having finished the series, I was as free as a bird until the next semester. It was only the middle of August, and there was plenty of summer waiting to be summered. When you live in Canada, summer has a special meaning for you. I was a visiting professor in Boston, one year, and asked my Canadian compatriot what was summer like in Montreal that year. He replied he didn't know because he went to Toronto that day.

Actually, that's not quite true. We do have winters that last up to six months, but our summers are as hot and humid, and as unpleasant as anywhere.

Ambrosia, of course, was mistress of her own time. She'd created her own program and could carry it out more or less at her own pace.

Upstairs, leaning against each other, letting our eyes wander over the deep greens of late summer foliage, Ambrosia told me another story about her mother. Sometimes I wondered if her mother was real, or a creation of Ambrosia's imagination. Then I pulled her onto the sofa.

"It is not true what we said about the perception of our senses not being real," she said. "Or that our senses do not perceive reality. Our senses are fine, it is the reality that seems elusive."

"Care to elaborate?"

"Well, it's back again to my mother. She said that the input she receives from her senses, when in an out of body experience, is vastly more intense than what we get here, in the physical reality."

"It sounds as if the unreal was more real than the real."

"What she said was that what we experience here is not only very restricted, but also diluted, as though seen through a veil."

"For now we see through a glass, darkly…"

"What's that, darling?"

"Paul's letter to the Corinthians. I don't remember the rest, but it tells of us seeing like children, of understanding little, and that later we shall see face to face, I think."

She looked up at me. "Do you think Paul was referring to an out of body experience?"

"I'm hardly in a position to know, but your mother obviously was. And there is a similarity. In the descriptions, I mean."

And then Ambrosia sat up.

"You don't suppose that all this talk of heaven and paradise and such exotic forms of existence are reference to little more than a condition of an astral projection?"

"Under perfectly controlled, reasonably permanent conditions?" I smiled wistfully. "I wouldn't be surprised."

"B-b-but that would make it possible for us all to…"

"I know of no one, darling, who can project, astrally or otherwise," I hated to dampen her excitement. "Shouldn't you ask your mother?"

Silence stretched. She just sat there, staring, unseeing, at the mountain. Judging by the concentration on her face, she was solving some heavy cerebral problems.

"I need three days, four at the most," she said at last.

"And then you'll project?"

"No, silly. And then I'll take you to Milos."

To say that I was in mild shock would be an understatement. I was resigned to spending the most tedious, oppressively humid months in Montreal, and now I was in serious danger of being whisked off to Greek Islands. Isn't life beautiful?

"There is a snag though," her face oscillated between euphoric, a minute ago, to utter hell, right now.

"What is it, for heaven's sake, tell me…"

Her bottom lip began to tremble. "Oh, darling," she barely uttered.

"What is it?" I repeated, now seriously worried.

"My father will kill us. Yes, both of us," she whimpered.

"But why?"

"If he caught us sleeping together…"

I took a deep—a very deep breath.

This could, or could not, have been, or could shortly become, a serious problem. There are hotels, of course, with interconnecting rooms. All we'd have to learn to do would be to lie like everybody else. After all, lies were what made all politics go round; it was no longer a social stigma.

Unless we stayed with her parents.

Unless we stayed with… I gasped, terrified.

Glory be! Now alarm bell rang in my head.

Then, I suppose, truth, like beauty, would have to be in the eyes of the beholder. After all, there is shallow truth, and deep truth, and half-truth. And some truths are not true at all, like people who swear at the altar that they would never leave each other. I don't even know what will happen tomorrow, never mind the day after.

I wondered what sort of truth Mr. Milos believed in.

"We'll take separate rooms," she said. "On different floors," she added, after due consideration. "You don't suppose it would be necessary to stay at different hotels, do you?" She seemed to be grasping at straws.

"Or we could get married?" I offered.

"Darling, I thought you'd never ask!"

"Here or there?" I asked.

"You mean we could get married on Milos? That would be nice," she continued, breathing hard, but I could see her wheels turning at an astonishing speed. "But wouldn't we miss the first night?"

"Yes, darling, we might miss the first night of sleeping together. On the other hand, you'd have both your parents present at the ceremony."

"That's a lot of plates…" she mused.

I gave up hope of keeping up with her. She looked surprised.

"Darling, you should read more. First we smashed plates as an expression of grief, at funerals. Then the restaurateurs took it up to attract attention, ergo customers. Now we do it just for the fun of it…"

"You mean everybody does it?"

"Well, not in the cities among the aristocratic families. Their china is too expensive. But out on the islands…"

"…we'll have to smash plates." I hated noise.

"I'll call them this afternoon. We must think this out. I suggest small, family only, local Greek Orthodox Church, and…" she gave me one of her looks, "honeymoon right on the spot."

"I'll drink to that. But, I insist," I put on my grave face, "without your father."

"My father doesn't drink. Not since his last brush with his heart problem," she said.

"Sorry."

"Or mother, or the priest. Just imagine, Simon, you and I, alone, on a Greek Island. Just imagine…"

"You can't call them this afternoon. It's night there, right now. We have to wait."

We did. We ended up on the bed. Again. Just for practice, I suppose?

"Oh, my God! I have nothing to wear…"

"That's the way I like you best," I murmured.

We had some heavy shopping to do. Actually, Ambrosia was the least spoiled woman I'd ever met. She also told me that her mother would probably insist that she'd wear the wedding dress her mother wore at her wedding. After all, it had only been worn once. Or did her grandmother wear it too?

"Oh, I don't know, darling. There is so much to do."

"Will it fit?" I asked.

That was a mistake. Obviously it would fit. When her mother got married she had a perfect figure. She still had it. I decided against inquiring about her grandmother's figure.

"Sorry," I said contritely. "Of course it will fit."

"You've never seen my mother, have you?" There was a threat in her voice.

"No, darling, I haven't. I'm sure she has a perfect figure, just like you."

"You like my figure?" Her tone changed substantially.

"I adore your figure…"

I thought it best to show her. Actions are so much better than words.

By one a.m., our time, it was all settled. Ambrosia's mother was ecstatic that we chose to include them in the ceremony. She promised to keep it very private. They would book a hotel for us, nearby their home, for our honeymoon.

Ambrosia's parents lived in Plaka, which housed the Municipality of Milos. Since 1989, the municipality of Milos was also the administrative centre of nearby islands, those of Serifos, Sifnos and Kimolos.

Father, Mr. Milos, whose voice Ambrosia heard throughout the conversations interrupting her mother's, would take care of all the papers and other formalities. Father had connections. He's been a member of the council for two years, and the mayor of Milos for eight years. He had clout. He knew how to twist arms.

We'd arrive on the eve of the wedding, a week from yesterday. An airplane would take us to Athens International Airport, and from there we would take any of a dozen small airlines servicing the islands. We would land directly on a brand new airstrip just built on Milos.

Since breakfast, until she left for her lab, Ambrosia was dancing Greek national dances in the living room. She insisted on teaching me some of the steps. I was glad she didn't smash any plates. When she left, I collapsed, exhausted. It's been awhile since I've played rugby.

***

Chapter 10
The Micro and the Macro

I was sitting on the throne, as we used to call it, in my bathroom. My lack of movement, lack of any sport of any nature, brought about a certain reticence on the part of my stomach to make room for the meals, which I loved taking with Ambrosia. Actually she joked that the only movement I indulged in was the peristaltic movement.

"I'll teach you dancing, 'darling. That will make you move all over," she promised. "And then, we'll take up tennis!" she threatened.

No matter. I sat and I thought of all the philosophical problems that plagued the world. It is the right place, my mother often told me, to cogitate the foibles of life; also on our personal shortcomings.

"Better there," she'd say, "than imposing it on others, elsewhere." She probably had a point.

And then I saw it.

It was a tiny bug, a little like a centipede only much smaller, thinner, and black. It was the sort you'd normally squash under your foot, or wrap it in a bit of toilet paper and wash it down the loo. It might have been asleep; at any rate, it seemed to mind its own business. After a period of rest, it continued its stroll, which must have been interrupted by my entry into the temple of thoughtful consideration, or by my switching on the light. It now moved along the floor in a purposeful manner.

Its body was no more than half a centimeter in length and about a tenth of that in height and width.

It was tiny.

After a stroll of about two feet, suddenly, for no reason that I could discern, it turned its trajectory at a right angle, and continued, at about the same speed, to walk up the vertical, slippery, tiled wall of my bathtub. It walked, or was it climbed, to within an inch of the top, changed its mind, and descended almost to the floor. Just before reaching a horizontal surface it suddenly unfurled its tiny wings, and took off, what must have been a flight of pure joy. I don't know why, but it just looked like joy to me. Perhaps I was thinking of William Blake wondering about a bird in flight and later about a tiny winged fly. The second verse of Blake's poem, the lesser known one, applied to my own experience:

> *Seest thou the little winged fly,*
> *smaller than a grain of sand?*
> *It has a heart like thee,*
> *a brain open to heaven and hell,*
> *within side wondrous and expansive;*
> *its gates are not closed;*
> *I hope thine are not.*

I never saw it again.

Since I was nowhere near to having finished fulfilling the purpose for which I entered this particular station, I continued my philosophical perambulations.

In many ways that bug, I thought, is vastly superior to me. I cannot climb the slick, slippery vertical walls with equal alacrity to walking flat surfaces. I cannot fly, taking off from neither horizontal nor vertical surface. The bug must have fed itself, without ever leaving my apartment. It must have defecated in places I haven't seen or suspected. Since the lifespan of a bug is short, there was a good chance that it has already procreated itself, perhaps many times. It might well have flown to feed its children.

I haven't. I haven't accomplished any of those feats.

Ergo, in many ways, the bug was, is, and for all I know will forever remain, vastly superior to me. At least within the sphere of its operations. It had the advantage, however, of living in a vastly smaller universe—although that could be just my ego speaking.

"We live in an enormous universe," Ambrosia said, without any preambles.

She breathed in, as usual, on a trot. She gave me a cursory kiss, *en passant,* on her way to the window. She stopped inches from the glass, and spread her arms as if to embrace this vast universe; or, at least, the Mount Royal.

"Today," she announced, "we've published a new paper. We have new evidence that we not only share infinity with a great many universes, but that, at some level, those universes are all integral to a single whole."

I left the bathroom only about five minutes ago. My mind was elsewhere.

"Tell that to the bug," I murmured, still lost in my thoughts.

"Bang?" she asked, then finished her previous thought. "Mega-universe," she affirmed proudly, as though taking responsibility for its creation.

"What ever happened to the Big Bug, ah, Bang?"

And then the life cycle of the little bug is over and its progeny continues the cycles, perhaps reincarnating its tiny consciousness, or, equally as likely, it takes another step, upwards, onto a larger bug, with bigger brain, which can visualize a larger universe which, like us, humans, it cannot touch, except with its thoughts.

"I really haven't thought about it, though, if the universe is infinite, than we'd have serious problems with the Big Crunch, so beloved by all the searchers for dark matter."

"You lost me," I confessed.

"You are not alone. That is why I chose the micro over the macro. They are both essentially invisible, but I find the micro easier to visualize."

Yes, but can you walk up a vertical, slick, polished surface?

"I wonder though, why so many physicists have spent so much time looking for this dark matter..." she sounded dreamy.

Tiny bugs. Bigger bugs. Much bigger bugs. Enormous bugs?

"It's an incredible world we live in," she practically exclaimed.

And in this never-ending cavalcade of Egyptian, Chinese, Hindu, Greek and Roman gods, I wondered how big must bugs be to invent gods in their own image?

"It's an incredible world we live in," I said.

"Yes, Simon, it's an incredible world," she concluded and with four quick steps chose me over the window. I, too, preferred to be the centre of her universe—even if for a little while. Before she discovers a bigger one?

Were the bugs faithful to each other?

"Shouldn't you have proposed to me, officially?"

"You mean with two witnesses and a notary?"

"That's not funny," she said turning away from me.

While Ambrosia was working in her lab I occupied myself by visiting a few jeweler boutiques at the Bonaventure. By the time she turned to me, I was on one knee, holding a tiny box for her to behold.

"Oh, Simon, I was only kidding..." Her eyes managed to turn twice their usual size.

The solitaire fitted perfectly. Just luck, I suppose. She

twisted her hand and wrist in a dozen different directions examining the ring, then repeated the same exercise in front of the bathroom mirror. Apparently satisfied, she ran back and threw her arms around my neck. Guess where we ended up.

Once there, (much, much later), she helped me with my hypnotic regression. I've been practicing it, on my own, with a micro-recorder on my computer switched on, just in case my post-hypnotic suggestions produced something audible.

They say that beginnings are always frustrating. Well, less so if you've dedicated your life to delve into the esoteric to which there are seldom, if ever, any positive answers. In a way, Ambrosia would probably lay the same claim regarding her theoretical physics. The gulf between theoretical and actual, or real, or physical, was probably as wide as in my profession.

Anyway, after a number of days of practice, she asked me questions, while I put myself under my own spell. No, this is not a form of masturbation. It is a very precise state of mind, which bypasses the critical part of your mind, and allows you to recall the past as though it was today. In a way, it erases the critical factor of time. When you recall events from the past, you don't just remember them, you relive them, engaging all your senses. What is more, you relive them as though they happened for the very first time.

We began with simple tasks, like remembering, or reliving, parts of our first dinner. Then—the walk we had on the mountain. The last time, she asked me to give her a head count of the people present at my last lecture. She said that I was actually counting the "heads", twice getting annoyed at someone seemingly hiding behind someone else. Whether my answer was correct or not was of little consequence. The vital thing was that I was actually counting, there and then. I wasn't just remembering.

I drew the curtains, went through my relaxation

exercises, and counted myself from ten down to zero. Then I told myself that with each breath I took I'd sink into a deeper and deeper state of relaxation.

Then I heard her voice; quite distinct, yet as though coming from a considerable distance.

"Tell me about it…"

I ran over the whole session on the recording I made on my computer. It turned out that it paid to have a precise record. Ambrosia kept her voice level, unemotional, talking as she would to a stranger. For a moment I thought of Dr. Steiger, but quickly dismissed that notion. Her voice was still familiar enough to be friendly, not just polite.

There was a moment of silence, then I heard myself talking in a surprisingly normal tone of voice.

The field is well trodden; not at all like the football fields of the professional clubs in London. When I visited Arsenal at Highbury, with my father, the field was like a billiard table. You could see the ball bounce, at a perfect angle.

What happened?

Nothing happened. Well, not much, ha, ha, Gonzales just scored a goal and the crowd went wild…

At the college. Rugby. Your ankle?

What happened to my ankle? Why nothing, why should something happen to my ankle. My ankle?

Yes, there is something about my ankle. I am running, the ball tightly under my left arm. I manage to swerve past George and Steve, and… and now I am lying down with my face in the dirt. Funny that. My ankle doesn't even hurt.

How did your ankle feel?

I told you, it doesn't even hurt…

She counted me back.

Three… two… one… and snapped her fingers. I rubbed my eyes.

"What happened," I asked.

"You fell flat on your face. That's all. Oh, yes. And Gonzales scored a goal for Arsenal. I think it was for the Arsenal at High-something-or-rather. Is that a name of a team?

I nodded.

"At least we got a *bona fide* regression," I mused. "I am making progress. I wonder if there is a way to remember it when I come to."

"If there is, then you'll find it, my love," she dismissed the matter as inconsequential. "There was one interesting thing, however. When I questioned you about the ankle, you replied in the present tense. I wonder if that means anything."

I had to determine if my response, or reaction to Ambrosia's question, in the present tense was already on the verge of my coming out of my self-induced trance, or if the whole affair was just a memory strengthened by my hypnotic state. I'd rather that I relived the event, thus giving greater weight to the ankle problem. I checked, again, the recording on my computer. Unfortunately, my other answers were in past tense. Except for those dealing with the ankle. That showed promise. I was too inexperienced to be sure which tense applied.

When I didn't comment, she must have assumed that the hypnosis session was over. There was much work I had to do before I could dream of deep regression into the murky past. I could see myself roaming the historical eras, picking up the points of interest, leaving my mark in history books. And not just in religious texts, although those probably needed more attention than many others, but in history of the world. It was an incredible challenge. I had to practice.

Practice makes perfect.

Ambrosia looked at me from under her long, superbly curved, eyelashes. "Want to do some more practice? We have less then a week…"

Whatever practice may have done to my ego, or any

other aspect of my wellbeing, one thing must be noted with great solemnity. Since we started practicing, not a single time did my errant ankle act up. That didn't absolve me from trying to determine what caused the original *articulatio talocruralis* (yes, I looked up the words) malfunction, but it did a great deal to encourage putting in as much practice as we could.

***

PART TWO

As Good as it Gets

Go to Heaven for the climate, Hell for the company.

Mark Twain

Chapter 11
The Nectar

Wedding notwithstanding, I had to go to Milos. Soon. Ambrosia told me so much about her mother, about Metria, that my heart was already there. Only my work had stopped me from catching the first plane to the Greek Islands. On the other hand, I haven't been invited.

Anyway, it would be soon now. Less than a week.

People have been searching for the elixir of life, or of health and longevity, of fame and fortune, from the day man learned to dream. I know. My dreams have been growing in interest and complexity. At least once a week I succeeded in, what is referred in my book on OBE, the Out of Body Experience, as a lucid dream. It is not a dream, which you decide on, as in hypnosis, but one you join in progress, and then, having become aware that you are dreaming, you take it in a new direction.

Enter alchemists.

The middle ages were replete with them. Overflowing.

Alchemy is a very broad subject. Originally it referred to the quest of the magical *kimia*, an Old Persian word for elixir, later turned by the Arabs into *alchemy*. Its original purpose was to turn base metals into gold. Only later they must have decided that once you'll get so filthy rich, you might as well live longer to enjoy it. It became a quest for longevity. I presume the attainment of wisdom was supposed to be the byproduct of both.

What I found interesting was that in days when, surely,

the vast majority of people lived rather inauspicious lives, they all seemed bent on extending it, nevertheless, for as long as possible.

Of course, as I mentioned, over the years, the elixir was to deliver not only health, but also mammon. Gold. They all wanted to indulge in Midas pursuits. The other premise being that, if you can't live forever, you might as well be rich. It worked either way.

We haven't changed much, have we?

I suppose it's all right if you can get it; but aren't there things more important then both of them? Than life and mammon? Socrates, who really had something to offer, preferred drinking hemlock to giving up his cherished principles. At one time, the early Christians were moved by similar predilections. Later, when poverty swept the vast majority of Europeans, they held onto their lives. Only the church was rich, in those days. The church and a few kings.

No. The few at the top, be they secular or ecclesiastical, were the followers of neither Socrates nor the Christ. Perhaps that was where our forefathers went wrong. They missed the secret of life. It is not in what you can get, that makes you rich, but what you can give. What you have to offer. On the other hand, surely, you cannot give what you haven't got. Right?

Hey, perhaps I should be teaching this! Maybe my mother was right—I could make a half-decent monk.

I asked Ambrosia what is the most important thing in her life.

"There are so many," she replied after considerable thought, "but if I lose all I hold dear, then I would survive if I had interesting work."

"You value work above all else?"

"You can't say that. I'd give up my work to be with you. I'd give it up if I had to look after my parents. But, it is as I already said, should I lose it all, work would keep me going." Then she added, "I simply love my work."

I wondered how many people felt the same way. Didn't the Catholic doctrine teach that work is the punishment for the original sin? You don't believe me? Read John Paul II's encyclical on human work. In Latin its called *Laborum Exercens.* In English it's called "On Human Work".

This was our last walk on the Mountain before our departure for Milos. Though I never suspected it would affect me, I was becoming nervous. What if her parents didn't accept me? What if they thought I was too old for her? I probably was. By the time she gets to be my age, I'll be a lot older.

At least that pearl of wisdom made me laugh, although my logic was impeccable. Usually, in my field, in Comparative Religion, logic is not a *sine qua non* requirement. Lucky me.

We strolled, hand in hand, trying to etch in our memories the effulgence of green that seems to explode every year, right here, in the middle of our city, with unrestrained generosity. During the working week (people doing their penance?) there was hardly anyone there. The main alleyways still showed some pedestrian traffic, with an occasional mounted policeman displaying his commanding presence, but the smaller paths were truly deserted. At least we thought so, until Ambrosia noticed that an inconspicuous looking tramp has chosen to travel exactly the same convoluted path, we did.

Coincidence?

I lived by the Mount Royal for the last eight years. The mountain rises some 233 meters above mean sea level, that's 764 feet for out visitors from the south, who usually prefer to hire a horse carriage, a *caléch*, to take them to the top and back again.

I prefer to wander on foot. After all, the mountain hardly qualifies to rise above the denomination of a 'hill' yet, with

200 hectares of densely treed terrain, with luck, once or twice, I contrived to get lost in its entrails.

By the time I met Ambrosia I knew just about every nook and cranny of its array of pathways. Long before I met her, I'd wandered the twisted trodden tracks up, down, and laterally, just to find out where they would take me. I met lone strangers, like me, seemingly seeking solitude, or, perhaps, trying to lose themselves, away from their feeling of loneliness.

Now, I'll never know.

I told Ambrosia to keep walking, to the top, rest a moment of two, and then start walking back.

"But why?" she looked surprised.

"You will have a surprise," I assured her.

Ten steps later, I took off at an angle behind two conifers, which made me virtually invisible to anyone coming behind us. Within less than thirty seconds, the man passed me. He didn't look like any CIA man I've ever seen, not that I've ever seen many. Any? Of course, one can't be sure. They're secret servants, so they're probably at least semi-invisible. The man was about five-foot-ten, a bit past middle-aged, also a bit on the shabby side, and certainly did not give the appearance of being an expert at unarmed combat. That last observation precipitated a long, silent expulsion of air from my lungs.

In fact, I could breathe, again.

With equal stealth that the man appeared to have been attempting, I followed him, assuming that he'd follow the path we, Ambrosia and I, usually took. That is to say, if he was really following Ambrosia. He did. And he was. At the top of the path Ambrosia stopped and waited. Then she turned and slowly began to descend the way she'd come. The man stopped, turned, and in no time at all ended up I my widely spread arms.

"Haven't we met?" I inquired politely. "It's George, isn't it?"

"No, Sir, I'm John, and we certainly haven't…" he was trying to nudge past me on the narrow path.

"Of course, John, how nice to see you again!" I grabbed his hand and continued to shake it most amicably.

By now Ambrosia was upon us and greeted John with a big smile.

"John, how are you. Long time no see?"

The man was close to tears.

"All right. You've got me. I meant no harm," he said quietly. "Please, don't tell them, please, Sir."

"Them?" I played dumb, which wasn't difficult as at that moment I really was.

"They told me to follow Miss Milos, Sir. Just to make sure she'd come to no harm."

Ambrosia left the initiative to me. I scratched my head.

"Then why don't you join us, John? At the top we can have a coffee together, and you can make sure it isn't poisoned. OK?"

"Yes, Sir. Just as you say, Sir. And it's Bob, Sir, not John. Robert, if you like."

On the way up I couldn't help wondering how could our friends down south, boasting a $14 trillion deficit, afford to play spying games. It weren't as though Canada and the USA were about to enter a state of war. Nor, to my knowledge, did Ambrosia work on anything that could possibly be of any value to the Pentagon.

The Lord works in mysterious ways, I thought; even more so do the Americans.

I found an empty table on the first floor terrace of the cafeteria overlooking the Beaver Lake. During the winter months the lake served Montrealers as a skating ring. On that day, we saw a multitude of ducks ducking to catch plentiful fish—that's if ducks eat fish—though as the water looked fairly polluted I couldn't vouch for the taste of their catch. No matter, the view was pastoral and thoroughly peaceful, in contrast to our cat and mouse game.

We sat down at a table hidden from general view by two splendid pine trees and a shorter cedar, conveniently growing just outside the balcony. Ambrosia offered to bring us coffees, while I made sure that our intrepid spy wouldn't give us a slip.

The man's story was neither threatening nor very exciting. It wasn't even very hush-hush. When Ambrosia signed the document in the Dean's office, the CIA agents followed her for a day or two, and when they didn't find any suspicious elements in her life, except for yours truly, *moi*, they delegated a local PI service to keep an eye on her. For obvious reasons they didn't approach any large, established firms of private investigators, but preferred a retired policeman, who was keen to make an extra buck. Less publicity and it still paid to play safe. Evidently the Dean had been right that the whole matter was a question of formality.

But then enter Robert, known to his friends as Bob. Since we saved him arduous climbs all over the Mount Royal, we have been upgraded to the status of his instant friends. At least, I thought so.

"Just what did they tell you, Bob?"

"It's as I told you, Sir. Just to make sure Miss comes to no harm."

"And did they tell you why?"

The man scratched his head, once again looking frazzled.

"They still check daily if there is anything to report, Sir," Bob said, once again looking none too happy about the turn of events.

"That's all right, Bob. You are among friends." I thought that was a rather good line. Then I added, "We'll keep you informed."

"That's really decent of you, Sir."

"So why do you think you were *really* following Miss Milos, Bob?"

"Well, Sir, I have to have some data, whenever I work for the government. Just to cover my own tracks, you understand, in case RCMP got involved, or something. So they told me that she, I mean Miss Milos, was working on some devise that would make spying dead easy. That's not exactly how they put it, but that was the gist of it."

I looked at Ambrosia and nodded. She tried hard to hide her smile.

"Hush-hush, eh?" I said that with my best Canadian accent. No reason why I shouldn't keep the fellow confused.

"Oh, yes, Sir. I'm not supposed to talk about it to anyone."

"Nor should you, Bob. We'll let this remain between just the three of us, eh?"

"Thank you, Sir. That would be nice."

"I'll tell you what, Bob. You give me your card, and I'll personally keep you informed if we want to go somewhere special. I won't use my name, but say that it's George calling. If you're not on the line, I'll leave a message. OK?"

The man weighed that in his tired head. He had to process of lot of unexpected stuff in a very short time.

"Thank you, Sir," he repeated, and finished his coffee in one gulp. Then he reached into his inner pocked, and extracted a card from his tired looking wallet.

"You won't lose it, will you, Sir?"

"I'll tell you what, Bob. Let's play safe and you give one to, ah, Miss Milos, also."

He did so without a word. He gave an impression that he was more afraid of tiny Ambrosia than the little, six-foot-one, me. He gave me a final once-over, looked at Ambrosia, again, then rose, nodded, bowed slightly, and within seconds only his smell lingered behind.

Moments later that was gone, too.

"I thought that went rather well, don't you?" I asked when the air cleared.

"It could have been different if he was the real McCoy..." she mused, her smile a little uncertain.

I simply didn't want to think what might have happened if the man was a real, highly-trained, expert killer-with-bare-hands, CIA operative. I had no way of knowing if they were anything like the types one saw on TV imports from down south. I could scream, of course—it might have saved my life—but it wouldn't have presented a very macho image on the woman I was about to marry. I counted my lucky stars.

I read, somewhere, that by law, the CIA are specifically forbidden from collecting intelligence on the domestic activities of the US citizen. Their mission was to collect information related to foreign intelligence and foreign counterintelligence. But if so, even if we were a good forty-five miles from the US border, what did any of this have to do with Ambrosia?

On the other hand only the president could direct the CIA to undertake a covert action. That would place Ambrosia's activities pretty high, although Madam President's directions may have been pretty general.

"I saw how he looked," I said, with a nonchalant wave of hand. "If he were a man from CIA, he could have made a fortune in Hollywood."

That last was perfectly true. I couldn't imagine a man looking less like a secret agent. On the other hand, I doubt they are supposed to look like professional killers.

We said our goodbyes to the Beaver Pond gracing the top of the mountain and made our way back. George, John or Bob was nowhere to be seen. But I'm fairly sure I caught a whiff of him close to the bottom of the trail.

"Bye, Bob," I said, but no one answered.

***

Chapter 12
At Thirty-three Thousand Feet

Ll right. It's only a bit over 10,000 meters. But when you fly in an airplane you can close your eyes, and pretend that you are flying on your own, without the metal coffin, sorry, metal box, surrounding you. Not that you couldn't do it flying higher or lower. With a little bit of imagination you could pretend that the air you feel washing over your face from the overhead air-conditioning jet is the air you feel outside. After all, ten percent of it is; you must just disregard the remaining 90% of the recycled, stale miasma that people use to breathe in the airplanes. Yes, including the recycled flatulence of some 400 passengers—less 10%, of course.

Try holding your breath, for a few hours. I read somewhere that some yogis can do it.

"I strongly suggest you try it. It's bound to make you feel better," I murmured to Ambrosia who, even here, on the wide, first class seats, managed to hang on to my arm.

"I'm feeling just fine," she assured me, squeezing my arm even harder. "I don't really like flying," she added.

Thankfully she hasn't heard my musings; although I was referring, of course, to pretending you're airborne outside, not to holding your breath.

Back to my imagination.

You have to relax, completely, then eliminate the noise of the jets. That last, frankly, is a pain I used to get way down, in the cattle section. On the other hand, if you succeed,

in some ways it is like falling asleep. In others it's good if
you've practiced self-hypnosis for a while.

This was the first time in my life that I flew first class.
While the armchairs were a very welcome improvement on
the stalls the tourists were herded into by the dozen, I hardly
took advantage of free booze. Before I met Ambrosia I
hardly even touched wine. In England wine was not that
popular, and I never acquired taste for the bitterness of bitter.
When others drank pints of ale, I compensated by drinking
cider. There was a reasonable choice. There was vintage and
green and rough and half'n'half. There were also some
special concoctions, which claimed to have been distilled
from apples. Sometimes I believed them. Those from
Jamaica were 140 proof. Those, I didn't drink.

On closer examination, I decided that the whole matter
of imaginary flying was of little consequence. I could fly as
easily lying on my bed, at home, with equal amount of
relaxation and without the need for eliminating the annoying
noise.

Voilà. Problem solved.

Ambrosia left teaching me the rudimentary elements of
politeness I'd need in Greece till the very last moment.
Words like please, thank you, good morning, bye, so long,
and a short list of other linguistic accouterments of everyday
living.

Half an hour later my lips were dry, my tongue twisted
in a Gordian knot, but my Greek vocabulary has increased by
between one and two-dozen words and expressions. The fact
that I didn't have any idea, which words or phrases meant
what—I managed to forget them at the rate at which they
penetrated my memory cells—was of academic interest only.
Ambrosia assured me that that would come with repeated
use. I could now bump into someone on the street and have a
good chance of escaping without loosing my teeth.

"Those little things make life more enjoyable,"

Ambrosia assured me.

I had no idea if she was referring to my newly acquired linguistic skills, or my teeth remaining in my mouth. Both prospects were highly desirable.

"Remember, Simon, when you meet my parents you must bow, not just shake hands. I know it's old fashioned but, well, my parents are of the previous generation.

"You mean like to Her Majesty the Queen, or at the hip?" I asked innocently.

"You just bow," she said, her voice threatening.

I bowed there and then—the luscious luxury of first class allowing me such elegance. Both my head and from the hips. I accomplished this trick without getting up.

"Just practicing," I said, when Ambrosia gave me a quizzical look.

I think my wife-to-be approved.

And then, suddenly, I felt very, very uncomfortable. It stuck me there and then, that I didn't so much as mention my impending marriage to my parents. Nor to my sister. I felt like a prodigal, ungrateful son who shortchanged his own mother and father. And this was me, a professor of Comparative Religion. Teaching the history of the Good Stuff. I felt disgusted with myself.

The next moment my mind was flooded with a million excuses. Time factor, the suddenness of it all, my nerves torn apart, the last few lectures at McGill, the meeting with Dr. Steiger, the CIA trappings, the… my falling in love, which did things to my mind that I didn't know existed. My belated loss of virginity.

Hi Mother, I'm no longer a virgin!

That's not the sort of thing you want to report to your mother. I was almost ready to blame Ambrosia. Or the Olympus. Anyone?

I'm sorry, Mother. I'm sorry, Dad. I really am. I'll make it up to you. Truly, I will…

I couldn't sleep after that. Not even a wink.

Before leaving, at my instigation, we decided to play a little
trick on the men in gray. The CIA guys. Frankly, after the
incident in the park, we were both just a little fed up with
them. Ambrosia argued that it was hardly Bob's fault. He
was carrying out his orders, no matter how illogical. On the
other hand, she could not deny that should she succeed with
her experiments on a larger scale, the application for the
Pentagon would be undeniable. I refused to discuss it. I
couldn't deny it, however, that I could imagine tiny spy-
microphones that could traverse solid objects like walls,
floors, or ceilings, and that such could yield valuable
intelligence. Nevertheless, according to Ambrosia, we were
still years away from such applications.

As for our Bob, he hasn't been seen by either of us
during the last three days before our departure. I had vague
hopes that they, the ungodly, gave up their vigil of Ambrosia,
and more recently, spying on my own movements also.
Assuming they ever began to take interest in me.

Before leaving, I kept my promise. I called Bob and told
him to tell the men who hired him that he, Bob, would be
unavoidably detained for the next day or two, and that they,
themselves, ought to put their own men on the job. Bob
agreed.

"I'm sure you have a good reason, Sir?"

"Yes, Bob. Saving your skin."

With that I hung up.

I asked one of my buddies, an associate professor of
astrophysics, to get for me, as you already know, two first
class tickets to Athens. Apparently, for stays shorter than
three months, no visas were required for visitors from
Canada. My buddy got the tickets, then parked in my garage
(I had a spot but no car as yet), and drove us both to the
Pierre Elliot Trudeau International Airport. If the man in gray
was watching then he must have had X-ray eyes. We both

ducked low until we cleared the immediate district.

"Eat your heart out, CIA," I chuckled.

I like to chuckle. In my line of work there is seldom occasion to do so. For some reason people take their religions very seriously.

By the time we reached A20, Ambrosia and I felt like kids who were getting away with being naughty.

In the second half of our flight, we tried to get some sleep. At least Ambrosia did, I couldn't get my parents out of my mind. It is not often that one has room enough, when six-foot-one, on an airplane. I took full advantage of the space, while Ambrosia drew her legs up on her seat, and used me as a pillow. I found the arrangement quite equitable.

For a while I tried to formulate things I would say to Mr. and Mrs. Milos. Somehow, nothing came to mind, to set me at ease. The formulas Ambrosia taught me seemed to turn into Hungarian goulash. I reverted to English, with little more success.

"How do you do, Mr. Milos. I came to take your daughter off your hands. I hope you don't mind?"

"No, Mrs. Milos. I am not rich. I barely make enough to support myself. But we won't starve, I promise. There's a cheap cafeteria at the McGill University. We can eat there, if need be."

What actually never crossed my mind was that I could, God forbid, but I could, lose my position at the McGill. Associate professorship was not equivalent to a tenure, which usually was a lifelong engagement, with a pension tacked on at the end of it. Of course I could work like a slave and try to get full professorship. Yet even then, there were no guarantees. There were not that many people interested in Comparative Religions. Most people I knew preferred to stick to their own, and remain obedient sheep. Safer that way. If you went to hell, at least it wouldn't have been your fault.

My mind was getting fatigued.

Sorry mother, sorry dad...

Then it happened. Behind closed eyelids, I saw my mother's smile. For months I've been trying to experience a lucid dream, and here, in these hardly most congenial circumstances, let alone conditions, I succeeded against all expectations. Actually, I wasn't even trying.

There is a fundamental difference between a dream and a lucid dream. I don't just mean that in the latter you are actually aware that you are dreaming, but there is also a physiological difference. Most people know that during dream period we all experience REM. This stands for "rapid eye movement", but it also means that the dreaming takes place in the shallowest part of your sleep. Likewise, few people realize that the dream part of the sleep, in essence, finds itself about halfway between deep sleep and the waken state. It is, so to speak, a no-man's land, where strange things can happen, including manifestations of various stages of hypnosis.

Another characteristic of a lucid dream is the richness of its detail. The shapes are sharper, the colours—richer, the sounds—more precise. If you touch a texture, you can virtually tell what it is that you are touching. It's a different reality. And finally, your recall of a lucid dream is vastly superior to remembering an ordinary dream. Assuming that any dream can be counted as ordinary.

I became aware of having a lucid dream when I realized that I am floating some inches above my seat. I asked myself if I am dreaming. The very question confers the state of lucidity on the dreamer. Once I realized my state, I took steps to deepen it, and then proceeded to exploit the situation.

My mother's smile was gone, but so was my anguish and my sense of guilt. Perhaps one can't feel guilty in a lucid dream?

I walked-floated to the cockpit. My legs moved, but I didn't have the sensation of touching the cabin floor.

Crossing the security doors created no problem. I merely closed my eyes, and the next instant I was on the other side. Tight as the cockpit was, I made it accommodate an extra armchair, which gave me a commanding view of the clouds below me. The view was breathtaking. Neither the captain nor the co-pilot seemed to be aware of my presence. If they were, they didn't say anything.

That is another characteristic of lucid dreams. You can see them, and they don't necessarily see you. Quite an advantage.

For a while I amused myself by spinning the various dials left and right, then by adding flexibility to the wings of the Boeing 747, and flapping them up and down. Amusing though it was, it neither affected the velocity of the airplane, nor its stability. Nor has it been detected by any of the flight officers. I wondered if they were sleeping on the job. They ignored not only me, but also all my antics.

"If you don't want to play then I'm going," I said, the same instant finding myself in the first class compartment, reposing happily in my seat.

Ambrosia's arm just slid from my chest and landed perilously close to the spot where rapid descent even of such a light, feminine arm, might have proven painful. By some miracle I came awake just in time to move my legs together and catch the descending forearm. It seemed that in lucid dreams we were protected by some powers of which, heretofore, I remained ignorant.

Nevertheless, I made a mental note not to attempt to induce lucid dreams in circumstances that might prove hazardous to the protection of my family jewels.

And then it hit me. Again. No. Not her hand. It hit me that in all the rush and hustle of our departure, I not only haven't notified my parents, but I didn't invite them, either. I didn't invite them to my own wedding.

It was too late now.

"I must call them the moment we get to Milos," I said

through clenched teeth.

Throughout all this, Ambrosia slept like a newborn baby. She almost looked like one. All pink, creamy complexioned, if slightly darker than most babies I've seen, but just as innocent. I could sit for hours, just looking at her. There was no lovelier sight in the world, certainly not at thirty-three thousand feet. I wondered what she would look like in a lucid dream. I've already seen her in ordinary ones, and believe me she wasn't ordinary. In any reality.

And then a strange thought stuck me. I've never seen Ambrosia when angry. I saw her concerned, slightly hysterical when thinking about her father killing us both, but not angry. Could angels be angry? If for some reason that question refused to become clear, I was determined not to let it happen. Something told me that it wouldn't be a pretty sight. It's just that I had no idea why. Why I thought so.

The next time I closed my eyes, it was with full commitment to dream a most normal, ordinary, everyday type of dream. I have no idea if I'd succeeded or not.

**

Chapter 13
Milos

We **landed in Athens** and were soon whisked off by a local airline to our destination. Ambrosia told me, proudly, that the new Milos airport was one of her father's pet projects. The airport and the new harbour. The new airport received us with grace and blue skies.

Milos, like its neighbours, is mainly a volcanic island. Volcanism on Milos began in upper Pliocene and continued until late Pleistocene era. Today, the island is a lot more peaceful. In fact, its serenity is almost palpable. The last volcanic eruptions on Milos is said to have taken place around 90,000 B.C., and even that was hard to believe. The calm permeating the air felt eternal.

Both her parents were waiting for us on the tarmac.

I veered to one side and pulled out my cell phone. Breathing hard, I dialed my parents' number. I counted the rings. After five, my father's voice advised me of their absence. "… if you leave your message…"

I was desperate. What else could I do?

"Dad? This is me. Simon." I hoped to make some kind of sense. "I'm getting married. Her name is Ambrosia. We eloped. We'll call when we get back! Love you Dad, Mom!" And I cut the connection. It was only a partial lie. We did elope from Canada. I felt better, now, but not much.

I turned to face Mr. Milos who was staring at me, questions in his eyes. At the same moment I remembered that

I forgot all about my sister. Later, I promised myself. Why am I such a scatterbrain? Momentarily I wondered if all men about to get married are like that?

Mr. Milos, a man quite tall, fairly thick set, reminiscent of Marlon Brando in the actor's better days. His white hair combed straight back, added to the impression of a commanding figure that does not tolerate refusals easily. He stuck me as a man who expects others to obey him. After all, he was the mayor, presumably used to giving orders. Perhaps his posture and expression went with the territory.

By contrast, his wife, Mrs. Milos, couldn't be more different. Small, practically diminutive, beautiful, not a single gray hair on her head, could easily be Ambrosia's elder sister. Even her open, inviting smile was an exact copy of her daughter's. Of course, it was the other way round. Ambrosia was a faithful copy of her mother.

I bowed deeply, probably a little too deep, but better low than sorry, I thought. To my surprise I have been embraced by Mr. and Mrs. Milos in turn, and hugged to within an inch of my life. This impromptu wrestling match was followed by an avalanche of kisses, more hugs, then more kisses.

"Look, mother, our new son," Mr. Milos said proudly.

His English was flawless, if accented as if he'd learned it in the UK. I found the echoes of my homeland rather nice. Then Mr. Milos followed his declaration with another squeeze. He must have been a wrestler in his younger days. Greco-Roman?

Ambrosia, who went through the greeting ceremony first, now stood a few steps away, obviously enjoying the spectacle unfolding before her eyes. It must have seemed to her that I have passed some sort of exam. In a way I have. So far they'd only heard about me from their only daughter, who obviously must have painted me with heavy pink strokes of her amorous brush. Now, they both saw me, examined me from all sides, squeezed me, then squeezed me again, and finally saw the way I looked at Ambrosia. That last did it, I think.

Evidently, I'd passed the entrance exam.

The car was small but fitted us all in very nicely. You really didn't want a large car for the island roads. You want one that will turn on a penny and stop on a dime. The Fiat was all of that. Father and I sat in front, the ladies in the back, with hand baggage on Ambrosia's lap. As I said, it was a small car. In spite of its inconspicuous appearance, the car sported the Greek and the Municipal flags, one on each front bumper. I felt very VIP. I have never been driven, anywhere, by the mayor in his official limousine. No matter what size.

Within minutes we were home. At the touch of an electronic button, the large wrought-iron gate opened silently, inviting us inside a beautiful driveway. We stopped at the steps leading to the front door. This was a glorious entry.

"Time for your hotel later, now we must eat, yes?"

We all nodded. The moment we stepped inside the villa, there followed another series of hugs, squeezes, and kisses. Ambrosia took it in her stride. I hailed from England. We call each other Mister plus surname for the first year, by the first name the next, until we mature to a serious relationship and revert to surnames, but, by then, without the Mister designation.

Here I was Simon before we left the airport. I tried Mr. and Mrs. Milos but have been quickly corrected. Just before we landed, Ambrosia tutored me about the manner of addressing her father. We went through babaás, pateras, pappas, papa and baba. Evidently, in Greece, they have a multitude of fathers. In Canada, and even more so in the US, they are often hard put to find even one. There are TV programs devoted exclusively to finding fathers for a multitude of children. No matter. We were in Greece.

Within minutes of arrival Mr. Milos became Papa, and Mrs. Milos, after a short stint as Mother, settled gracefully to being addressed as Mama.

"Life is too short," Mrs. Milos, ah, Mother, ah, Mama said. "Why waste time on formality?"

Her accent was only a little stronger than Papa's, but it had a Mediterranean lilt to it. She was also a very beautiful woman. Papa Milos has done well for himself. And now it was my turn.

The table had already been laid out. We landed at noon, so by that time we were just about ripe for a light lunch. Only, I soon learned, you didn't ever have anything light in Greece. Every meal is an occasion, practically a celebration.

Luckily for us, at this first get-together—only Ambrosia's parents and two cousins, who happened to be staying with them at the time—were present. The cousins, both men, took a week off from the heat of Athens to enjoy the breath of the sea. They seemed to be giving me warning looks, evidently placing themselves in the role of protectors of Ambrosia's innocence. Poor guys! If only they knew? If anything, it was me they should have been protecting, but even for that it was too late. Weren't I lucky?

The 'light' meal finished about 3 p.m.

I have been asked if we'd like to take our first dip in the sea, an activity which the islanders do daily, if not more than once. I was given strange looks when I dallied about my swimming costume. Finally, Ambrosia was given keys to the Fiat, and we were told not to be late for supper. We drove to our hotel, less then ten minutes away. Ambrosia already knew the place. Her various cousins had been put up there over the years, when visiting Milos. Milos Island, and Milos household.

I was amazed to find two adjoining rooms with interconnecting doors at our disposal. Apparently, Papa Milos was not as murderously inclined as Ambrosia had implied. After all, his daughter was 26, and a Ph.D., and a hell of a lot of other things, about which her father would never find out. And Papa Milos was not only a mayor but also a very wise man.

Within fifteen minutes we have changed into our swimming gear, and Ambrosia drove me to her favourite beach, less then fifteen minutes out of town.

Unbeknownst to me, topless swimming and sunbathing is practiced on virtually all Greek beaches, with some restrictions only on beaches within the boundaries of small towns. In Greece, including on the islands, secluded beaches are not hard to find.

On Ambrosia's beach there were five or six other couples, women topless. I was grateful for little mercies. I said little, as I have been warned that nude beaches were quite popular here.

"Only in designated areas," Ambrosia explained. "We can go there tomorrow," she added, with a dirty wink. "Today you have to be satisfied with the top half only."

I should add that both Ambrosia's top halves were perfect. Later she saw me looking at a couple some distance away. Yes, a couple, they were both women.

Ambrosia sighed deeply, then proceeded to explain the problem.

"In the murky past," she said, "French ladies, and I can only speculate some Greek ones also, who wished to preserve the curvature of their secondary sexual characteristics, hired professional nurses for their children to suckle. That must have helped," she nodded to herself knowingly.

"But the laws of gravity continue to assault their, ah, curvature?"

"Well, with time a woman's breasts gets fuller," Ambrosia defended her own species. Her own sex.

I looked around.

"Both of them," I commented. "It seems to me, darling, that with age women's secondary sexual characteristics don't get fuller but, well, longer."

I was lucky that Ambrosia had years of safety on her side. The way she looked now, she'd be likely to defy the laws of gravity forever.

The water was fantastic. No, it was glorious. No wonder the Greek gods adored this island. Looking at the sea bottom, some twenty feet down, I could see every pebble, practically every grain of sand. We swam, we luxuriated, we inhaled the nectar of the gods.

Surely, the air qualified as such.

A little farther north the sea carved from rock formations shapes that stirred my imagination. Was that why ancient Greeks produced such incredible sculptures? Nature was on their side. Nature and the gods. Which made me wonder just how the gods became immortal. I began to suspect that before I leave this miniscule heaven, I'd find out.

"This indeed is the home of the gods, darling," I whispered, licking the salt from her arm.

She didn't say anything but pressed her almost naked body to mine. It's been a while. Not since Montreal, two nights ago. I looked around.

"This way," she said.

Some forty or fifty paces away she pointed to an indentation in the rock. It was hardly visible from the rest of the beach. We had to climb some six or seven feet up to get to it. By some miracle it was made smooth by the water or wind. Or it could have been made smooth by the backs of mermaids who rested here, waiting for their mates. Their mermen?

For a moment I wondered if this was a designated area. The next moment, I didn't care. My mermaid was waiting. A gentleman doesn't make a lady wait.

I decided to be a gentleman.

Later we swam again, this time with slow, rhythmic strokes, that took us way out into the sea. Ambrosia was an excellent swimmer, much better than I; as I suspected all the Greeks must have been. We, British, are sons of the isles, too, but unfortunately our islands are surrounded by water that is only inviting during about three months of a year. The rest of the time it is positively freezing.

Some time later, Ambrosia drove us back to the hotel. We showered, changed, and drove back to the Milos residence. After the drinks, we sat down to our first family dinner. There were toasts, stories, and a brief description of tomorrow's wedding.

"Since you've obviously enjoyed your first day on the beach, we have a little surprise for you." Mrs. Milos, Mama, said with a whimsical smile.

No matter how we prodded, she refused to give up her secret. "It wouldn't be a surprise anymore, would it," she insisted.

It is hard to argue with Greek logic. It dates back to the stoics who had been seldom upset by prodding, or any other forms of persuasion. Nevertheless, it was a thoroughly pleasant dinner, with the two cousins providing a diversion by attempting to utter some words in English. I was amazed how many people spoke English on the Greek Islands.

"Many, many more do it in bigland," one of the cousins assured me. "Even on percentage."

I believe him. On mainland, business had its demands, here, I suspected, tourism.

We broke off early. Ambrosia and I were both tired from the flight, and the expectation of tomorrow also took its toll on our emotions. Although neither of us have ever been married before, we were both old enough to be well aware that even these days, when divorces were almost as common as wedding ceremonies, marriage was a big step that is much easier to take going forward. When all was said and done, we only knew each other a very, very short time. Neither of us could explain why we found each other so compatible.

At the same time, even at this early stage, I simply

couldn't imagine life without Ambrosia. We seemed to share something elusive, that only time would help us define, to put it into words. For now we seemed satisfied with a touch of a hand, a kiss, or just being together. Love is as intangible as any emotions, but it is equally as demanding. I seemed to regard the whole world, at least partially, through her eyes. And I would not have it any other way.

* * *

Chapter 14
The Wedding

If **you've never attended** a Greek wedding... keep it that way. What I mean is, well, don't!

It's not easy.

First, our wedding was supposed to be small. Family *only* affair. In that respect the Milos were truthful. It just so happened though that, by my reckoning, the whole island, with the ancillary islands thrown in for good measure, was related to the Milos. I mean it. The whole something-something island. Give or take a few hundred.

We have been picked up at the appointed hour by a limousine decorated in most festive way, and deposited on the beach.

Ahhh, a quick swim, just what I need...

Ah, ah, no such luck.

It never crossed my mind that they may have chosen the beach to save on tableware. After all, it would be hard to smash plates by throwing them into the sand. Nevertheless, a bunch of people must have worked day and probably half the night to build a raised altar, seating arrangements, and all sorts of ancillary bits and pieces required for a proper Greek wedding. I think Ambrosia and I fitted somewhere there, though frankly, to this day I'm not sure where.

Then came the ceremony. Correction, ceremonies. Lots of them. And I don't mean eating, dancing and all the subsequent joyful activities. I mean the official part.

First there was the exchange of rings. Luckily, someone thought of getting them. I, well, I just forgot. I felt I was already married, and Ambrosia gave me an impression that she felt the same way.

"It's all for Mama and Papa," she whispered to me, her face registering self-control only just winning, marginally, over an attack of hysteria.

Then the priest blessed the rings. Then us. We then placed the rings on Ambrosia's and mine the third finger of her and my right hand. Then, the Koumbaro—our religious sponsor whom I've met about ten minutes earlier— exchanged the rings three times on our fingers. Really, three times! This was intended to symbolize the strength of the married couple. That's us, only officially, we weren't married yet.

Confused? Me too.

"It won't be long now," I heard a whisper in my ear. She was lying. It only just began.

Apparently the Sacrament of Marriage consists of many, many parts—all as important. After the priest concluded his prayers, he tied our hands together, and kept us so restrained for the duration of the ceremony. It was either to signify the union of the couple, or to make sure that we couldn't escape before it was all over. Speaking for myself, I was ready to run.

Finished?

Ha, ha! If you don't like the ceremony, you shouldn't have let me begin.

"Love you," came another whisper.

Then we got crowned. Then they read excerpts from the Epistle and the Gospel. I didn't understand a single word.

"It was from the marriage of Cana at Galilee, which was blessed by Christ," Ambrosia informed me.

"Where he later performed his first miracle of converting water into wine," I completed the lecture. "Got any water?" I tried to help out.

Success! We were given a sip of the wine as a remembrance. I thought we deserved a lot more than a sip.

The priest then led Ambrosia and me three times around the table. I lost the meaning of this particular liturgy. I'm sure it was as profound as everything else.

Following the Walk, the priest blessed us. Again? I thought he'd already done that. No matter, you can't have too much of a good thing. Then the priest removed crowns from our heads, and said something about a long and happy life together. I was ready to drink to that, but nobody offered me any wine. My throat was parched. Probably nerves.

Can you blame me? The Greeks surrounded me on all sides, from the rocks on the landside down to the waves lapping the shore. There was nowhere to run. Nowhere!

At long last the priest untied our joined hands, which I thought was the right moment to make my escape. The padre stopped us.

"He's reminding us that only God can separate us from one another, so watch it!" Ambrosia also said that she was just translating the priest's words. Her tone said otherwise.

"I've had it!" I said.

"So do I," she affirmed.

Which was just as well. Apparently Ambrosia and I were now officially married.

And then, yes, and then came... and it went on and on...and on... I'm not quite sure what came next, but it did go on and on and on...

Mr. & Mrs. Simon Jones have been toasted one hundred twenty-seven times. Or, at least, so I've been told the very next morning. About noon. I still had a headache.

I would be more than happy to share with you the festivities that followed the religious ceremonies. Regrettably, by the time I woke up, I didn't remember much of the previous night. But I have been told that I had been one of the best dancers that ever came from outside the island. Ambrosia, for some reason refused to talk about it. To this day, I have no idea why.

There was one other thing that will, at least to me, remain a minor mystery. I also have been told that there had been a number of speeches delivered by various members of my, as of now, very extensive family.

But that wasn't the point.

The point was that—and this I know from a number of people—that mine had been not only the best, but the longest. I received, so they swore, the biggest applause.

Apparently I talked a great deal about my parents who couldn't come for a number of reasons I made up on the spot. It's amazing how inspiring the Greek wine is. You can make up almost any stories right there and then.

Now this wouldn't really be a mystery, if it weren't for one little detail. I don't speak Greek. And the Greeks, with a few notable exceptions, didn't speak English. Or maybe some did?

Must have, I suppose.

It must have been like deaf people applauding a concert pianist. A mystery?

The following afternoon we joined Mama and Papa in their villa for a late lunch. I have been welcomed as their favourite son. Piled on one side of the living room was a stack of presents from people I've never seen, probably never met, though I cannot be held responsible for who or what I may have met or witnessed yesterday. I suppose I'll have to write a lot of thank-you notes. In Greek?

Poor Ambrosia, she'll be busy for a year.

Mr. & Mrs. Milos' home was about five times larger than my apartment in Montreal. Not that it was ostentatious, but the hosts were ready to receive any number of relations, who, probably for financial reasons, have been compelled to move to mainland. Nevertheless, no matter how long they stayed away, Milos was their home. And if their actual home was no longer there, well, there was always Mr. & Mrs.

Milos who, as the name indicates, were synonymous with the Greek Island.

If Greeks had their way all houses would be all white. Actually, most of them are. Maintenance was no problem, as with the absence of industry and a steady breeze from the sea, there was no pollution to speak of.

They, (the houses—not the Greeks) were white from inside and out. The barrel arches, which often served as ceilings, gave wonderful diffused, indirect light that made you think you were outside. Strategically placed vases overflowing with bougainvilleas exploded against the enticing white background. There were lots of vases. There were lots of flamboyant, red explosions. It was all very breathtaking.

It was all quite amazing. It was Ambrosia's home!

"How could you ever leave this place," I asked her.

Momentarily my memories retreated to good-old England, bathed in fog, smog, and for the most part of the year, in drizzle, which often changed to rain. Sun was something we were given to enjoy only on special occasions. Rare occasions.

"How could you ever leave this place," I repeated.

I got a gentle shrug, an enigmatic smile, but no answer.

We ate sparingly. After the feast yesterday, we all needed a little rest. Even gastronomical rest. It seemed that in spite of my oratorical talents yesterday, my hosts, my parents-in-law, wanted to know a great deal more about me, about my parents, about the way we lived in Montreal, before that in England.

It was a typical get to know you get-together. Not even for the nearest family. Just for the four of us.

"We shared you both yesterday. Today you are both all ours?" Mama Milos announced the moment we arrived.

We talked the whole afternoon, and into the early evening. This was exactly what Ambrosia and I needed. To start feeling like part of the family. Nothing was too small, too insignificant to share. We talked, and we sipped wine, gently, and we nibbled on Greek *petit fours*, nuts and other *amuse-gueules*, between stories from both sides. I've learned that Ambrosia had a brother, who'd lost his life waterskiing. A motorboat had run into him.

"The man was drunk," Ambrosia told me. "For two years my father didn't touch a drop of wine," she added, giving Papa a loving look.

And then Papa came up with a corker.

"How would you like, Simon my son, to move to Milos?" he asked.

I looked at Ambrosia, not knowing how to handle this question. Mr. Milos looked and sounded perfectly sober. She was about to say something when Papa waved her down.

"Look, Simon. I don't mean today or tomorrow. But we have this house, this place that was in the family for a few generations. Ah, yes, a few generations..." his eyes wandered over the whitewashed contours, then, seemingly, over the rest of the island. "And you see, you and Ambrosia are our only children. When we go, this will be all yours. If you like it, that is."

Ambrosia got up and embraced her father. I stood in line to follow suit, but Mama Milos took me in her arms, instead.

"We saw the way Ambrosia is looking at you. We already love you, just for that," she said, wiping a tear forming at the corner of her eye.

That got me all soft. The next few minutes we were all embracing each other, kissing, and wiping off tears of emotion. Never in my life have I felt so accepted, almost wanted, as during the latter part of that afternoon. I knew they meant every word. I also knew that I'd do whatever Ambrosia wanted. At any time. Now or in the future.

But most of all I realized that my own future has opened wide, new horizons. As wide and as blue as the Aegean Sea. And I liked it. I liked it a lot.

Of course, by then I was tipsy, again.

Back in the hotel, I found it hard to accept that only yesterday morning I was, at least officially, a bachelor, who, on a spur of a moment, flew over the Atlantic, on a whim to get married. In my late teens and early twenties, I'd hung out, as we used to call it, with my own age group. We'd go to pubs, sometimes movies—we called them cinemas— sometimes we'd raid local dancehalls; yes, there had been such places—always in search of "chicks". Gradually the group would come of age, mature, most would get jobs, get married, and develop their own lives, apart from the original group. Some contacts would continue to linger for some time, but with less intensity and certainly with less emotional commitment.

My friends have grown up.

And then, one day, I found myself completely alone. For some reason I remained single, detached, without any lasting friendship. Couples invited couples to dinner, parties; single men or women were no longer in great demand. I've learned to be self-sufficient, independent. I've learned to like it, to find satisfaction in my work, my interests, which I no longer needed to share with others. I've learned to enjoy my self-imposed freedom.

And then happened… Ambrosia.

She literally happened. She was minding her own business, as had been I, and then I was lying at her feet, embarrassed, desperately trying to extricate myself from the folds of her skirt. Yes, she was that rare bird that still wore loose skirts below her knee.

My life was never the same since.

I now had a wife, a brand new pair of most definitely loving parents, and the prospect of being welcome here, on Milos, in this heaven of Earth, whenever my heart or soul would so dictate.

I saw Ambrosia stealing glances at me, her eyes proud, as if I'd accomplished something beyond the reach of mere mortals. After studying me for some time, at last she came close, pressed herself against me and stayed that way for a little while. Then she looked up.

"Thank you," she said.

"You thank me?" I was dumbfounded.

"You made both my parents very happy," she explained.

"How about you, my pet?"

"Come and I'll show you, my husband."

And she did. Until the early hours. There were brief moments when I was hoping that her mother was not looking over us in her 'other' body. You never know with mothers.

Less so with mothers-in-law.

***

Chapter 15
Mitera

Having my head already full of countless myths, I was keen to learn about Ambrosia's mother's reputed ability to project her inner self outside of her physical body. We haven't yet established what that inner self is, but I hoped that a chat with Mitera would clarify this question.

Mitera already became Mama, pronounced Ma-mah, with accent on the second syllable. Except when referred to in third person. Mitera, or Mother, did this or that, but Mama when addressing her directly. With Mama and Papa around, I felt integrated into Ambrosia's family. And family meant, I found, three cousins, two uncles, an aunt (others were on the mainland), and an ancient grandma we briefly visited (just to pay our respects) on the first day of our arrival. She was no longer ambulatory but made up for it with a wicked sense of humor, which made everyone laugh hysterically, and I couldn't understand a single word. That was the "immediate" family. The rest were "distant" cousins, who qualified by living, of having sometimes lived, on Milos.

Later that day, I managed to get Mama alone. I brought up the subject of Out of Body Experience. The Phase. Capital P to match the OBE. At first she was reticent to talk about it. Apparently very few people took her seriously, and she was tired of being ridiculed.

"You know what happened to Shirley MacLaine," she said, looking slightly embarrassed.

I had no idea what happened to Shirley MacLane, but then Ambrosia joined us and Mama relaxed. I learned later that the famed actress was well into spirituality and the attendant experiences.

"I still remember the first time it happened," Mama began, slowly. "It was by accident. I was standing at the side of my bed, looking at my own body, which was seemingly asleep. I was actually afraid to touch it, in case I, or it, was dead. A thoroughly unpleasant experience."

We both waited.

"Well, I did touch it. It was warm and pliable. It felt like the body of a person that's alive. For some strange reason I found comfort in that. The moment I became happy, I found myself back in my body. My physical body, I mean. I felt almost as though I've passed an exam of some sort. A week later I knew what it was. I was out of my body, again, only this time I wasn't afraid."

"And now," I asked, not quite knowing what I was supposed to say.

"Now I know that an out of body experience is a perfectly natural condition of being, accessible to anyone who wants to go to the trouble of learning it."

I waited a moment and then asked, "I don't want to be impolite, Mama, but, well, why would anyone want to, you know… why would one want to be outside of one's body."

She looked at me with a mixture of compassion and disbelief.

"It is like asking the Prisoner of Zenda if he'd rather be outside of his prison."

I looked at Mama with, what must have been an expression of disbelief. "Zenda…?"

"Count of Monte Cristo. Anyone who's been imprisoned for a very, very long time." When I still must have given an impression of a dumb dodo, she added: "The freedom you experience out of your physical body cannot be described in words. It wouldn't make sense."

This time Ambrosia came to her mother's rescue. She joined us quietly, and until now just listened.

"Mama told me that in OBE you are outside the confines

of time and space, and that you could even manipulate the shape or colour or density of objects around you."

"In a way, the reality is malleable," Mrs. Milos confirmed. "It is as though it were in the process of creation. Of being created. Something like that."

I didn't ask any more questions. For now, if Mama was to be believed, I had plenty to chew on. Among other things, I wondered if there was any parallel between, what they called OBE, an Out of Body Experience, and a deep state of hypnosis. But at that particular time, I was in great need of talking about the weather or any other innocuous subject. Better still, I asked Ambrosia if she felt like a quick dip in the sea. Mama Milos smiled her understanding.

"The subject had the same effect on me, some years ago. Enjoy yourself children. That's essentially what life is for."

Evidently, Mama was a Hedonist. Like most Greeks. Like I became from the moment I met Ambrosia.

We came back to the subject only after we got back to our hotel. That night, and for the next three nights, we tried to enter into the spirit of out of body projection. In spite of our best intentions, we got absolutely nowhere. In the OBE department, that is. The problem was that when we were both reclining on our bed, we were both thinking of other bodies then those, reputedly, encountered on an astral journey.

"Do you think one can make love out there?" Ambrosia was the first to ask.

"Will you ask your mother?"

"Would you ask yours?"

"Don't be silly. My mother is a virgin."

"And which star announced your arrival?"

"You don't need a star. You just need an ignorant, slightly retarded, emotionally underdeveloped son."

"So that's why you're continuously trying to catch up with your education."

"Meeeee?"

Our OBE exercises didn't work that night. We've decided that in order to succeed, at least one of us has to take it seriously. That, and we'd have to ask Ambrosia's mother how to go about it. After three days of unsuccessful attempts, we decided to seek Mama's help.

"Mother," Ambrosia began without any preambles, "Simon and I need your help." When she addresses Mama as Mother that meant business.

She then proceeded to explain that she, Mama, had made the experience of out of body projection sound so exciting, that we were both determined to try it.

Mother looked at us for what seemed like a long time. At last she addressed us both.

"Do you both believe that it can be done?"

I looked at Ambrosia—she looked at me.

"I'm a scientist, Mama. I need some proof to put all my money on it. Some proof…"

Even as she talked, Mrs. Milos sank deeper into her armchair, closed her eyes, and appeared to fall asleep. Moments later her eyes opened.

"For the last three nights you attempted to project, and ended up making love. If you don't take the matter seriously, you'll never succeed."

I opened my mouth, wide, and closed it even faster. Ambrosia seemed busy looking away and trying to scratch her neck at the same time. Silence stretched. After a good minute, Mrs. Milos said one word.

"Well?"

"How did you know, Mother?"

"I was there, dear. No, I wasn't peeking last night or any other night. I was there just now."

"Peeking?"

"Looking without permission."

"Peeking, Mother. You weren't peeking?" Ambrosia corrected. "I suppose that's your, ah, proof?"

Ambrosia was still hesitant, but she recovered from her momentary embarrassment.

"Would you prefer me to give you details?"

"No, Mama, no. NO. Please… I was just asking…?"

"Then ask away, but don't be a doubting Thomas. And remember, in the Phase, I can see you as you are. But I can also change you. Hence the need for free will."

Both, Ambrosia and I needed a little while to collect our thoughts. That last sentence of her threw a spanner into my idea of what OBE might be like. Wasn't free will a gift the gods granted to their creation? It was obvious that by some means or another, Mrs. Milos knew what was happening in our bedroom. She almost implied that she could have changed it, changed our behaviour, but she respected our privacy. That didn't quite meld. Of course, it has been only a few days since our wedding. We could hardly be expected to be doing something else. On the other hand, she did guess right that we began, each night, with unsuccessful attempts to project our consciousness outside our bodies. Could she have guessed that also? We could have been practicing my exercises in self-hypnosis, which we did some days ago, before attempting the OBE. We didn't.

Guesswork or not, neither Ambrosia nor I doubted Mama sufficiently to ask her for more proof.

Or… details.

Mrs. Milos gathered from our expressions that we were both contrite and interested. She made herself comfortable, but sat straight, as if in an attentive position. It was evident from her posture alone, that she took the subject seriously. Perhaps more so than we ever imagined.

"First, my children, you must believe me when I say that there is nothing unnatural about out of body projection. It has been practiced for as long as humanity walked his earth. The various prophets, saviours, mystics, probably saints, they all practiced it under different names, under different guises. So, believe me, the only thing that keeps you from succeeding is ignorance. That and lack of technique and... faith."

We neither dared nor wished to interrupt. Her voice was quiet, perfectly relaxed, without any apparent wish to convince us of anything. She was merely sharing her knowledge. With her children.

"There is only one thing you must learn," she resumed with a slight smile. "The condition necessary to leave physical consciousness is neither sleep, nor waken state. It is exactly in the middle. You must achieve, what is called, a free-floating state. A state of mind from which you can move into any direction you wish. Up or down. To a waken state or to sleep. It is only, however, if you maintain the in-between state that you will achieve liberation."

Mama continued talking, while Ambrosia and I, gradually, became more and more relaxed. She talked of images behind closed eyes, about listening to the sounds inside our heads, about phantom movement of our limbs. After a while, her voice seems to have been coming from a small distance, yet a distance not defined by space alone.

Then I felt vibrations. It was like a gentle electric current passing through my body. A very strange, and not an unpleasant feeling.

I don't know what happened next. I do know, that for a little while I was not there, not with my wife and mother-in-law, but I was enwrapped in darkness that changed to gray mist. I moved my hand to ward off any danger, and in that moment I saw my hand in front of my face. The next moment I was sitting opposite Mama, with Ambrosia giving me strange looks. For a second I remembered my experience in the airplane. Were all these things manifestations of the same thing?

Mama was looking at me with a lopsided smile. "I don't know what happened, Simon, but I think that you'd be a natural. Did you ever practice self-hypnosis?"

I told her the story of my heel, and of Ambrosia's help in

removing the condition imbedded in my subconscious. She listened attentively. Then nodded her understanding.

"I don't have to tell you anything more. The techniques, as such, you'll find on the Internet. There are, literally, hundreds of them. Don't expect great experiences to be yours without commitment and practice. But if you can learn self-hypnotism on your own, then you'll find learning to enter the Phase much easier."

"The Phase?"

"The Phase," she made it sound like a proper name. "Astral travel, astral projection, out of body experience, OBE, and a dozen other names. I prefer 'the Phase' because it removes esoteric connotations. It makes it something we can study, not just believe in."

"I like that," Ambrosia approved.

Mama rose to her feet.

"I have to go and see Papa. Just remember, that reality is yours to conquer. Astral projection, soul travel, the Phase, out of body experience, they are all one and the same. They are the gift that gods left for us to enjoy."

With that she embraced Ambrosia, then me, and then left us to consider her words. We had a great deal to consider. Mrs. Milos was a very wise woman.

It was less than a ten-minute walk back to our hotel. Yet, by the time we got there, my left arm carried blue reminders where Ambrosia's fingers dug in with all her might. She seemed quite unaware of having done so.

"What is the matter, darling," I asked, when we finally got there.

She looked at me with a mixture of disdain and apprehension.

"I don't want to go there," she almost whimpered. "Not without you," she added, reaching once more for my arm.

This wasn't like her. "Where?" I asked.

"There," she said, making it all very clear. I looked down at her questioningly. "Where Mama said we should go. That place is empty," she added. "Quite empty."

I didn't know Ambrosia had previous experience with OBE. Apparently she realized that she had, without recognizing it for what it was. Actually, only then it dawned on me that Ambrosia was referring to the Phase. Indeed, from what Mama had said, the reality into which we might be able to find our way, was not, it seemed, fully developed. We'd enter into a no man's land, and it would be up to us to create the world we wished to have. Again, it seemed, that Mama was right. The gods have left us a gift. What she forgot to mention was that gods looked after their own. They left their gift for other gods to follow in their footsteps. There may be echoes, there, of previous inhabitants, but that was all. The reality had to be built anew, almost from scratch. Like God did, in the Garden of Eden.

Or… I could be completely wrong!

On our return, I clicked on the Internet. I wrote "out of body experience" in the Google space. The next moment I fell back against the back of my chair. Within 0.12 seconds there appeared 24,500,000 million results. Mama was right. Again. This was going to be a long journey.

That night we didn't make love for a long, long time. Not until we tried again and again to follow Mama's scant instructions. At long last we gave up, again, without success.

"There are different ways to get to heaven," I said at last. Ambrosia agreed.

I suppose we have to thank gods for that also. We both did.

***

Chapter 16
Echoes

"**T**here were wars, and echoes of wars,"** I mused aloud, while Ambrosia was trying to read.

The world was falling apart. It all started, in earnest, a good while ago. Year after year I heard of one or the other banana republic losing its president, or some other honcho with an inflated ego and a few pounds of glittering crosses and medals adorning his meager chest, was strung up, or shot, by people searching for freedom. Just a few months later, the great liberator declared himself generalissimo, and clamped down on his comrades just a hard as his predecessor. This went on for a few years.

It's quite easy being judgmental when stretched out under an umbrella, listening to gentle waves lapping the pristine sandy beaches.

"There were wars, and echoes of wars," I repeated aloud.

"Yes, dear," she nodded, without looking up from her book. She obviously found it more interesting than my mental acrobatics.

Then came the Arabs. While during the last fifteen years virtually all dictatorships seemed to have been dissolved by people at large, the citizenry—variously called the ordinary or common people, rabble, rebels, and a number of less flattering names used by those deposed of power—gained that elusive virtue called freedom. The ordinary people, however, who have gained the power, had absolutely no idea how to use it.

When you hold the stick, ignorance is not bliss.

That was precisely why the previous potentiates had lost control. That ignorance, and the well-known fact that power corrupts. Always.

This was true of not just the civil authorities. About ten years after the churches lost their tax-exemption status, the tithing went by the wayside. The churches could still register as non-profit organizations, but, alas, for a while at least, they all made substantial profits. At least, some of them did. Particularly those that managed to induce their congregations to congregate in front of TV sets. The easily fooled ones? At any rate, once tithing went out of style, the sacerdotal community lost weight. And not just financial. They lost clout in more ways than one.

They lost the authority.

The individual countries, states, provinces, boroughs and municipal politicians followed. Their pensions became aligned with the taxpayers' own. Soon they all began driving Fiats. Papa Milos just beat them to it.

The last to go were the CEOs' bonuses.

Specialty banks, which began with those dedicated to small loans, began in India. Within a few years the idea caught on first in Africa, and soon after, in the West. Europe and Canada led the way, the USA reluctantly brought up the rear. They had to. People refused to support multimillionaires with their meager holdings. The big international banks lost billions of dollars in capital. Since they were still lending at least $20 for each dollar they held in reserve, their profits tumbled astronomically. It meant that for every dollar they lost, they effectively lost $20 of business. No small matter when you're dealing with hundreds of billions.

Soon the small banks grew sufficiently to begin financing larger projects. That was the nail in the coffins of the big boys. The bonuses were gone.

And now we heard echoes and echoes of echoes.

Daily.

Sometimes there were rumours that affected us directly, interfering with the delivery of oil or bananas, or other valuable commodities or comestibles, which kept us fat and happy. Well, fat anyway. Obese. Most of us.

Yet here, on Milos, there were no signs of Greece being bailed out from international debt a few times. No one talked money here. No one talked much about work, either. Perhaps the tourists took care of that.

On the other hand the USA, although their dollar, after a few financial hiccups, fell well below its previous value, no one offered to bail out. They seemed to struggle under their staggering national debt. They said that it already exceeded $14 trillion and was continually mounting.

Wars and echoes of wars…?

Apart from the wars and other military actions, there were the veterans to take care of, the infrastructure was crumbling, the prisons were overflowing, the population was not only aging but living longer…

In England we had a saying, it never rains, it pours. Well, on the good old USA it did just that. Drastic measures were called for, but not many people were listening. It is much easier to get spoiled than to accept responsibility for one's actions. And the population was spoiled to the extreme. They assumed they all had a "right" to almost everything. Almost—without paying for it.

I'm sure, in time, they'd overcome it, they always did, but it would not be easy. I wondered if Ambrosia ever thought about such things. She seemed quite contented within her own, mysterious universe. I was hoping I'd fit in somewhere between her quarks and bosons. It atoms were mostly empty space then there ought to be room for me. Somewhere, there…

Yet, on Milos, those rumours, or echoes, did not strike

anyone's ears. Here people lived in a world apart, content
with what they had, hardly wishing for more. They appeared
to have reached a certain, inexplicable state of balance. A
stasis? Perhaps. A haven in the turbulent world all around
them.

But isn't life defined by change?

We, Ambrosia and I, had access to news, of course, but
the bulletins seemed to concern only the world outside. Here
the gods extended their aegis with generosity that reached
beyond the ordinary. The beauty of the islands was such that
it precluded people's ability to accept that the rest of the
world could be full of strife. Listening to the news was more
like watching another Hollywood movie about Armageddon,
that wasn't real, but it balanced the truth that was full of
beauty and delight.

"You must always maintain a state of balance," Papa
said. "It helps if you accept what we have as real, and the rest
of the world as imaginary."

Isn't this something like what Buddha had said? A state
of balance? The Middle Path?

Within a week of our arrival, Ambrosia and I shed the
remnants of the imaginary reality whence we came. The
climate, the temperature of the water, the wine, the fresh
breeze, the smiling people, the… the list went on.

"Why did you ever leave this place to come to Canada,"
I asked, stretching on a deckchair to adjust the umbrella.

Even on beaches farther from town there were
deckchairs, arranged in pairs under the accompanying
umbrellas, waiting to be occupied by people who always
seemed to have enough time. Sooner or later someone would
come and ask for a few Euros for the rental, and if not, they
would leave it until the next time. After all, on an island,
where could you go?

"I never imagined that the rest of the world could be
different," she replied. When I looked at her with disbelief,
she added, "Until I'd studied in Athens. It was like a halfway

house."

A halfway house between heaven and prison. Only her ship was pointing the wrong way. She must have seen that her answer didn't satisfy me. She looked away, as though doubting her own words.

"I really can't explain it, Simon... there was something that drew me to Montreal. Just there, to Montreal."

I waited for her to continue. The silence enveloping us with intimacy was shared only by a couple of birds balanced precariously on a crag pointing into the sea. I suspected that Ambrosia's actions continued to place demands on her confession. Or the other way round? I don't know why this was the right time to bring back the subject of her departure from Milos.

"I sometimes wonder if we really are propelled along our journey by free will, or by forces completely beyond our control," she continued to muse aloud. "I knew I had to go there, yes, even to the McGill. I just didn't know why..."

Only now she looked up and held my eyes.

"And then I saw you, and I knew why."

This time silence stretched for a little longer. Ambrosia put her book away and let her eyes follow a lone sail silhouetted against the distant horizon. "There were echoes and echoes of echoes," she said at last. Then she looked at me again.

"There were echoes of long distant past," she said very softly. "I can still feel them..."

I wondered what past she was referring to.

"I had the same feeling," she said, "when I was helping you to solve your ankle dilemma. I thought I had something to do with it."

"You're beginning to sound a bit like your mother," I commented quietly.

She smiled. "My mother is a very gifted woman. I lay no such claims. But I do wonder if what she says, about her soul travel, could really be true."

"You doubt it?"

"I don't doubt that she believes it, that she considers her experiences real, I only wonder if they are purely subjective."

That got me thinking. The same was true when I first heard about self-hypnosis. It seemed only for "other" people. Not something one would try oneself.

"Did you ever try it, yourself?"

"What, to have an out of body experience?" She smiled again, this time a little sadly. "I wouldn't know where to begin."

"Wouldn't your mother help you?"

"I don't know. I never asked her. Mother doesn't impose. It is fa…"

She stopped short, as though disturbed. I suspected that the rest of the word would spell out "father". That it was father's prerogative to impose.

I assumed that for a Ph.D. in physics such claims as her mother made were a lot harder to swallow than for a fellow who was teaching comparative religion. My life was so filled with various myths that, most of the time, I seemed to hover between them and physical reality.

Ambrosia leaned back and closed her eyes.

"Also, for the most part, she does make it sound very inviting," she said after a while.

"The ultimate escape?"

"She makes it sound more like a return to true reality, rather then escape from ours."

I could see that Ambrosia was still hovering between the quarks and quirks of her mother's philosophy. "Who knows," she said at last. Perhaps I'll try it someday."

It was obvious that she ignored our attempts to-date. I suspected that if she'd really put her heart in it, she'd succeed. Like with everything else. Then she turned her eyes towards me.

"But only if you come with me."

I didn't know one could book double tickets for those

trips. But I'd follow her to hell and back, if need be.

"What do you think?" I asked. "What do you think?"

We were growing ready to begin in earnest.

"Now remember what Mama has said," we both said almost simultaneously.

We didn't.

Neither of us was willing to treat Mama's words very seriously. Not yet. After all, weren't we on holidays? Whatever Mama said was probably true, but it required work, or at least a high degree of concentration. We were not in the mood.

We didn't come to Milos for sightseeing or tourist reasons. We came to get married. But after all, one cannot be in the Aegean Sea and not visit Santorini. A local ferry took us, bright and early, to Port Athinos, where we were unceremoniously packed into a tourist bus, which almost immediately took off on a hair-raising zigzagging, serpentine climb to the edge of the caldera. Eastwards, to our right extended flat fields, apparently devoted to the cultivation of Greek favourite nectar—wine. Brusko, Nichteri, Vissando, all acquired their strong, unique taste thanks to the volcanic soil and relative lack of water. We had occasion to taste some later.

Simultaneously, towards the West, our left, extended the caldera itself which, according to our guide:

"...erupted in 1650 BC with biggest fireworks in the last 10,000 years!"

Our guide, made his announcement in a heavily accented English. He sounded delighted at this cataclysmic eruption, which, obviously, was responsible for his livelihood.

"It was the same eruption that destroyed the Minoan civilization," he added proudly, as though he was personally responsible for the devastating effect.

The bus kept rolling. What the guide didn't mention were the stunning views we enjoyed, which displayed below us not only the flat waters of the caldera but three small islands, one of them Nea Kameni, the newly forming volcano which, in the fullness of time, would probably provide new fireworks to satisfy a new generation of tourist guides. It, the island, was growing already, though, as was the rest of evolution, at snail's pace. As I looked down at the peaceful atoll I wondered how many people had once clustered on the slopes of the original mountain, the volcano, before it erupted. Were they like the Incas, at the top of their empire? Or have they reached the nadir of their existence, and, like the Minoans, arrived at their fulfillment in their timely demise. The humans seldom realize how very fragile is our existence. We are covered by ashes, swept by Tsunamis, or discarded like yesterday's trash by whirling tornadoes. Who are we? Why do we cling to this inhospitable globe with such tenacity?

Or are we little more than envelopes worn by gods, who deny us even the awareness of their presence. And yet, simultaneously, my eyes feasted on indescribable beauty. Had it all been created just for us?

Or were we all but echoes of our long gone past.

By noon we arrived in Oia. I begun humming Oia-oia-oh, but was quickly silenced by my… wife. I think this was the first time that I actually thought of Ambrosia as my wife. After all, we lived together for some time, and then followed the wedding ceremony, which I managed to relegate to foggy memory, and now, she was shushing me. Like a wife should, I thought.

Oia was splendid.

Located on the top of the western tip of the island, it offered a view to die for. Oia, virtually a one-horse town, though I haven't seen any horses (there were a few donkeys strutting around) at all, claimed to sport 40 hotels, each precariously glued to the slopes of the caldera. Forty hotels seemed like a lot, but not if you consider that Oia is the Santorini's showpiece, and the whole island counts 175 hotels. It seemed to me, that the Greeks really liked tourists.

In Oia we took our lunch. We sat there, contemplating the new volcano slowly making its way, to the surface. We had Tzatsiki. It consisted of yogurt with finely chopped cucumber, garlic and olive oil. We topped it off with bread and fried potatoes. Lately we lost taste for meats, particularly red meats. It was also here that we tasted the local wines. An experience like no other.

On the way back, our ferry advanced to Fira. We arrived early, to look the town over. A beautiful place. Whitewashed facades perched on top of a volcanic island. The ever-present steps and cobbled alleyways led us from one shop to another, displaying jewelry made from lava.

From there we descended about 600 steps, down to the harbour, and boarded our little ship. Each time the steps zigzagged left or right, we'd stop to feast our eyes on the view that seemed to change at each landing. A few times we have been passed by donkeys, which descended to the port below, carrying passengers on their aching backs. The donkeys were not many, but the stench of their sweat permeated every step we descended. That wasn't all. Some parts of the road were smeared with piles of donkey dung.

Ambrosia refused to blame them, the passengers, not the donkeys, as she did actually climb all those steps, up and down, some years ago.

"And trust me, darling, nothing would induce me to do it again. It's utter agony."

On the way up there was the alternative of taking a *telepherique*, but modern conveniences do not offer old world charm. Not even a whiff of donkey dung.

We felt exhausted, elated, and still had the return trip to

enjoy. No wonder the Greeks were a happy people. So were we. We took a bottle of cool Nichteri with us. They were right. It was white, it was strong and it was very dry. With just a few olives and local bread, it kept us going all the way home.

∗∗∗

Chapter 17
The Lost Secret

Throughout their ancient history, Greeks had been obsessed with immortality. When they couldn't get it for themselves, they assigned it to their gods. They forgot that that which is immortal has neither beginning nor end. Thus, if you are to become immortal, it means that you already are. This led to the natural philosophical conclusion that that which is immortal is, somehow, trapped or contained within the envelope of that that wishes to experience that immortality.

Ambrosia, the nectar, came later. But it had come out of desire for immortality.

Later, the Christians began the same cycle with the soul. *"He who eats this bread will live forever."* They, the Christians, had a lot of problems with this soul business. Did animals have one? If so, were they also immortal? Was soul an integral part of God, or did God create souls and distribute them around for His own amusement. *Nephesh*, in Hebrew, means animal soul. The biblical scholars translated the word as soul, without assigning its characteristics.

To my knowledge those questions remain unanswered to this day.

A few thousand years ago, however, the Greeks did not have to face such problems. There had been no church, as yet, no infallible ecclesiastical authority, to tell them when, and/or how, and in what they ought to believe in. They had been forced to make up their own myths, and, as far as I am concerned, they've done a great job.

Just look at their pantheon.

The last time I'd counted them just before delivering one of my lectures at McGill. There were forty of them. Not bad, considering that around 1250 BC, the gods had to look after about one million people. Forty gods and goddesses.

Not counting my Ambrosia.

They truly created a pantheon to be proud of. They had the First Born Gods that formed the very fabric of the universe. They also created the spirits that nurtured life in the four elements. Then came the spirits, which included love and hate, and joy and fear, and most of our emotions. Next came the class of Gods that controlled the sky and the sun, the winds and the sea, and all the forces of nature and of civilized arts of mankind.

Only then we come to the Olympian Gods, the ones we all heard about—the gods that later migrated to Rome. Of those, the most familiar to us are Zeus, Hera, Poseidon, Demeter, Artemis, Apollo, Ares, Athene, Aphrodite, Hephaistos, Hermes, Dionysos, and Hestia. The marble statues of most of them adorn our museums to this day.

The sixth group of divinities comprised the constellations that ruled the night-sky, including all the signs of the Zodiac. Way down below them was a group of monsters and beasts, and dragons and sirens… they enhanced our fables.

Finally came those that didn't quite make the grade, the semi-gods; yet they gave hope for us; that we too might ascend to their level.

But let us not forget that, one way or another most, if not all, of these divinities personified elements and attributes only for the masses; traits to look up to, to worship, to give meaning to life. Men like Socrates rose above such trifles. Above the gods?

So it seemed.

Yet that is not how it all began.

Mrs. Milos was sitting on the terrace overlooking the distant bay. Her relaxed manner was contagious. There were no servants in the house, yet the house was spotless, the meals were on time, tasty, and the shopping must have been done by teleportation. Whenever we visited the Milos villa, Mrs. Milos was invariably on the terrace, under a huge umbrella, reading a book. There was total privacy there. The villa has been built so high that, barring gods and airplanes, nobody could overlook it from above. It was a fortress secure from peeping eyes.

God only knows when and how Mrs. Milos ran her household. I've learned later that there was a girl who came once a week to clean, and a man who seemed to be in charge of making sure that neither walls, inside or out, nor ceilings, nor parapets nor even a solitary column, would lose any of its pristine whiteness. Someone must have done the cooking though, having partaken in clearing the table on a number of occasions, I've never met a cook, nor anyone resembling a cook. Two other men seemed busy keeping the garden in a tip-top condition. There must have been others who, for some reason, and probably by magic, remained invisible. To add to this invisibility, a six-foot wall, as white as the rest of the house and most furniture, surrounded the house and garden, offering privacy within and without, though I never saw either of my parents-in-law walking its manicured lawns.

Perhaps they floated in their invisible cloaks.

Mama, Ambrosia and I were alone. She promised to tell us about the long lost secrets.

"At first," she began, "There were no gods in Greece. There was the sky and the sea, and the rest was just life. And then people found that it was not enough. They began searching. For years they searched, and they found nothing. Nothing except ambrosia. A nectar that did strange thing to their mind."

She looked at us making sure she held our attention. I've

spent years studying the subject. I was beginning to suspect what was coming.

"In our times, people experimented with LSD and other mind altering drugs. Those chemicals affected both, their minds and their bodies, not always for the best. In time, the authorities began to control access to the psychedelic drugs and people lost interest."

This was a twist I wasn't counting on. I was more inclined to study myths. Ambrosia looked relaxed, her eyes on the activities of fishermen, down below, in the bay. They always seemed busy with something, yet never hurried.

"Modern man had made a number of attempts to rediscover the lost secret. Aldous Huxley, experimented with mescaline, Carlos Castaneda explored the ancient teachings of shamans or sorcerers, who were reputedly capable of shape-shifting into animal or other forms. They did it partially through magic rituals or shamanism, but also through experiences with psychoactive drugs, such as peyote and jimson weed."

Ambrosia got up to top up our glasses with *frape*, iced cold Nescafe, which balanced the wine we sipped slowly.

"So that, my children, is what's left of our ancient search for ambrosia, although there are a few amongst us, today, who claim that the nectar still exists, and that there are very secret societies who both, produce it, and indulge their need for immortality with them."

She gave no indication if she believed any of her stories. She delivered them, however, in such a neutral voice that she'd obviously left it up to us whether or not we'd give them credence. It was then that Ambrosia came to life.

"And then," she took over the account, "someone came up with the idea that ambrosia, the nectar that turns you into an immortal, is hidden in the depth of some bottles of wine. It seems, that the Greeks, at least on Milos, never tired of looking for it. They are, still, all really keen on becoming immortal."

We laughed, but I was keen to discuss the matter further.

"Would you say, Mama, that immortality is a state of mind?" Then I hesitated. "In fact, or at least in the eyes of those people you discussed."

Mrs. Milos considered that for a moment.

"I'd say, Simon, that whatever is incomplete cannot be immortal. We all, men and women, are incomplete. We'd have to become androgynous to aspire to immortality."

"Hermaphrodites?"

"I suspect so. Don't you? You're the expert."

"I find this just a little embarrassing, Mama. A wise man once said that there are liars, bad liars and experts. I aspire to neither."

We both laughed, but I could see that she agreed with me. Or, with the wise man. We agreed to continue our discussion later.

Ambrosia and I decided to spend the evening in our own place, at the hotel. We wanted to have an early supper, more like a snack, and try to recover from the last few days of overeating and overdrinking, which on Milos was a hazard we had to face daily. We indulged ourselves a lot more here than we did in Montreal. A lot more.

Just out of interest, Ambrosia telephoned McGill. She thought that if the Scientist, American Scientist or the Nature, the International Journal of Science, looked at the articles she'd submitted then, by now, there should have been some reaction at the McGill. Some feedback. Positive or otherwise.

First she called her physics supervisor, Dr. Leblanc, and when that bore no fruit, she decided to contact the Dean.

The Dean was out. She asked if there were any messages for her. No. There were no messages. None at all? Not even from any publications? For her attention?

"No, Miss Milos. Not to my knowledge. I'm sorry."

Ambrosia replaced the receiver without saying goodbye or thank you. This was not like her. Then she just stood there, looking through the window.

"She was lying," Ambrosia said, after a short while.

"Who?" I asked.

"Miss Jones, Dean McGinnis' secretary. She knew there was input and she was told not to tell me what it was."

I looked up, hardly believing my ears. "How could you possibly know that?" And then I softened. "Why would she, or they, do that?" I wondered aloud.

"That, my dear husband, we shall find out on our return."

Hardly a satisfying answer, but Ambrosia dismissed the matter for now. She wouldn't say anything else but I thought I witnessed the first signs of my wife being angry. It was like a long dormant volcano slowly coming alive. The first wisps of smoke rising into still blue skies. I was close to feeling sorry for Dr. McGinnis. On the other hand, if he deserved her wrath, if wrath it was, then it would serve him right. I wondered how it would develop.

A few minutes later Ambrosia recovered her usual, delightful disposition. Nevertheless, I made a mental note to avoid the subject of McGill for the next day or two. Just to play safe.

But then, the following day she received a telegram from the university. It was delivered to her parent's house, which was registered at McGill University as her usual domicile. The wording was short though not very sweet.

Regrets. Article refused. Regards McGinnis.

She handed me the paper without a word. I was still trying to formulate some words of regrets when she spun on her heel to face me.

"It's them," she said. "They are getting even." The

second sentence came out through her clenched teeth.

"Them? Even?" I must have sounded retarded.

"The boys playing spies and robbers have just robbed me of my publication. You may or may not know it, Simon, but in my field publications are very important. Without them I cannot win grants to advance my work."

"I thought McGinnis said you got a million for keeping quiet?" This was supposed to be a question.

"McGinnis is a functionary. An administrator. He says things he finds convenient to say at any particular moment. If I don't come up with publications I might as well pack my bags."

"I thought McGill was keen to keep you," I reminded her.

"Of course they are. I've had seven publications in two years. I am good for their image. And now…"

"I think I am getting your point. Nobody's indispensible it's just that some people are a little more indispensible than others." I was never sure if it should be a little *more*, or a little *less* indispensible. Anyway, she got the point.

"Right in one," she replied.

I mulled that over in my head. It wasn't all that easy; not as easy as it sounded. I knew that Ambrosia loved her work. Whatever she did, she did it on the cutting edge. She was as good as they got. I was beginning to suspect that she might have been right; that the ungodly have been attempting to get even with her for her surreptitious disappearance. By the time we left, they probably checked the passenger lists at J-P Trudeau International Airport, and her name would figure there, in the first class.

We had our fun. Now they had theirs.

"Is there anything you can do?"

"The whole thing is a farce. Two principal and a few secondary scientific publications cannot reject you, simultaneously. The odds are just too great against it. No. They must have gotten to McGinnis. And he bent over and kissed their…"

"He would do this to you?"

"What, kiss their…"

"No darling, not that."

She shrugged. "For money? He'd sell his own mother. It's only a question of how much."

I heard stories about how universities are run, but, frankly, I didn't believe them. I knew that the competition was great and that, in spite of the austerity program in the US, the Pentagon had a bigger budget than all the universities put together, but this was still hard to accept.

I let Ambrosia simmer for a while then took her out for a walk. Milos, at night, looks even more enchanting than during the day. I must have seen it on my wedding night, if only I'd been sober enough to appreciate it. The few times we walked home from the parents' villa, we didn't really look around that much. Now, as though for the first time, my eyes were opened to the moon casting it's magical shadows, to the twinkling of lights on the boats anchored in the bay, to the sounds of two flutes having a lonesome discussion, echoing between white-washed walls.

It was romantic, enchanting, Greek.

"Love you," she whispered when the magic caught up with her.

"Love you too, Pet," I affirmed also. "In the end, you know, the good always wins."

"I know," she said. "But sometimes the end is just a bit too far in the future."

***

Chapter 18
The Wall

I **really didn't care** if it was just fantasy, magic, myths or on the periphery of science. My ankle was cured. Healed. I was as sure of it as I was of having two legs to stand on; two good, healthy legs. And, even as my hypnotic exercises had also been intended, I began to discern the invisible line between myths and reality. It seemed, even then, that I've hit two birds with a single stone. Or was it grasped...?

The bird in hand, and all that...

Wait. That was later. I'm jumping ahead of myself.

I was lying on our bed, in the hotel, doing my thing with self-hypnosis. I was relaxed. After the initial shock Ambrosia seemed to have settled down, also. She still had moments when her eyes smouldered with unholy fires, but less often.

As apart from frequent trips to the beach, getting stuffed at the Ambrosia's parents, or sampling Greek wine—and not just Retsina—most of the time we had little else to do, I began practicing my hypnosis every day; sometimes morning and evening. We decided, together, to leave OBE for later. Soul travel, or astral projection, needed not only mental but emotional inner peace. Ambrosia was not quite there.

As for self-hypnosis, I've reached the level of being able to stick pins in my thigh and feel no pain, other than awareness that I have actually done it. It was an achievement

I was particularly proud of, and which Ambrosia dismissed as an unusual perversion.

"You like sticking things in, don't you," she commented dryly.

I thought silence would be the better part of valour.

She may have been right, but for me it was a means to an end—a way of finding out just how hypnosis worked. And work it did, in more ways than one.

The actual healing took place just yesterday. I was alone in my hotel room. Ambrosia slipped out to get something, she didn't tell me what. I went through my usual relaxation exercises, putting myself in as deep a state as I was capable of at the time. My intention was to try regression on my own, recording the whole procedure on my portable computer.

I'd speak aloud, describing all I did, hoping to study the recording later and learn from it.

I was already well under when I heard her voice.

"You will continue to relax. With each breath you take, you will go deeper and deeper..."

We've done this before. I was used to her voice. After a while, she said with calm confident tone, "Now you are going to pull your heel out without hurting it."

My immediate environment changed abruptly. I was sitting on hard ground, my back against a rough stone wall. The room was small, dark and damp. Next to me a bearded fellow looked worried. I looked around. The only way into the cell, for it looked no better than a prison cell, was through a heavily barred wood and metal door. Quietly I got to my feet, and approached the door. Through a small opening, I could see three or four slobbery looking men, either drunk, or sleeping, just outside, on the ground. As rundown as the men looked, they bore the signs of remnants of some uniforms that once must have represented some powers that be. It was too dark to see whose insignia they wore. Empty clay pots, presumably of wine, lay scattered about. Whatever the men's condition, they, and not the door, presented an impenetrable barrier. I walked back, silently, and slid down on my hunches next to my companion.

"Well, John, have faith and follow me," I said rising.

The ridiculous thing was that I knew what I was saying, though I said it in a language I neither knew nor understood.

I stood up and faced the wall.

"There is an open field in front of you. Just close your eyes and walk towards it. I am always with you," I said softly. That last sentence I borrowed from my Master.

Then I closed my eyes and walked forward towards where the wall used to be. A moment later I heard a muted shout of joy. My friend was outside. Unfortunately this expression of joy deprived me of my concentration. I felt a tremendous weight attached to my left leg. I yanked as hard as I could. It would not give. Finally I closed my eyes and repeated again the last phrase.

"I am always with you." It was a promise I'd never forget.

The same instant I felt my ankle give a strange crackling sound and clear the wall. We were indeed standing in an open field. I closed my eyes and whispered words of thanks.

Then, surrounded by silence, we walked into the dark, moonless night.

"What happened?"

Ambrosia was staring down at me, looking worried.

I was still in the process of finding my orientation. I recognized her face, then the room, finally the bed.

"Were you here long?" I asked.

"I forgot to count you back…"

"Never mind. I am back," even to my ears, I sounded a little uncertain.

"You screamed," she said. "Screamed and looked as if you're in a wrestling match with someone. What happened?"

"Don't you know? I seem to have carried out your

instructions."

"What happened, Simon?" Her voice was assuming threatening overtones with an admix of desperation.

"I was saving my ankle," I said quietly.

And even as I said it I realized that that was exactly what I was doing. I looked down at my left leg. There was not the slightest indication of any change. Yet, there and then, I knew, without the slightest shadow of doubt that my long-suffering ankle was healed.

"So it really works?" Ambrosia's face was a picture of surprise, consternation, and hope.

Maybe all Greeks are like that, but her expressions changed in quick succession.

"What, hypnosis?"

"No. Regression," she said. "Regression!"

"Yes," I said. I was quite confident. "Yes, my love, it works. You made it work." I really meant it. I have had little doubt that on my own I would not have succeeded.

Suddenly I felt I had to leave the bed. I had to get up, move physically away from where I was. There was something pulling me up and away in a manner that a cigarette pulls a man who just gave up smoking. We went on the balcony. It was tiny but we managed to get two chairs on it, facing each other.

As though through a thick, yet slowly dissipating fog, I began to recall images of what had happened. The images came as you sometimes see them on TV, when a digital broadcast goes wrong. Snippets, fragments, images overlapping each other, not in any coherent order.

"I think you'll have to put me under to find out exactly what happened. I only have the vaguest recollection."

"Not today. Today you need a rest."

"I tend to agree with you. Whatever it was, it must have been quite an experience. I feel, well, frankly, I feel washed out."

Two days have passed before we've discussed it again. First Ambrosia, with my help and dare I say expertise, put me under and asked me pointed questions. This time I did not experience images I took part in two days earlier, but I had a much better spectator's seat over the whole affair.

We both learned that I was either a follower or even an apostle of Christ. Could it have it Simon, normally known as Peter, or was this just a coincidence? The drunken guards could have been Romans, or some rabble rousers on the payroll of the Pharisees. Either way, they were of little consequence. What mattered was that I appear to have walked through a wall, leaving my heel behind in a moment of distraction or weakness.

There was one major problem. I knew from my work in Montreal that there was no mention of a 'live' apostle or follower of Christ ever walking through any walls.

Something was amiss.

Then I remembered that the principle reason for my hypnotic exercises was no longer my ankle, but my desire to attempt to separate myths from reality. Not just the myths recorded in the various scriptures, but an attempt to examine the reality that was not available to be witnessed, except, perhaps, by personal regression. If what I experienced under the hypnotic regression were true, then regardless whether the event had or had not been recorded in the scriptures, it could be taken as real. After all, while we do not question the veracity of events in the scriptures, no one ever claimed that the writings were the complete sum total of all events that had taken place at the time described in those scriptures. To have done so, the Bible would have to have had a million or more pages.

This reasoning sounded convoluting, but the essence was there.

Thus, while the scriptures used historical events to present spiritual truth, events that did not lend themselves to such illustrations would simply be omitted. They would not be used. Hence, the wall incident.

"It is as I've always thought," I said, gazing at Ambrosia's body turning dark bronze under the Grecian sun.

To be quite earnest, I sniggered to myself, as Oscar Wild would say: "the colour's immaterial." A goddess is a goddess by any other name. Or any other colour. Sorry, must give Shakespeare a break, too.

"What I am trying to say… is… that the scriptures are a compendium of, ah, spiritual truth, ah, hung on historical events, for, ah, the lack of any other."

"You're mumbling," was her intellectual comment.

"What I am trying to say," I began again, "is that anyone who interprets scriptures as essentially historical events is a fundamentalist. It is an attempt to convey the spiritual truth that could be understood by the widest or most common denominator."

"Like in politics?" the goddess inquired.

"As in politics. To do good, you must get elected. The only way you can get elected is to appeal to the majority. And majority is invariably the lowest common denominator."

"So you can make promises, lie, twist the truth, so that you get elected, so that you can do good for the people."

"Which is precisely what the church has been doing for two-thousand years. Hence, this time I'll call on Iago to explain, the eternal folly of heaven."

"Iago said that?"

"In Italian. *La Morte e il Nulla. E vecchia fola il Ciel.*"

"He really said that? Isn't that blasphemy?"

"Well, we'll have to dispatch Shakespeare, Verdi and Boîto to hell together. I'd settle for their company for a while."

"…a long while," Ambrosia commented dryly.

People who don't actually study religion tend to take

some concepts too literarily.

"Hell, my darling, is a state of consciousness. Like heaven," I offered.

"Just how do you know?"

"Well, for a start I believe the mystics. Usually they speak from personal experience. They claim, universally, that Kingdom of God is within you. I suppose if I were immortal, then it could remain within me forever. There is no mention of the same being available on the other side of the equation."

She looked at me, and, unless I'm very much mistaken, there was just a smidgen of admiration in her eyes.

"It all gets me a bit confused. The mystics say that god is in heaven and heaven is within you. That places god within you, too. Furthermore, if god is ubiquitous, then you must also be within god, who or which is also already within you. Get my point? It doesn't leave much room for hell, does it?"

"All this talk of hell makes me hot," she said. "The last one in will fry on a spit," she threw over her shoulder and sprinted for the water.

Now, that I have a good ankle, I mused, *I'd probably follow her anywhere, even to hell; though if she were there, I'm sure lots of angels would move there also. It could be rather nice. Ambrosia, Shakespeare, Verdi, Boîto and a bunch of angels. Who needs heaven?*

And then I had a very strange feeling that she'd heard everyone of my thoughts. That was impossible, of course. But for some reason she stopped, sprinted back to me, put her arms around my neck and planted a very romantic, saucy kiss right on my mouth. There must have been a reason for it.

Mustn't there?

In Montreal we hardly ever went out. Having only met recently, we were both hungry for each other's company. We both left going to parties, balls or dances behind us, mostly in the years when we were both students.

Yet here, on Milos, hardly a day passed without some curious friends dropping in; an *ad hoc* party would drag on into the early hours. Alternatively, we would be invited by some of Ambrosia's old friends, for a get-together, with wine, song, and some good old-fashioned smoochy dancing. We enjoyed all of it but, frankly, while the sun-soaked days on Milos left us with wonder, Ambrosia and I were already missing our balcony, in Montreal, where just the two of us could shut out the world outside, and drink life from each other's eyes.

One day our relationship would mature into, perhaps, unconditional love. Right now, I suppose, we were *in* love— absurdly, inexplicably, irrationally in love. Each moment we shared with others, detracted from the joy of being alone.

Just the two us.

Soon.

***

Chapter 19
Devolution

We were sitting on the terrace at the Milos villa. Contrary to the balcony at our hotel, the villa had a large terrace that could accommodate five or six deckchairs, a table or two, with enough room left over for a couple to dance *Tango Greco*.

Mama and Papa's deckchairs were facing us, leaving Ambrosia and myself to enjoy the splendid view that seemed to change with each hour. It was that part of the day when the sun was losing its battle with the sea, which was about to embrace and swallow the fiery countenance. Peace in the air was palpable. Even the gray herons, the buzzards and the ever-cackling crows have stilled their joyful exchanges.

Nature held her breath. She was bidding silent farewell to yet another day.

Indeed, there was a strange silence after the guests had left. Greeks are naturally boisterous, socially active, engaging in lively exchanges on virtually any subject. On the departure of a gathering of English speaking contingent of Mr. & Mrs. Milos' friends, no one wanted to invade the silence that engulfed our foursome.

We inhaled the silence.

A good while later, I was asked to tell them about the courses I was giving at McGill. Rather then give them the exact program I have been delivering for some years now on Comparative Religion, I decided to share with them my latest thoughts on spiritual evolution, which, as it turns out, at least in my opinion, has been devolving for a few thousand years.

It so happened that I intended to make that the underlying subject of my new semester.

"Yes, *devolving*," I stressed the word.

There was mild surprise on my hosts' faces.

"According to the Hindus, devolution began some millions of years ago," I continued, none too sure of my ground. "The Bible began with the Paradise, and devolved to our present state of affairs. What people do not seem to understand is that the more advanced our civilization, the more we advance technologically, the more we regress spiritually. Now this may not mean much to people who are not inclined towards spiritual life, but it means more and more to scientists, who are amassing vast stores of information which proves that the physical world is little more than empty space."

I looked around, hoping that someone would jump in and relieve me from having to carry on the, what must have sounded like, apocalyptic monologue.

"Spirit being omnipresent is *per force* static—it's already there, so to speak." I continued, getting slightly hot under the collar. "The allegory of spirit, as the energy of life, needs to be attached to something that is transient; to us *inter alia*. To us—human beings."

They listened attentively, without a single interruption. Finally, Papa withdrew his eyes from the distant horizon and looked directly at his daughter.

"Is that so, *mikro koritsi*?"

I later learned that those incomprehensible words were the way Papa often addressed his daughter. They meant, roughly, 'little girl.' I knew he was asking her to confirm or deny my empty space postulate.

The Little Girl nodded.

"Yes, Papa. I'm afraid it's true." She then proceeded to give her father the story about an orange and the football field. "About 99.9999% of matter is empty space. That's four nines after the ninety-nine," she added to play safe.

Mr. Milos remained silent for a while.

"So what is it that we see with our eyes?" He didn't sound convinced.

"Mostly photons reflected off clouds of electrons."

That didn't mean much to non-physicists.

"So what you are saying, son," he now turned towards me, "is that the more we rely on our senses the further we drift away from the true, or spiritual nature or our world?"

"You could put it that way." In fact, I was amazed how quickly Papa got the general idea that I was attempting to present. "Hence the devolution," I added, almost as an afterthought.

"But aren't we intended to develop physically also?"

Mrs. Milos looked worried. After all, women are more or less designated to carry the responsibility of maintaining the human race at a sustainable rate of replacement, and maintain it in reasonable numbers. Such programming is, I have been told, in their genes. Of late, they carried out this responsibility in slightly too large numbers, I feared, but that, too, was a matter of opinion.

"Physical evolution advances at a pace of a sleeping three-toed sloth," I murmured.

"What we recognize as progress, Mama, is the invention of lazy man." At last Ambrosia came to my rescue. "The lazier he is, the more he wants to have gadgets to do the work for him. And what does he do with his newly gained free time? Contemplate? Meditate? Compose timeless poetry? Or even attempt to fulfill the dictum posed by Socrates? No, Mama. He watches TV, preferably professional sports, while guzzling cans of beer and downing tons of potato chips. That, I contend, is not progress."

There. I gave her a grateful look. Only native Greeks would know what she meant by Socrates' dictum: *The unexamined life is not worth living.* People seldom placed thinking, self-criticism or even just self-examination at the top of their lists of priorities. She got it off her own, and fortuitously, also off my chest. I would not be able to say such things in my lectures, but I needed to share them with someone. In a way it sounded a little phony since, lately, most of my time I've spent on the beach, or sipping wine. Or… making love. Of course, this was our honeymoon. Honey-fortnight.

At least I did not switch on the TV.

"I never thought about it in just those terms," Papa admitted. Then he looked at his daughter with a raised eyebrow.

She smiled, a little sadly. "We can only be responsible for our own actions, Papa. I firmly believe that whatever is the destiny of the human race as a whole, it does not affect the individual."

"Carl Jung would drink to that," I said, raising my own glass. "He recognized the individual as the only reality. And, as little as I know of his philosophy, I very much doubt he was referring to his physical body."

For a few minutes we all contemplated the nectar of the gods shimmering in our glasses. The last rays of the sun gave the wine an unearthly glow. Perhaps wine really was the origin of their famed ambrosia? After a few glasses one felt quite divine.

There is an incredible variety to Greek wines. I learned yesterday that the Greeks produced wines for more than 6,500 years. By the fundamentalists' reckoning, that must have been long before God created heaven and earth. Well, the planet Earth, anyway. And that would have made wine divine, wouldn't it?

I also suspected that their wine was singularly responsible for the Saturnalia. After all, Cronus was there before Saturn emigrated to Rome. Furthermore, if it hadn't been for Greek wine, the Roman Empire would probably still be around. After all, it was only after the Greek colonization that wine began to flourish in Italy. Until they developed their own, the Romans tried to run their empire on Greek wine. The Americans are trying to run theirs on Arab oil. It doesn't work, either way.

You need your own ambrosia, so to speak.

Nevertheless, I was in grave danger of falling under its spell. First Ambrosia, now Greek wine. I wouldn't be surprised if they all dabbled in magic. The Greeks, I mean. Just for fun, of course. The Greeks are very good at fun.

"So we are all pointing our ships the wrong way..." Papa interrupted my thoughts.

"Not all, Papa. Just the masses. We are all hosting the divine potential, but only as individuals. Not as members of any club."

Mr. Milos nodded a few times, sighed, but still appeared unconvinced. It's not easy to change directions when you're already in Paradise.

I think the wine was beginning to affect my speech. I'm fairly sure I said 'matheth' not masses. I put my glass down, leaned back, and run my eyes over my three companions. They all seemed far away, each lost in her or his own thoughts. Perhaps they were carrying out the advise of their great Master, wondering if their life was worth living. Looking at Ambrosia I knew that mine was. And how! Perhaps not in my recent past, but today it was definitely worth every breath...

Today I shall get as close as I can to ambrosia. Not my Ambrosia, but the nectar hiding at the bottom of my glass. I leaned forward and picked up the remnants of my wine. Perhaps Papa was right. What else can you do in Paradise?

The following day we spent on the beach. We sat in the shade of our umbrella, with occasional lazy strolls on warm, almost hot, sand, to dip our bodies in lukewarm water of the bay. Three days ago Ambrosia found an old snorkeling mask, which we shared until she bought me my own. We wiled away time just by lying flat, suspended on the lustrous surface, peering down at the underwater life.

Masses of it.

The fish, like us, didn't seem to have much to do. They swam to and fro, occasionally tasting a morsel of this or that, rather as we did for these last few days.

For the life of me I couldn't think of anything that made us superior to those fish. They only ate when hungry; they didn't accumulate food for old age; they didn't worry about tomorrow. When nature roiled their world, they simply dove deeper, and continued to have fun.

Were they evolving?

Perhaps not. Not much. But for all I've seen they also weren't devolving. Time for them, fish-time, seemed to travel laterally, not forward or backwards. Given enough of it, they would travel a similar road they did yesterday, or the day before. The road their parents traveled. Round and round, yet never the same identical road. Also their paths led up and down, not just in cardinal directions. Like birds. They could swerve at any angle without fear of veering off the permitted pathway. They were free. A lot freer than we were.

The concept of freedom, among us, humans, was becoming a farce. We were controlled by masses of laws and bylaws, rules and regulations that would make Hammurabi green with envy.

Our concept of freedom was becoming a farce.

Before we left Montreal, I'd made notes on a news flash about the cost of incarceration in the USA. By 2008, one in every 48 working-age men was in prison or jail. That added up to 2.3 million inmates, or 753 per 100,000 people. As this was 240% more than in 1980, by now, by today, the prison population must have been considerably higher. I don't remember the precise figures, but I recall that the cost of incarceration, already in 2008, run into billions of dollars. Over the years, trillions.

Trillions!

And that in a World Power that was struggling with its budgetary deficit. Yet, the USA had by far the biggest *per capita* prison population in the world.

And talking of trillions they have to add more trillions for the costs associated with the veterans of the wars and military actions they conducted over the last few decades. And then, there is all that money in China. American money, the money America owes them. It's not easy being an American. None of this should bother me, I'm a Canadian, but the US is our Big Brother.

A very Big Brother.

I'd rather be a fish.

At least they seemed to stick to their own territory; they didn't impose on anyone; they didn't treat their neighbours badly. They didn't bully each other, didn't start wars or invent weapons of mass destruction. I am not talking about sharks, obviously. Sharks are the same everywhere, in the sea and on land.

OK. Occasionally, when hungry, the fish ate each other. On the other hand, we eat everyone else. Hungry or not.

How much closer were they to Paradise that we escaped from, but for the want of a single apple?

In some ways, the people of Milos were a little like those fish. They were free, or at least much more free than we were, in Montreal, in the highly technologically advanced civilization. They lived closer to nature, in greater harmony with it, with greater regard and respect for its demands. There seemed a strange symbiosis between the islanders and the island that supported them. They seemed contented with the relatively simple life. Were they making progress? Were they evolving? Certainly no less so than we were. But if a life of contentment and harmony is any guideline, then they left us ages behind. They were much closer to heaven.

In my religious studies, I came across dozens of empires that were born, scaled the crags of fame, and wealth, and power, mostly on the backs of others. For the briefest fragment of history they ruled their realms, only to collapse into anonymity.

I wondered if Ambrosia had any views on the transiency of fame and fortune.

"You know, darling, ever since we visited Santorini, and the big hole their predecessors left in the sea, it made me wonder about the Minoan Empire. Wasn't it Atlantis? And then I thought, Empires come and go; the ancient Egyptian, later the Roman, the British Empire, the Communist Oligarchy, the power wielded by the Vatican during the Middle Ages..."

She looked at me with those wondrous eyes as though trying to bring me back from my wandering mind.

"How many of us," I asked, "can name but a few past empires? I recall Wikipedia lists more than 150 of them— alphabetically. Can you name ten?"

And then she surprised me. Again.

"We don't remember them. We don't have to. No one does. They do not matter. Few things, in this world, do matter. The trick is to find out which ones do."

For a moment I wondered if she was still thinking of the articles she wrote which, but for the fickle fate, or the greed of a dean of a single university, might never be published; might never be made available to other scientists, who might, just might, advance the theory of what we are all about a step further. For the glory of man? For evolution?

Perhaps the Greeks had the right idea.

***

Chapter 20
Goodbyes

She didn't give me an apple. We decided to leave Paradise, together, before we would get thrown out. Yes, as long as we were together we could face the outside world and pretend that we are still here, on Milos. Ambrosia's parents came to pick us up at our hotel, in their minuscule, official Fiat, and take us to the airport.

There were tears.

"Will you visit us more often, Simon? Remember, you're our son now."

"Yes, Mama, yes, Papa. I feel at home here. You made me feel at home." I felt practically like a thirty-eight year old kid going back to school.

I saw contentment and acceptance in the faces of my new parents. But there was also something more, something I didn't understand at the time.

"We are leaving Ambrosia in your hands. Promise me you'll not let her come to any harm."

There was gravity in his voice that went beyond the unusual words of departure. I had to make him feel confident in me.

"That I swear, Papa. That I swear."

I don't know why I used those very words, but at the time they seemed appropriate. Later, I thought them pompous. Ambrosia didn't think so.

"He puts great trust in you, Simon. I know you won't disappoint him."

I certainly hoped not, though that too, I thought, was a strange thing to say.

Having packed I went downstairs to pay for the hotel only to find that the account had been settled. The payer remained anonymous. After some prodding, the desk clerk divulged that it was the owner of the hotel who settled the bill. What he refused to say was who the owner is.

"I've never met him, Sir, it's all done through the accountants."

"And who are the accountants?"

"They're a large firm in Athens, Sir. I can give you their name, if you like."

A Mystery? Just then Ambrosia joined me at the counter. She was no help at all.

"A time will come when you'll have a chance to reciprocate. That's how it works in Greece. It's probably something to do with taxes. They hate taxes here."

She sounded as if her statement left nothing unsaid, but it went a long way to explain the state of finances the Greek government was in. The "ordinary people" were tired of supporting the fat cats who lived off the taxes.

I smiled. There was a group in the USA, some time ago, which hated taxes also. They believed that you could have all the goodies of civilization for free. They called themselves the "Coffee Party", or something like that. On the other hand, I've never met anyone who liked paying taxes.

"That's makes it all perfectly clear," I murmured.

"There," she smiled. "I'm glad you're happy now."

Was she being sarcastic? Were my eyes blinded by her beauty, charm, sparkling intelligence, and all the other attributes I'd normally assign to a Greek goddess? Or did she know something she was not prepared to share with me.

"Very well," I nodded, "we'll leave it for now. But just for future reference, I don't like debts of any sort."

Perhaps I said it in a tone of voice she wasn't used to, but she turned and walked away. This was the first time since we've met that there was a slight coolness between us. Or, perhaps, I imagined it, too? I did absolutely nothing for two weeks; I was virtually a kept man—a condition I was not used to. I like to make my own way, no matter how humble.

I joined Ambrosia at the front door where our baggage was already waiting. She seemed relaxed.

"Ah, parting sweet sorrow!" Mr. Milos said with a Shakespearian theatrical gesture. He swept the steps with his white panama hat.

"Not yet, Papa. You're stuck with us all the way to the airport."

"Yes, I guess I'm still lucky," he admitted.

Mrs. Milos stood by, regarding us with a mixture of sadness and contentment. "I'll miss you," she said as we all squeezed into the car. "I'll miss you both," she added.

Moments later we were nestled, for the last time, in the tiny Fiat.

Whether it was the two tiny flags, or just coincidence, the uniformed people at the airport saluted on our approach, and let us through directly onto the tarmac. I assumed that the mayor carried a lot of weight in a place as small as this island. He must have been the biggest fish.

A Cessna 208 Caravan was already warming up its engines. We embraced and kissed with hardly a word. The emotional part was left behind, when we had more privacy.

The plane, I was told, could carry nine passengers. Today we were alone, with just the pilot and two assistants who behaved more like stewards than copilot and navigator. Perhaps they were both. Or all three? Flight time was just over 30 minutes, hardly worth sitting down.

Nevertheless we did, and one of the stewards made sure our seat belts were tight.

"It can be windy here, Sir. Mustn't take any unnecessary risks," he explained.

Then there was the last wave through the window and

the little Fiat disappeared from view. The holidays were over.

I looked at Ambrosia. She was still looking out of the porthole. It couldn't have been easy for her to leave the place she loved so much.

"I'm sorry," I said.

She didn't turn away from the window, but leaned back against me. I needed that. I felt there have been things unsaid. Now her touch told me it was all right.

"I don't know what I'd do without you, Simon." She snuggled even closer. "You don't begin to realize how much I need you."

This sudden out-flowing confession coincided with the roar of the take off. The skipper dipped his wings slightly to the right, towards west-northwest, and settled to a steady hum. The white island was behind us. I felt a strange disquiet, which I couldn't define. I had no idea if it was the future or the past that gave me this feeling of vague, undefined apprehension. Perhaps Adam and Eve felt it after they were expelled from Eden.

Ambrosia leaned her head on my shoulder.

Past or future, it had something to do with this goddess resting by my side. I hoped my shoulders were broad enough.

The Air Canada 747 looked as comfortable as the KLM that brought us here. This time in Business Class, we were still offered sufficient comfort for us to enjoy the whole trip. The seats did not recline to a flat position, but it did not matter. Time enough to sleep when we'd get home. The food was acceptable, an aspect of flying which deteriorated of late badly. No matter, we were going home, and though I knew I'd miss Greece, I looked forward to getting down to serious business with my experiments with hypnotic regression. I felt certain, that one way or another I'd incorporate them into my lecture program at McGill, hopefully without loosing my job.

But most of all, loving and generous as the Milos were,

we were looking forward to being alone.

After the whirlwind of parties, dancing and laughter, we could at last retreat into a womb-made-for-two, our small, one-bedroom apartment, our own, very private terrace, where we could and would spin dreams of out of body travel to fabulous places, of regressing into times which fascinated both of us. I wanted to retrace the steps of the Old Masters, Ambrosia to meet the gods of Olympus, face to face, perhaps on equal terms.

That is what we were looking forward to. That, and not sharing each other with anyone. Not for a while. At least, not for a little while.

My, or really our, combined effort, which took me to and then out of the cell that wasn't even mentioned in the Bible, gave me a lot to think about. If I could do it, then, surely, one could organize a group of people, perhaps students, who could attempt to regress, under hypnosis, to a number of historical periods, and either confirm or refute our present knowledge. If two or more people would confirm the same event, one could accept with a fair degree of confidence that the event really happened.

This sounded like a completely new field of research. There was a good chance that we could expand our history-books by masses of factual details, which, in turn, would shed light on how we'd want to behave today.

My ego already envisioned Dr. Simon Jones, PhD, as the leading authority on regression into heretofore-unknown historical periods. My name was embossed, or was it engraved, on a large plaque, over a magnificent mahogany door in my new, large office, that made my colleagues green with envy.

And then I started laughing. I envisioned a number of my students having their heels caught in the wall.

Dr. Simon Jones, PhD, the celebrated heel trapper, didn't sound as good.

There was only one way not to repeat mistakes of the past, and that was to study them. Otherwise, we would continue to walk in circles, getting nowhere very fast—or very slowly. It simply wouldn't make the slightest difference. Perhaps this accounts for the rate of our evolution to date— our continuous repetition of the same errors.

But first I had to return to the discipline, which kept me going before the Greece interlude.

"I think I fell asleep," Ambrosia's sleepy voice announced.

"We have to get pretty serious about it," I answered.

"Of course we should," she obliged.

"A glass of wine?" I asked.

"I thought you'd never ask."

At that she closed her eyes and rested her head on my shoulder. I liked her head there. At least I'd know where to find her if I needed her. It seemed that that would be quite often. There was no way I could do the regressions on my own. And she already had some experience. Also, my subconscious was familiar with her voice. I suspected that might prove pretty important.

I clicked on TV and ran through the channels. Quite a choice, but my mind was too full of impressions to digest, to mull over, to pay any attention. I watched three movies, about five minutes each, before I switched off.

Just then I felt a stir on my shoulder.

"I think I'll take a swim now." Her voice was still very much asleep.

"Wouldn't you rather have a glass of wine," I countered.

She rubbed her eyes with the back of her fists.

"We're not on the beach any more, are we?" She sounded surprised—her eyes remained closed. "I love those waves washing ashore..."

The hum of the engines.

I waved to a stewardess and ask her for "two red and dry, preferably wine" and left it at that. You have to be in first class to specify vintage; if you're very lucky you might get it.

By now Ambrosia was sitting up. "What a pity one cannot sleep the whole trip. I'd probably have taken a dip or two, then dried myself in the sun…"

"And then went to Mama and Papa's for a great dinner, drank a lot of wine, then went to our hotel, and showed me how much you love me. Right?"

"Do you see anything particularly wrong with this sequence of events?"

"I didn't for two weeks, almost daily," I assured her.

"And nightly," she added with just a tiny giggle.

Our wine arrived together with a tray of smoked almonds. We sipped it slowly, enjoying the taste of sun trapped in the grapes. It is hard to imagine that back home, in Montreal, we shall not experience the same amount of sun. Not that Canadian summer was not generous in that department, but we could hardly spend most of our time outdoors, let alone near-naked. I found it hard to believe that I, born in the British Isles, could become a heliophile, a sun-lover, after a single visit to Greece.

I also never imagined, that the offer Papa made close to two weeks ago, to move to Milos—the offer I thought at the time as ridiculous—would suddenly sound so attractive. There was only one problem. For the life of me, I couldn't imagine working on Milos. That would probably be the problem with heaven. Imagine spending eternity in paradise, doing nothing. It sounded like hell.

"Will you be busy the moment we get back?" I asked, just to tear myself from the dream that couldn't come true. At least, not yet.

"I have a couple of things to settle," she replied noncommittally. "Nothing much."

"I though we might call on Bob, just to find out what happened?"

"It would be interesting to hear his version," she said, but she didn't sound as if that matter interested her at all.

I let the subject rest. Frankly, organizing a research team that could experiment with regressive hypnosis interested me much more. I really wondered if such a thing were possible, or had our success on Milos been just an accident, just a bit of luck. Whichever it was, I wouldn't give up without a fight, though whom I was supposed to fight I wasn't sure.

"Will you help me with my regressions?" I must have sounded hopeful but uncertain.

Ambrosia turned towards me, her eyes wide. "How can you ask such a thing, Simon? Of course I will help you. I'll help you in anyway I can." Then her voice softened. "Frankly, darling, I must admit that I doubted your efforts when you first began, but now... Now I don't have to believe. Now I know that you can do it. At the same time, I am amazed that you're not afraid to play with your own mind. Are you sure that it's safe?"

What could I tell her?

"Well, sweetheart, I am here and so is my ankle. What more can I say?"

She nodded. Apparently, for now, it was enough. Also, it appeared, that I've crossed the first wall.

**

PART THREE

The Escape

"Become passers-by"

Nag Hammadi Library
Gospel of Thomas, logion # 42

Chapter 21
Little Girl

The actual payload that gives an atomic bomb its incredible explosive power, is very small, when compared to standard weapons of destruction. Relatively small bombs are equivalent to thousand of tons of TNT. As an illustration, the gravity bomb the USA dropped on Hiroshima, known affectionately as "Little Boy", had a yield of 12-15 kilotons of Trinitrotoluene, commonly known as TNT. A kiloton means 1000 tons. That makes the payload equivalent to 12,000 to 15,000 tons of TNT.

And that's an awful lot of explosive material for just one bomb. But all that is purely coincidental. I was merely trying to illustrate the explosive power of my darling wife's temper. What I also wanted to illustrate was that great explosive power comes in very small packages. And I don't just mean... atom bombs.

Trust me, I know.

I actually learned all that from Ambrosia about ten hours after her meeting with the dean, following which she'd spent the first night in her old apartment. She'd told me later, that she'd kept it for just such occasions.

"Were there to be others, I asked?" When she finally turned up the following day. She ignored me.

"You wouldn't like me, last night," she said, over a late breakfast. She'd calmed down by then, somewhat.

The moment we landed at J-P Trudeau Airport, I felt that the dormant volcano was showing renewed signs of life.

Once we cleared the customs, Ambrosia gave me, what I can only describe as, a cursory kiss, pushed two men out of her way, and grabbed a taxi. I was left stranded, standing at the curb with all the baggage. I concluded that she'd decided that, for now, she wouldn't be good company. Having observed the first wisps before, I was almost glad she'd made that decision. I really had no idea if I could handle another Santorini.

It just so happens that once I got over the initial surprise, I didn't mind her sudden departure, well… not that much. The moment the taxi deposited me at home I've spent the next half hour, probably longer, on the telephone to my parents. To my pleasant surprise they both forgave me. In fact, mother thought that the very concept of eloping was…

"Simply the most romantic thing anyone could do. I could just see you in Gretna Green…" she went on for a while. Quite a while.

I think way back when, mother must have dreamt of being whisked off to Scotland, to escape the drudge of her own wedding. My mother is the antithesis of a typical woman. She still thinks that marriage is between two people, not between two families and a few dozen friends.

To explain her (mistaken) aspirations, Gretna Green is a village in the south of Scotland famous for runaway weddings. It hosts an average of 5000 weddings every year, often for couples escaping some family disagreements. Its fame dates back to 1753, when Lord Hardwicke managed to pass a law requiring both parties in marriage to be at least 21 years old, or procure their parents' consent. As the Act did not apply in Scotland, many a youthful runaway took advantage of the Old Blacksmith's shop, which offered wedding ceremonies.

"Well, it was better than Vegas, anyway…" I could hear dad talking to himself in the background. I wondered how my father knew so much about Las Vegas. Perhaps he was a dreamer, too.

I wouldn't dream of dissuading mother's romantic ideas by reminding her that we went to the Greek Islands, instead of to the cold, foggy Scotland. After all, in a way, she had the right idea. We did elope, even if the assumed CIA were the culprits.

It appears that at her meeting with the Dean, Ambrosia's yield was equivalent to *mikro koritsi,* known to us in Greece as "Little Girl". For a moment I went as far as feeling sorry for Dean McGinnis.

These are the actual words she used to describe her meeting with the poor old man.

"I gave him a *mikro koritsi,* twice the size of Hiroshima and Nagasaki combined," she said, almost smiling, and then added, "Greek bombs, are particularly dirty, you know."

I didn't want to know. I supposed she might have been referring to fallout. As I said, I didn't want to know. I've read that Hera, when angry, could be quite nasty even to Zeus. By now, Ambrosia was just beginning to relax. Just beginning.

We were still officially on holidays, and, as of last night, Ambrosia was on a self-declared suspension. She told the Dean she'd have to think things over. She said he begged her to reconsider. She replied that he had one week to have her articles published or... else. The stupid thing was that the articles had not even been on the list of subjects defined by, and or dear to, our friends from the CIA.

For the next day or two, I tried to keep well out of Ambrosia's way. It's not that she'd turn nasty or even intentionally unpleasant to me, but her head was so full of scheming, devising ways for getting even with the offending dean, there was little else she was willing to talk about.

On Thursday after our return, the fourth day if I remember correctly, she began talking about tunneling. She'd go to her lab, return home, make notes, file them in *my* filing cabinet under lock and key, then run to her lab again. A number of times, when I returned home from the library, I'd catch her on the telephone, which she'd quickly replace as though having been caught flirting with a lover.

Her immediate assault on my lips, and a number of times on the rest of my body, dismissed that last possibility. In fact I was beginning to hope that I'd catch her "red-handed" on the telephone more often. What peeved me somewhat was that I had absolutely no idea what all the hush-hush stuff was about. By Friday, apart from her surreptitious phone calls, she got back to normal. Ambrosia's normal. A bundle of romantic emotions interrupted by mental gymnastic.

After all, goddesses are not supposed to behave like normal people. They wouldn't be goddesses it there did, would they?

By Friday afternoon, I began to make some phone calls myself. I wanted to test the ground if my ideas on hypnotism had a chance of success. In order not to be taken as loco, or a metaphysical crank, I had to tread gently. I couldn't mention, for instance, my own recent successes. That might have placed me under lock and key, in a nicely padded cell. Even assistant professors are expected to exhibit a modicum of sanity. I was playing close to the borderline.

I missed not having Ambrosia to bounce off my ideas. She struck me still as completely consumed with something which, at least for now, she was not disposed to share with me. As long as her distraction wasn't tall, dark and handsome, and wearing pants, I was willing to play along.

But not for long. OK. I was *hoping* it wouldn't be for long.

The responses I got from my contacts were mainly positive. A group of five had agreed to meet with me, to discuss the *modus operandi*. I wondered if we should involve a professional hypnotist, but I decided against it. After all, the purpose of my research was still intimately connected with my profession, with Comparative Religion. If there were to be peripheral benefits, those would come later.

The reason I needed a number of people to take part in my work on regression was that, at least in theory, you can only access your own past. What you haven't experienced yourself, presumably in some of your previous reincarnations, was not available to you. There was a ray of hope, however. If Carl Jung, the distinguished funder of Analytical Psychology was right, then we all might have access to some aspects of racial memory. Jung defined it under two headings: the Collective Unconscious and the Archetypes. The racial characteristics developed over ages of evolution.

At the moment we agreed that all five of us would download from the Internet a book of instructions dealing with self-hypnosis, and begin practicing its guidelines immediately. I gave them the title and the author, and we agreed to meet within three days, to compare notes.

It was only the first step, but even the tallest mountains begin way down in the valley. I had to start somewhere.

As for myself, I added another post-hypnotic suggestion to my exercises. I attempted to program my subconscious to make the necessary adjustments in my mind/body connection to assure the best possible results for the fulfillment of my purpose in this life. A tall order, but... *Qui ne risque rien* n'a *rien.*

Actually I prefer the Polish version of this proverb: Who doesn't take a risk, doesn't go to jail. I find the Polish version more inspiring.

I'd just put down my receiver, having made the last call, when Ambrosia blew in. She was all-smiles. Immediately, I smelled a rat.

It was evening. I got a bottle of wine and poured both glasses. I preferred not to ask her what happened. She'd tell me in her own good time. I didn't have to wait long.

"Well, darling, I ought to tell you, that once again, I'm on holidays," she said as we sat to dinner.

No fireworks, no tears, not even sadness.

In fact, Ambrosia made the announcement without any emotion. It was her way of saying that she'd resigned from McGill, the place she loved. I thought it wiser not ask her about the details. They could wait. And frankly, after what I've heard already, I could well guess what happened.

The following day I told her about my plans for the group I was forming. She got instantly interested.

"What, and you didn't include me?"

"You are integral component of my success. Without you I'd have to start from scratch. I just didn't feel empowered to mention your name to my team."

"Thank you, my Lord, but I don't have any secrets, and I'm extremely proud of our success with your ankle. Did you tell them about it?"

I raised one eyebrow at the "no secrets" statement, and was glad that she hadn't noticed.

"Not in as many words. I want them to learn the principles of autohypnosis before I'll get them involved in actual regression."

"So how did you get them excited?"

"I gave them the theoretical possibility that we might be able to rewrite history books, once we master the techniques of hypnotic regression."

"Hmmm, how humble!" she laughed. Yes. This was the first time she laughed since we got back from Milos. I patted myself on my back.

"I told them we have to start somewhere..." I added, trying to look as self-deprecatory as I could.

"So why not at the top?"

"That's not what I told them, darling. You know that," this time I tried to look crestfallen. I still had no idea if her humour was here to stay.

She stopped eating, put down her knife and fork, and looked at me.

"Darling. I'm all right. You don't have to humour me. I'm all right, really. I'm only mad when I feel helpless. I'm not any more." For now, she didn't volunteer any more information on her solution to her problems.

To my pleasant surprise we spent the rest of supper discussing various aspects of my own work. Later we tried to make a list of the most fascinating periods of history that might benefit from closer scrutiny. To my surprise, Ambrosia was very conversant with the New Testament, particularly the parts dealing with Paul's travels and good works in Greece. Apparently Greeks felt very proud of carrying the heritage of the early days of Christendom. I made a mental note to reread the Acts of the Apostles, before she'd embarrass me.

Each time I talked to Ambrosia, I was surprised what a very orderly mind she had. It seemed at odds with her apparently explosive character. Or perhaps she'd learned to channel her emotional energies into her work. Most of the time.

Next morning she was up well before I got out of bed. After all, I was still on holidays, though, I was under an impression that so was she. When I finished my shower, I found her on the balcony, the telephone in hand, making notes. She was so preoccupied with whatever she was doing that she hadn't noticed me approaching with a mug of coffee. When she saw me, she looked almost flustered.

"I didn't want to wake you up, darling. Thank you. Thank you very much. I could do with a cuppa-java.

"Strong, full-bodied and freshly brewed," I said, wondering if she'd notice that it was instant from a jar. I also wondered if I should pull up a chair and sit next to her.

"You sit right here, and I'll make the eggs. Just the way you like them." She disappeared inside the living room.

The morning was perfect. No longer humid, like last month, but warm with just a touch of freshness. That last was probably due to the elevation we were at. The steady breeze helped. It blew from the side of the mountain, giving us the benefit of oxygenated air. At least, I hoped so. Downtown's fresh air is at a premium.

My mind returned to Ambrosia. She seemed busy, but no longer tense. Just busy. I wondered when she'd share with me her latest endeavours.

The next two days were strange to say the least.

I spent every evening attempting to enter a state of self-induced hypnosis, and then to attempt imposing on myself post-hypnotic suggestions, recorded with my own voice on my recording machine. While the system worked a few times with reasonable results, I needed to advance further. For that I needed an outside person to monitor my results while under hypnosis. In the past, before we left for Milos, Ambrosia assisted me almost every day. Since our return, I didn't feel I could ask her for help. Though lately she refused to admit it, she was deeply preoccupied with something which, at least for now, she refused to share with me. She also developed a habit of popping out of the apartment for fifteen or twenty minutes at a time, four or five times a day, and then returning as if nothing had happed at all.

While I trusted her that whatever she'd do would be for the best, most probably for the both of us, her reticence to discuss it was beginning to weigh more heavily on me with each coming day.

Ambrosia would also get up in the middle of the night to make phone calls. Not that I was spying on her, but her voice sometimes took tones of persuasion, which sounded a lot louder in the still of the night than it would have during the day.

Tomorrow, I told myself, I'm going to put my foot down.

The moment I've decided to act, Ambrosia demonstrated

her sixth sense. I have no idea what else it might have been.

For some reason, she chose to repeat, word for word, movement by movement, the first night we'd spent together in my apartment. It was like reliving the experience under hypnosis. Her words still ring in my ears.

"Make love to me, Simon. Make love to me like you've never made love before…"

I did. Only this time I had no idea if this was an echo of a wonderful past, or the beginning of a painful goodbye.

***

Chapter 22
Home?

"There is something** I haven't told you, Simon. I hope you'll forgive me," Ambrosia said, her face a picture of misery. "I really wanted to, but, then... you made me so happy, so very happy... oh, Simon, I simply couldn't risk losing you."

As she talked, her words came out softer and slower, like a *diminuendo* as well as *rallentando*, performed by a practiced musician. I reached for her and held her close. To my credit, I must confess that I had no idea what she was talking about. Even the weather, for once, was just as miserable as her voice. They promised sunshine in late afternoon, but none came.

After wiping a tear, I noticed that she continued to avoid my eyes. I still had no idea what got her into this state.

"There was another reason why I had to leave Milos for Athens, and then go as far away from Greece as I could."

This came up with her normal, controlled voice. At last, we were getting somewhere. I didn't want to interrupt in case she'd seize up on me again.

"It was my father," she whispered. "My dear, loving father."

She was all right now. In control. I left her on the settee and went to open a bottle of wine. "It has to be dry, it has to be red," she'd once told me. "The name's immaterial." I'm sure some *connoisseurs* would be deeply offended but for me, it made shopping much easier.

I was about to open it when she stood up.

"Before you open it, come with me. If you'll still want to drink it with me when we get back..." she didn't finish.

She took hold of my elbow and led me to my front door.

Then she pressed the "UP" button on the elevators. There were only three floors above me. What the hell, I mused? What if she has friends?

The cab door slid open on the penthouse floor. That's where instead of four, they have only two apartments per floor. On *the* floor, there's only one penthouse. And large, magnificent terraces, reminiscent of the Milos' villa. I looked one of them over when I was first moving in. Just for fun. I knew I'd never afford it. Not on associate professor's salary.

She put her key into the door of the door facing southwest. Then she stood back to let me pass.

"What's this?" I asked.

For a moment she remained silent. Then she cleared her throat and said softly.

"This is my father's wedding present for us."

"B-b-but this would cost a fortune..." I couldn't help stammering.

"It did. And I might as well tell you. The other side of this floor is reserved for your office and my private lab."

I had to sit down. There were deep armchairs and two settees ready to take the load of my rapidly weakening legs. Even as I let myself slide down, my eyes roved around the living room. It was at least twice the size of the one we lived in below. You could entertain royalty here and be proud of your pad. Pad? More like a palace.

"He is that rich?" I muttered at last.

Ambrosia was slowly recovering her usual wonderful composure.

"And this is why you had to leave Milos for Athens... and beyond?"

"No, silly. Do you remember I told you that my father would kill both of us if he caught us, well... he'd call it fornicating?"

"You were joking, of course."

She gave me a long, slightly uncertain look. "Don't be so sure, Simon. In Greece we, or should I say they, have different ways of expressing their displeasure."

I suddenly felt a cold shiver. I remembered her eyes, which, at the time, I put down to a slight attack of hysteria. This sounded more like Mafia than Municipal Government. In spite of my mental condition, and my nerves that seemed stretched to the limit of their elasticity, I made a mental note to look up "Greek Mafia" on the Internet.

She took my arm and led me on a tour of the apartment. It was splendid. Then we crossed over to the lab. Two thirds were already showing signs of future computer terminals, as well as other electronic gadgets. The remaining one-third was fitted with wall-to-wall shelving, a desk with two portable computers, printer, telephone, and the usual peripherals of a well-appointed office. A large archway led to a sitting area, which opened to the terrace.

"If thou therefore wilt worship me, all shall be thine..." I mused, too softly for her to hear. I was beginning to put two and two together.

"Do you like it?"

After a while I turned. "Let's go and have that wine, in *my* place." I must have stressed the adjective "my" a little too much. We left without another word. What was there to say? Her face clouded, but she maintained a tight grip on my elbow on our way out, and all the way to *my* place. I was waiting for my breathing to return to normal.

The penthouse was magnificent. Compared to my own apartment, it was a palace. And I certainly never had an office such a size, with such a library and such equipment on my desk. Yes, I glanced at the books. There was a selection of subjects that were available in my specialty. For reference purposes mostly, I supposed. Lately I used principally my computer—for research, that is. Books? Books I liked. No. I loved books. I liked their feel, their smell, and their timeless quality. You can click off a computer; you can't click off a book. It is still there, with you, like a faithful companion.

On our way down I noted an additional elevator door.

That's right. The penthouses had a private elevator.

Ambrosia sat on the settee, facing the mountain.

I poured wine into two glasses, brought them over, and sat next to her.

"Your view would be identical," she said.

For some unknown reason I felt angry. I wanted to hurt her. I offered her my apartment, the best I could afford, and now this. Perhaps it wasn't her fault but she must have had her hand in it. Her father couldn't have done it all on his own. And her father must have been stinky rich. I mean *really* rich. The Montreal downtown penthouses went for lots more than a million. A double one would probably be priceless. He must have bought somebody out, to make room for hers and my office.

"We didn't want to hurt you, Simon," she began, halfway through the second glass. "It's just, well, you see, there is a good chance that I'll have to resign within a few days. I simply cannot stop my research in mid-step. I truly believe that it's that important."

She looked up at me for understanding. I decided to keep pouting just a little longer.

"We can continue living right here, darling. Really." Then she gave me that special look. "It is here that I have my most precious memories…"

She wasn't playing fair and she was winning. After all, she was a goddess. My god, was she ever a goddess!

It took another while, but we ended up on the bed on which she had all those precious memories. She wasn't the only one. I wonder if she knew that I'd been a virgin when I met her? I still didn't have the courage to tell her. Could she tell, anyway? Can women tell? I never even imagined that she could have been one. With such looks, such brains, such figure…

Later we lay, side by side, the curtain drawn wide, in full daylight. Somehow whatever happened upstairs seem less important now. She was my wife, my lover, my goddess. I would follow her to hell and back, never mind upstairs to the penthouse.

"It's all right, darling. It's alright."

I'll never figure women out. Now, that I told her that it was all right, she started crying. Big, gut wrenching sobs.

"I w-w-as s-s-so w-worried…" she mumbled. "I w-was so w-worried you w-wouldn't love me any m-more…"

"It would take a lot more than a gorgeous penthouse apartment, with a breathtaking view, a splendid office and a private elevator, for me to stop loving you," I assured her.

"And my father isn't a crook, Simon. He's just very rich. Each time a member of our family wanted to leave the island, he bought them out. Bit by bit. We used to have a large family, for hundreds and hundreds of years. Now, he owns virtually the whole island. He's not a crook, Simon, but he does wield a lot of influence."

I never implied he was a crook but there must have been something in my eyes, I suppose. Ambrosia was a very, very smart lady. And even if she weren't, I'd still love her just as much.

"I'd love you even if he were," I assured her. "I'd love you if he were the devil himself." That came out a bit strong, "instead of an angel which he is," I corrected quickly, and collapsed on the pillows.

Believe me, with all those emotions and, well, you know what, I was really tired. No exercises tonight.

Later, when yours truly calmed down somewhat, we went back upstairs. During the rest of the afternoon, evening by then, she confessed, that the whole penthouse business had begun before we left for Milos. As the matter hadn't been settled, not legally, she wanted to wait until the papers had been signed, so as not to bother me unnecessarily, in case nothing came of it.

Later, once the furnishings were in place, she wanted to inspect the place, again, before bothering me. All furnishings except for my king-size bed.

"I had to move things around to make sure you'd like it there. You do understand, don't you?"

I was beginning to. Ambrosia was a most extraordinary woman. She even suspected that I might be sorry to leave my old place. After all, no man likes to be a kept man.

"Papa thought the new place ought to be in your name."

With that she got up, opened a drawer in my new desk, and pulled out a folder. In it, some very legally looking papers certified that the Penthouse (at such and such), is the property of one Simon Jones, referred to hereinafter as the owner...

I hated legalese.

This went on for seven pages, some of which I could understand. There were even clauses "in the event of death," which, for some reason at moments like this, I felt fast approaching. Lawyers are not all bad—it's just that 95% of them make the rest look bad. I remembered the phrase.

At the bottom of the last page I noted that the Montreal firm of lawyers were hired by a firm of accountants in Athens. They must have been busy boys, those accountants.

I put down the file and got up. First, I looked around just standing there. The walls were white, as was the ceiling, as was most furniture other than the parts made of wood. That, in turn, was highly polished, mostly rosewood, to which Ambrosia referred to as palisander. At that moment I still hated to admit it, but the place was beautiful. It was elegant, warm, inviting, almost embracing with, yes, with Greek generosity. If I hadn't been in such a foul mood the first time, I would have admitted it to myself there and then.

Also, there were Ambrosia's touches throughout the luxurious apartment. In the living part of the penthouse, there were four large vases of fresh bougainvilleas, their explosions of red demanding to be admired. This was no longer Montréal, this was Milos. This was the place where Ambrosia wanted to be; this was the place where her parents could visualize her, to feel that she's not that far away.

I suddenly felt embarrassed by my selfishness.

I read a book once, by Steinbeck. I can't be sure, but I think the book was titled Sea of Cortez. In it, I'm likewise not sure, but I think there was a character name Ed Ricketts. A marine biologist, ecologist, and philosopher, man of few possessions, but with a magnificent ability to receive with such grace that the giver felt exulted. I remember, at the time of reading, I had been most impressed by Ed, who rather than give, had learned to receive with such enormous grace.

It was at that moment, I realized, that I lacked this grace. That I must change my ways, must sublimate my ego, and rejoice in being part of such wonderful people as Ambrosia and her family.

Most people don't appreciate how lucky they are. Well, as of that minute, I decided to always, always count my blessings. I still do.

There is only one thing I must add to this event. We'd still spent the night in my old apartment. My king-size bed, looking lonely in spite of its size, was the only piece of furniture still there. The next morning, Ambrosia and I spent a good few hours transferring my king-size frame up to the penthouse. Ambrosia categorically refused to give up the memories she tied up with this mattress. I can't say that I blame her. There were many wonderful nights we've spent on it. But there was only one First Night. For that there is no substitute, there is no other.

We were black and blue by the time we managed to transfer the large monster up there, to the new bedroom, which in all other respects resembled my old one. Ambrosia saw to that. She was funny that way.

***

Chapter 23

More Walls

The man whose face filled the screen of my videophone connection to the lobby was a total stranger. Judging by the proximity and the angle his face presented to the camera he must have been tall; also he looked very tanned, and sported a flamboyant beard that covered most of his lower face. The mustache was trimmed short, and the hair on his head was cropped to look like a 1950 GI Joe action figure. If it weren't for his beard my first suspicion would have been CIA, but the beard, even if it was a disguise, was just too much of a good thing, even for a secret agent. It had to be real.

"Simon? It's me. Could you let me in, please?"

The voice was definitely familiar. Then the man leaned towards the camera so that only his eyes were filling the lens. I caught my breath.

"Pa…"

"Just let me in?"

I pressed the button and the door to the private elevator in the lobby opened. The man walked in without looking back, and the cab door shut behind him. Seventeen seconds later he walked out on the penthouse floor foyer. The disguise was perfect. Not even I, who saw him daily for two weeks, hours at a time, could possibly recognize him.

"Papa?" I couldn't help saying this with joy mixed with curiosity.

"Of course it is I. Who else would have made such a fool of himself just to see his only son and daughter?"

Papa Milos was standing in our private hall, trying to look over my shoulder.

"Is she in?"

Only then I heard a gentle giggle from the living room behind me. The next moment, Ambrosia run out with her usual lack of restrain, and dove into her father's open arms.

"Papa, Papa, Papa, you came!!!"

I concluded that she was pleased to see her father, even if he wasn't in the least bit recognizable. For some reason, Ambrosia didn't seem in the least surprised. After a prolonged hug, they walked arm in arm into the living room. A moment later she turned, ran back, and pulled me inside. She then walked to the window, turned and stared at us both.

"My two favourite men in the whole wide world!" she said, clapping her hands.

Then she ran to her father and hugged him again.

Some minutes later Papa asked, almost shyly.

"Can I see it?"

"Of course. It's quite wonderful. And it's all thanks to you, Papa. We are so grateful, aren't we Simon?"

I nodded repeatedly affirming my total agreement. I surmised that they were both talking about the apartment.

"Simon, you show Dad around, and I'll prepare some refreshments. You will stay for supper Dad, of course, won't you?"

It was a rhetorical question. Her father only smiled. I was about to take him on a tour of both sides of the penthouse, when he grabbed me in a bear hug I haven't felt since my rugby days.

"She's happy, my son. You made her happy!" he added, his smile beaming from ear to ear.

I was about to say "guilty but insane", but thought better of it. It was apparent that Mr. Milos was deadly serious. For a brief moment I wondered what would have happened to me if he'd thought otherwise.

I showed him our "living quarters", then, slowly at a leisurely pace, I took him to the other side of the penthouse to show him where we worked. I told him that the place was almost as new to us as it was to him; that we were just beginning to get used to it. Mr. Milos walked slowly, lagging a bit behind me, peeking at details of walls, and doors, and even examining the handrail on the terrace. He then looked at windows, how they opened and closed, then gave equal attention to the light fittings. He's acting as though he wanted to buy the place, I chuckled to myself.

"To tell you the truth, Papa, I've never lived, let alone worked, in such luxurious surrounding. Never," I added. I must have sounded as I felt, still in a slight daze.

"But do you like it, Son?"

What a strange question, I thought. It's like being asked do you like luxury, comfort, superb view, great air, lots and lots of space etc, etc.

"We are having a wine cellar installed next week. Then it will be perfect," I said instead. I felt the need to say something constructive. I thought that would stump him.

"Where," he said, "show me."

It was where the previous penthouse apartment, which we now used as offices, had its kitchen. I showed him.

"Good choice," he said. Then he smiled. "Something tells me that you like it," he said, staring directly into my eyes.

"I guess, you can tell, Papa. I also guess, I never really thanked you. Not properly…"

Before I could finish I was on the receiving end of yet another bear hug. One more of those and my ribs would need a long holiday in a sanatorium undergoing extensive physiotherapy. After that, nothing would induce me to pay Papa any more complements. Such show of gratitude might prove detrimental to my physical wellbeing. What did bother me, however, was the trouble he appeared to have taken to hide his identity. In the end I had to ask Ambrosia.

"It's a long story," she said, a little sadly. Then she added, "You'd better ask him yourself."

I was ready to do so, over dinner, when he became aware of the repeated curious looks I must have stolen in his direction, without actually saying a word. It wasn't just the beard, but I remember his hair having been combed straight back and being virtually pure white. His GI Joe coif was not only standing on its end, but it was darkish red, to match his beard.

"It's the colour, isn't it," he said at last, downing his third glass of wine. This was a night of celebration. He also tugged at the splendid growth, showing that it was his own.

I smiled, not quite knowing how to react.

"Oh, yes, he said. I started working on it the day you left Milos. I knew I'd want to visit you both, and this was the way I presented myself on my last trip."

"You were here before?"

"Just to sign all the documents. It wasn't nearly as long then," he laughed, still playing with his beard. I suspect his laughter was directed mostly at seeing my obvious confusion.

"Oh, all right, son, I guess you ought to know. The last time I was in the USA, some years ago, I did some deals, which, ha, ha, the CIA thought threatened the security of their country. It had only to do with tourism but the Pentagon has a bee in their bonnet that everybody lives for the sole purpose of killing them, preferably with weapons of mass destruction. They are daily torturing their own people with security measures that are absurdly exaggerated. They ought to be treated by an army of psychiatrists."

"Papa meant them no harm," Ambrosia put in.

"I merely found a way for the Greek expatriates to visit their homeland, and return to the USA, without going through the red tape rigmarole which they'd created. The fact that this also made it possible to smuggle some goodies, some of them not encouraged by the Surgeon General, was hardly of my concern." He raised his glass, and studied the refracted reds against the flickering flame of the candles.

Ambrosia was watching me. There must have been something in my eyes that worried her.

"No, Simon, not drugs. Well, not really," she added on due consideration.

"Greek wine, my son," Papa confessed. "Wine and ouzo. A bit of tsipouro. Nothing much. We are sick and tired of being upstaged by the French and the Italians in their exports. It's all to do with connections, with who knows who, not with the quality of wine. You can attest to the latter yourself. Yes? No wonder Greece is falling behind economically. I enabled my people to bring in fair quantities of our wine, without going through official channels."

"How?" I was flabbergasted.

"That, my son, will remain a secret even from you. Ambrosia doesn't know either. But I do know, and that is why I travel under an assumed name, passport, and appearance. There. Now you know. And if you brag about it, you'll send Papa to jail."

I wouldn't dream about it, but it did cast the CIA interest in Ambrosia Milos in a slightly different light. We already knew, on our own skins, that they did not like to be upstaged, let alone being made fools of.

We talked until the early hours. Papa had countless stories to recount, all from his own experiences. Now that apparently I've passed all the requisite tests, I was treated to stories I would amuse my grandchildren with for years. Of course, we would have to begin with children, Papa said, with a pointed look at Ambrosia's stomach.

"Papa!" she exclaimed, but her eyes were smiling.

Papa slept in our official guest bedroom. At last we found a use for it. Since England, I've never had more than one room dedicated to sleeping. If friends came to visit, they slept on the sofa. They never complained. But I was very glad that we could treat Papa royally, even if, let's face it, it was with his own money.

The next morning, I had yet another shock. I went to the kitchen early, to prepare fresh orange juice, which I knew he loved on Milos. I didn't have a proper squeezing machine, and had to do it manually, which wasn't that easy. At last I succeeded and was ready to present Papa with my *pièces de résistance*. Ambrosia caught me at the door. She looked sad.

"He's gone," she said, a tear forming at the corner of her eye. "He always does that," she added. "He hates goodbyes. They hurt too much, he told me." And then her tears came in abundance.

Those Greeks, I thought, sure are emotional people. On the other hand if I had to leave Ambrosia behind for any length of time, I'd be none to happy either.

"There, there," I said. I had no experience what one is suppose to do in such circumstances. "There," I repeated the third time, "you have his orange juice."

Somehow my freshly squeezed effort didn't help. In fact, it brought another flood. She turned and went back to the guest bedroom, only to return smiling.

"He'll be back," she said.

I looked up, still holding up the orange I prepared for Papa. "How do you know?"

"His travelling bag is still there. He hid it under the bed."

It was then that I remembered his words, last night, when Ambrosia was preparing dinner.

"This is all yours, my son, but you are too busy right now to look after my investment."

I wasn't aware I was that busy, but I had zero experience in investments, in real estate, or any other moneymaking enterprises. I've learned later that a number of subcontractors had to be paid the residual amounts, after the final inspection, which, apparently, Papa has carried out on arrival. I thought he was just admiring the place. I assumed that the luxury passed the test, or else he'd still be here.

For me, Papa will forever remain an enigmatic figure. Each time I met him, even on Milos, there was something new, something unexpected. Like that story he'd told me that he had to go all the way to Athens to get permission to rebuild the airport in Milos. Apparently, the other islands presented stiff competition. Jealousy or greed for the tourist dollar, I wondered? He did it, of course, mostly with his own money.

As Ambrosia already told me, he owned most of the island.

We were having second cups of coffee when, with a mischievous smile playing about her lips, she asked me, "So how did you like his cloak and dagger story?"

"You mean all that stuff about protecting the expatriates?

She nodded.

"Well..." I mused, "fairly convincing?"

"Just fairly?"

Then she couldn't hold it back any longer. She started laughing, then giggling, then laughing outright again.

"He tells everybody that story. It's his favourite!"

"And the truth is..." I urged.

"Oh, the story may be true. I have no idea. Papa can do just about anything he puts he heart to." Her speech was still interrupted by sporadic giggles.

I waited, not knowing if I should laugh with her, or feel offended.

"Oh, all right, darling." She wiped tears of merriment from her eyes. "Let's start at the beginning."

I nodded vigoruously.

"Have you heard about the Flower Children?"

"A little..."

"It was a hippie movement of idealistic young people who gathered in San Francisco around 1967. A little later they spread to England. That was when father was just finishing his LLB. He studied law at the University of London."

I topped our cups again. The story was beginning to draw me in.

"Well, please don't laugh, but dad's name, then, was Abioud Agamemnon Damokles Maripeloponissos. That last was his surname. He carries it in his passport to this day."

To say that I was stunned would be a considerable understatement. Ambrosia just smiled.

"So his real name must have been what he referred to as an assumed name," I mused, "and his appearance was to match his photo on the passport?"

She nodded. "Each time he renews his passport, he grows a beard. It's his way of making fun of rules and regulations, which he dislikes intensely. He dislikes anything that restricts the freedom of man. You might say he's the original libertarian."

My eyes were growing larger.

"Well," she continued, "according to dad, in England, when you come from an adjacent village, for the first five years you are called a bloody foreigner. For a man with my father's name, they've run out of offensive adjectives."

I could only nod. She was right, of course. This was before London became the Mecca for foreigners from all over the world.

"So… when asked where he came from he'd reply Milos. Within a week he became Milos. Mr. Milos. No first name, as often is the case in England."

"And what has that to do with the Flower Children?"

"In those days you needed a long beard to be accepted among the students. Now father had a long beard and a name they could pronounce. He was finally accepted. He was in! Where he drew a line, so to speak, was with the long hair. He had his cut into a GI Joe style, which you've just seen, and which still figures on his passport."

"So his name really is…"

"Unpronounceable to most people. His popularity in England inspired him to retain this moniker back home. There, especially after he became the principal landowner and sat on the council, they began referring to him as Papa Milos, a little after Papa Hemingway, dad's favourite author."

"And now, when he travels, he reverts to his true self?"

"Just for fun, darling. Just for fun! It makes him feel young again."

As I sat back downing my third cup of coffee, with all that happened, I found it hard to believe that Ambrosia and I have met less then two months ago. I could only wonder what the next month would bring.

Papa Milos was back in for dinner. He stayed with us another two days. Apparently he had three other buildings to inspect. After the Greek economy had begun to show signs of stress, he'd chosen Montreal to protect some of his money. It was much cheaper than Toronto, let alone the USA.

It seemed that Papa had also built a wall around Milos, and felt safe behind the crowds of people who regarded him as friend, and somewhat in a way that members of the Mafia reputedly regard their "Godfather". The difference was that while Papa would fight for the wellbeing of his own people, he would not break the laws of his own country to do so. If the USA decided to interfere with his plans that was their problem. With the Greeks, and with Greece, he was always above board. Still, I wouldn't like to be on the wrong side of him.

My ribs still felt his bear hug.

It came to me, however, that one of the reasons why Papa furnished us with these new palatial quarters, and particularly Ambrosia's private laboratory, was that he felt that he might have been at least partially responsible for the CIA giving her a hard time. He may have been right. Elephants never forget, nor does the CIA, and Ambrosia did carry her father's name. Until, at her father's request and her own pleasure, she changed it, officially, to Milos. To Ambrosia Milos.

Proudly, I might add.

***

Chapter 24
Prisons

"**H**ere, on Earth, we are all imprisoned** in our physical bodies. They are the walls we built around ourselves, to protect our egos from the vicissitudes of everyday life," I wrote. I had a great deal more work to do before the next series of lecture.

I was depressed—I had to get the negativity out of my system. I have been writing my opening lecture for the new semester for a week, now. While most of my material *per force* had to repeat itself, I always tried to start the season with something fresh.

"Some, if not most of us, are searching for a way out, or looking for gods or idols we can look up to, idols we can admire, perhaps envy, yet continue to treat as superior entities so that they might, by some means, miraculous or temporal, free us from our self-imposed prisons."

Not realizing, I thought, that that which is immortal is hidden within us, often trying desperately to get out, yes, from those very same, self-imposed prisons. Could I tell them that? I was not a preacher; I was an interpreter of what virtually all religions of the world have been attempting to teach us. Not religions so much as the myths from which they'd originated. I didn't tell people to listen. I told them what they were listening to.

Yet, people needed idols—people who'd look after them. People or gods.

I recall my sister composing a poem, some years ago, in

honour of one of the American or was it the UK Idol winner, or participator, I forget which, who must have been from Alaska.

> *My grunts vibrate over the North Pole,*
> *travelling right thro' the growing ozone hole,*
> *then bounce and rise to the silvery moon...*
> *I can scream, and howl, and sometimes even croon!*

> *Then I overdo acting, like the misbegotten hams,*
> *And I roar louder, to drown the deafening drums.*
> *I throw my weight around, jerk for all I'm worth!*
> *'Cause I'm the First, the Only, Idol of the North!*

I wondered if I should read it to them...

"That search for idols we can admire is the beginning of all religions. We wish to realign ourselves, to reconnect to that within us, which unbeknown to most of us already is immortal.

On the other hand, according to Webster's Collegiate Dictionary, the word religion goes back to old Latin *religio*, meaning "taboo restraint". If we dig deeper, we might split the word into *re* prefix of "return", and *ligare*, meaning to "bind". Doesn't it sound like yet another wall? A return to bondage? We spent most of our lives either trying to hide behind walls, or to escape from our need for their protection."

I took a sip of water.

"This season, we shall attempt to examine the precepts of Christianity, Judaism, Hinduism, Islam, Buddhism, Shinto, Sikhism, Bahai and Jainism. I think you'll find that all of them are motivated by the same desire: to break the walls which keep us from discovering our true nature."

I wondered if I was pushing them—my future audience—too far. On the other hand, it was my job to expose and attempt to explain various religions, not to judge them.

"We all seem to search for idols we can admire, exactly like the people of Moses, or Mohammad, or Buddha, who had to deal with their followers bowing to a different idol they've created for every week of the year. Not much has changed since those days. Perhaps it got worse. The ancients had some fifty-two gods to look up to; our youth is looking at hundreds of stars and starlets who seem to define their hunger for success. Those star and starlets became their idols, the idols they worship. Just listen to their screams and applause, when one of them appears in the periphery of their vision. They create a veritable pandemonium, and that, my friends, is how Milton in his *Paradise Lost*, named the capital of Hell. Yes, my friends, the Paradise that we have lost. Or, perhaps, we are not as lost as we seem to be. Perhaps, in essence, we bow to but two gods; their names are Fame and Fortune. The numberless idols serve them even as we do. They alone feed our egos."

Somehow, my bellyaching didn't make me feel any better.

How few of us, I mused, could see that this search to placate our egos is a sign of devolution? At our subliminal level we see the world collapsing all around us. No, not physically, although there are wars and rumours of wars— just like in the apocalypse of John. Yet, our world will not end physically. For that, according to Hindus, we have to wait another 400,000 years or so. Perhaps that's how long it will take for the Black Hole at the center of our galaxy to swallow us.

No. It is our spirit that seems imprisoned behind ever-thickening walls.

"And when we awaken from the onslaught of the media feeding us, daily, mayhem and destruction, degeneration and decadence, we begin to understand our need for gods, for idols of any kind. We realize that what we are really searching for is immortality, even vicarious immortality masquerading behind the faces of idols, men and women usurping fame, money, or political posturing."

"What a pity," Ambrosia murmured, looking over my shoulder. "Your next lecture?"

I hadn't heard her come in. Her hand, gently resting on my shoulder, was just the right medicine I needed for my disgruntled nerves.

The bold-lettered title at the top of the desktop was *Prisons in Scriptures.* I wondered if I was taking liberties. I seem to have pointed out the prisons we create in our everyday lives. Underneath I wrote a subtitle in smaller letters: *The Walls We Build.*

I looked up at Ambrosia, trying to read her thoughts.

"If they only knew that the walls they build between their egos and their true selves are mostly just empty space. Like the rest of physical reality," she added, after reading my last paragraph.

"Would you join me on the lectern to tell my listeners about the reality of empty space? They would not believe me, but they'd take it from a physicist."

"You are forgetting something…" she smiled sadly.

"Such as?"

"I'm blacklisted."

"In publications, not by the McGill, I thought."

"Sorry, darling, that's not a risk I am prepared to take. My ego has built a wall between me and McGill," she said smiling, but her eyes were unaccustomedly cold.

"Did something new happen that I should know about?"

"It may be nothing, I am not sure yet."

"Well?" I stopped writing and swiveled away from my keyboard. Ambrosia's voice showed signs of tiny wisps I've heard before.

"I didn't want to bother you. It's personal."

"Your parents?"

"No, silly. It's something I have to take care of myself."

"Come on, Ambrosia. I'm your husband!" She was beginning to act like her father.

"That's exactly why I didn't want to bother you. Oh... all right. Two days ago there were signs that someone was tinkering with electric cables leading to my computers. Since, I already had additional breakers installed, and tomorrow a generator is coming, which will be installed, under lock and a key, on the roof."

"And you thought you shouldn't bother me with that? Really, darling. You must learn to trust me that I can take little adversities in my stride."

She continued looking very serious.

"There is more. If we attempted tunneling..." she started and looked away.

"Ambrosia, please?"

"If the fluctuations in the current happened during the transfer of any living organism, such organism wouldn't arrive at the other side of the wall in one piece. Half of it might have, but not all of it."

"That's it?" I still wasn't quite sure of the possible consequences. I also had no idea that Ambrosia was already playing with the idea of tunneling living organisms.

"Well, there is also another danger," she looked away from me, unwilling to meet my eyes. "Last weekend, hackers managed to break into the McGill University website. An official from the dean's office said that the incident had been inconvenient, but had not compromised the security of the staff."

I was ahead of her.

"And McGill has access to the computer files you left behind?"

"Yes, Simon, they do. In all honesty, I could hardly have erased them all. After all, I developed them under the aegis of McGill."

Somehow this was reason enough for me to drop the subject.

I closed my computer and invited Ambrosia on the terrace. There were not that many sunny days left in the season for enjoying the outside. I took my shirt off and pretended I was on Milos.

"A swim?" she asked, joining me within a minute or two. She managed to slip into a bikini.

Actually there was a swimming pool in the building, but we didn't particularly enjoy sharing our bathtub with strangers. OK. It was larger than a bathtub, but not enough to make us forget the other people.

It was like with a glass of water. Take a mouthful, rinse your mouth, spit it back in the glass, and then drink it. I bet you won't do that. Nor would I. And I really have no idea why. That's how I feel about small swimming pools.

Actually, I wanted to ask Ambrosia a question. While Jesuits have brought me up, she had a good grounding in the Greek Orthodox version of Christianity.

"Do you think there may be a connection between the miracle makers and the OBE?"

"You'd have to ask my mother," she smiled sweetly, stretching herself suggestively on the other deckchair. That was part of the problem. Whenever we were alone, and not working, most of what Ambrosia did was, or at least seemed to me, to be suggestive. She was obviously determined to make sure that I wouldn't be shortchanged for the first 38 years of my life.

"Seriously," I tried again. "Since according to your mother there are virtually no impossibilities within the realm of the Phase, this would go a long way to explain the miracles. All you'd have needed would have been to make sure that the subjects acquired their shortcomings through a past event and not through some undefined genetic disorder."

"And then, presto, whisk them off into the Phase, perform the necessary repairs and restore them back to physical reality, whole and sound. Sounds good to me?"

"I'm serious..."

"Really, Simon, you don't expect me to solve the mysteries of reality lying half-naked on the terrace, do you?"

"I thought there was virtually nothing you couldn't do providing you were half-naked," I murmured.

"You'll pay for that," she murmured even softer.

I must have grinned like a teenager who was just let out of the cellar for the first time. "I know," I said. "I'm counting on it."

We returned to the subject after dinner. I was also concerned with the subject of resurrection. There were some sources that claimed that Jesus never died on Golgotha, but survived his crucifixion and spent the rest of his life in India—other sources said in the South of France. The India version was supported by no lesser figure than Saint Irenaeus. He was the second century bishop of Lyon, a Church Father, who with his celebrated book *Against Heresies* managed to destroy, almost singlehandedly, the Gnostics. This was particularly surprising since in the Gnostic First Apocalypse of James, Jesus declares, *"Never have I suffered in any way, nor have I been distressed..."* This would strongly imply not only his survival, but also that Jesus was either out of his body, in an OBE, or detached from it in some other way. It goes without saying that if he didn't die, the reports of his resurrection were *non sequitur*.

I wondered how would Ambrosia react to my research.

"What if..." Our discussions have lately began quite often with "what if..."

"What if," I began again making sure I had her attention, "what if during the eighteen years of Yeshûa's life missing from the Bible, he was practicing, wherever he was, the art of OBE? What if he became an absolute master of this state, making it possible for him to move in and out of this state at will?"

She was hooked. Ambrosia liked problems that although they seemed theoretical, yet might have practical applications. All she expected was logical progression of argument, even if the *a priori* sounded farfetched.

She nodded encouragement.

"What if he'd learned to stabilize his reality there? It would explain a great many things, including his statement, towards the end of his ministry *'You will look for me, but you will not find me: and where I am, you cannot come'*."

"Of course they could come if they'd learned the techniques of out of body projection," Ambrosia was getting into the spirit of the discussion.

"Yes, and no," that was one of my favourite answers in metaphysics. "It may be possible that, within the Phase, each one of us creates or, in fact is, a complete world of consciousness, in which we can create anyone and anything, and by the same token, be created by anyone else, who has knowledge of us."

"Mother did say that in the Phase there was nothing we couldn't do…" she put in wonderingly.

"That being so, this would go some way to explain the phrase in which Yeshûa expresses desire that his followers might be made one "in" him. I recall a statement in the King James Bible, *"I in them, and thou in me,"* *'thou'* being his OBE or Phase omnipotent entity, which, I claim, should be considered as his, and thus our, true self!"

I looked up and she was still listening.

"As my job is to separate, as best I can, myths from reality," I concluded triumphantly, "I'd suggest that even if we are talking of unity of consciousness, this, within the scope of our knowledge, would only be possible within the Phase."

"Wow! I bet you can't say that again!"

"I wouldn't even try. But the realm of OBE does open up an unprecedented field of research. We should really get your mother involved in this."

"Good luck," was her only laconic comment.

I sighed to show her my utter desperation. I don't believe she believed me. I tried a different tack.

"And now, allow me to remind you that here, in this wondrous material reality, we abide in Maya. In illusion. After all it is you, the physicists, who claim that we walk on, and are surrounded by empty space. Remember?"

"Are you suggesting that OBE is the "real" reality, and here, on Earth, in our physical reality, we, ah… we, our bodies don't really exist?"

"No, my Pet. I am not saying that. You are. Mrs. Ambrosia Milos, PhD. I just listen and obey."

"You never obeyed anything in your life unless you agreed with it."

"That's as it may be. But do you find my reasoning logical?"

"It might take a little longer to get my blessing as a physicist, but, well, I'll give it some serious thought."

"We mortals, can ask no more of a goddess," I said, bowing deeply.

The following day Ambrosia charged in, ignored me completely and ran, at her usual jog, to the bedroom.

"Is it something I said?" I asked. To my knowledge I was innocent of any marital transgressions.

In minutes she ran out of the bedroom wearing the shortest miniskirt I've ever seen. I think it's called a micro. She stood at the door to the bedroom, still as a statue.

"New?" I asked innocently.

Without a word she started gyrating her hips, then, facing away from me, she began to adjust her high-heeled shoes. I may not have sinned but I was beginning to feel guilty for the thoughts that began crowding my frontal lobe. Ambrosia never needed encouragement in the matters of boudoir, but this was exceptional even for her.

My collar was getting too tight for me.

"Is it something I said?" I repeated, this time hopefully.

"Last night?"

"What about last night, darling?"

"You don't remember!" This time her voice was threatening. She spun on her heel and flung herself on the bed exposing two perfect hemispheres.

"B-b-but you didn't make love to me, last night," she whimpered.

Goddesses extract heavy toll for the transgressions of the mortals. I spent the next three hours paying for my sin of omission. Also I had to swear that I would never commit such a sin again. Never!

***

Chapter 25
I did it my way

From the moment she got up Ambrosia was singing that old Paul Anka classic, "I did it my way." Sinatra may have done it better, but Ambrosia put more heart into it. Since she's gotten blacklisted in the scientific journals, she made sure that none of her work could leak out to those magazines that succumbed to non-scientific pressures from outside. She referred to them as *Les Vendus*, or *Quislings*.

While it would do great things for her ego to be able to wag her finger at all the English Journals on the American and European continents, as well as at the McGill University in general and Dean McGinnis in particular, for a while she didn't have any breakthroughs that would enable her to do so. As for her articles that had been reputedly refused, she now had a choice of German, French and Italian Journals, to mention but a few, who, expressed interest in her latest work. She intended to submit her articles before the Anglophone traitors (that's how she called them) got the wind of it.

Ergo, her bursts of joy.

"I did it myyyyy waaaaaay!" reached me from her lab, through the terrace to the living room where I was attempting to read a book. For a small person, she was endowed with quite a penetrating and sonorous mezzo. I got up quietly, and closed the doors to the terrace. It helped, but didn't eliminate her performance altogether. I put the book down and switched on the TV. I suddenly realized this was the first time this week that I clicked the ON button. I ran through the channels, then ran through them again, and pushed the OFF. I had enough for another week.

Thank heaven for the remote control, I thought. Now that was progress!

Only later that day I've learned the reason for Ambrosia's delight. It was implicitly connected with my own work. In fact, it filled me with equal joy, though in my case it was mixed with considerable, if inarticulate as yet, anxiety. The moment of truth was approaching us in hops and leaps.

Ambrosia said that she could reproduce, seemingly at will, the distinct brainwaves of any living creature. This in itself wasn't the real breakthrough.

"What really counts," she said, "that I can magnify them in a way that the psychokinetic tunneling is becoming a reality. Would you believe that? I did it! And I did it myyyyy wayyyy!"

She couldn't resist that last chorus.

I had to recall everything she's told me about quantum tunneling. If I remembered correctly, one could transfer a small number of electrons through a solid barrier, a wall, if those electrons were propelled on their way with psychokinetic energy. I may not be accurate in my description, but, to the best of my recollection, that was the general idea.

That was still a long haul to transmitting a biological structure, let alone a living organism.

She added, though, that should it be necessary, the restoration of the original atomic structure, if such were required, would be accomplished also by psychokinetic force, generated by yours truly, under a hypnotic trance. Though I failed to see what atomic structure the electrons are supposed to have, without the attendant neutrons and protons, i.e. complete atoms. Don't ask me if it makes any sense. Suffice that she was singing.

"And in what way does your latest magic differ from

previous postulates?" I asked innocently.

"Simon, don't you understand? Now I can move mountains!"

Not being an engineer I had no idea why she'd want to rearrange the landscapes. I liked the Mount Royal just were it was. Is. The last time I heard such claims was when I was still studying the Bible. Speaking from memory it went something like this, "If your faith is the size of a mustard seed, you can say to this mountain, 'Move from here to there,' and it will move." Not a bad trick if you can do it. Speaking for myself, I'd rather move a mustard seed than a mountain. Whichever it was, in my lectures I always assumed this was an allegory. The mountains referred to heaps of difficulties, of troubles, which powerful faith can remove. Now, it seems, Ambrosia had other ideas.

"Well, not exactly mountains, but..." she began, then her voice trailed off.

"You could have told me that before I subjected my mind to a wild goose chase," I complained, surely not without a reason.

"What I mean is that I can think in terms of more than just small quanta. I can actually work with objects. Real, *bona fide* objects."

"Like cars? Elephants?"

"Coins, pins, pencil stubs."

"That sounds like a good start," I approved. I had no idea how we'd get an elephant into our elevator and then into her lab.

"You don't seem to understand, Simon. Before we had to rely on the waves produced by the brain alone. We were talking of micro-voltaic waves, so tiny that little more than subatomic elements might be persuaded to tunnel their way among the atoms of what we call solid walls. Now? Now, theoretically, the sky is the limit. I can multiply the psychokinetic waves exponentially."

I was afraid we were returning to elephants. I was

hoping that, in time, she'd deign to grace some other laboratories; other than the ones that shared my floor with me. With us. I looked again through our splendid window with dire hope that she wouldn't temper with the mountain. If you may think that I was suffering from *prostraria*, the male version of hysteria, then think of *mikro koritsi*. Little Girls are not to be taken lightly.

Still, I sighed, Little Girls must have their toys.

During the next two days, I haven't seen much of Ambrosia. I continued working on my lectures, checking my references, updating my notes. My wife has incarcerated herself in her own office, next to her precious lab, madly feeding data to a battery of her computers. She went there after an early breakfast, broke for a sandwich on the terrace at noon, and continued until dinner.

I was trying to remind her that we've only just got married, but… to no avail. Her muse commanded, though among the nine of them, I couldn't find one that amused herself with science. Perhaps Ambrosia will be the tenth—by being the first. Clever, eh?

When we met, for minutes at a time, we discussed the weather, some politics, a little bit of family, and, peripherally, my forthcoming lectures. She refused to discuss her work, let alone her achievements.

"To do so would be to disperse the concentration at the subliminal level. Even as we talk, here and now, my subconscious continues to work on my problems."

Nothing would have been farther from my mind than to impose on my goddess's subconscious. I wouldn't dare tell her that two days ago she was singing "I did it my way," as though it were "mission accomplished". Actually, some years ago, this last expression got a very bad reputation on both sides of the Atlantic. I forget why.

Then, on Friday, she made breakfast. Cornflakes, eggs, toasts, cheese, marmalade, the whole shebang. The sort of breakfast we only had on very special occasions. Then she bowed slightly and ran out to her office.

She was back a couple of minutes later with a file held firmly under her arm. She sat down, cleared her throat, and presented me with five computer printouts. They were confirmations of acceptance of her articles by various European journals. There was more. What set me back were the last two. One from Russia, and one from China. Each was accompanied by a copy of a money transfer to her account in Athens.

"Athens?"

"Is that all you can say?"

I got up, walked round the table, kissed her hands, her lips and was getting down to her neck when she stopped me.

"It's OK. I forgive you!"

"Congratulations, darling. To an amateur like me, these look like tremendous achievements. Really, congratulations."

"To a scientist they are not bad either," she corrected.

"So… why Athens?"

"You must be aware that our friends from the Pentagon will not be happy about this. Particularly about Russia and China. But my old professor in Athens, dating back to the time when I was still doing my doctorate in physics, taught me that science belongs to the human race, as a whole, not to the rich and famous, even less so to the high and mighty."

"Your professor was a very wise man, Ambrosia. So why Athens?"

"Ah, sorry. I just thought it would be a lot more difficult for them to block my bank account there than here."

I smiled. Those scientists think of everything, not just how to move mountains, I mused.

"Very wise," I nodded my approval. "Very wise indeed."

Then I scratched my head.

"Did they give publication dates?"

"Yes. A week after my Canadian Citizenship papers are due to arrive."

"Your what???"

Only now I remembered that Ambrosia flew to Greece on a Greek passport. For some reason I assumed that she had dual citizenship papers. Then I recalled that she was here on a visitor's visa.

"I thought as my wife, that would be automatic?" I asked.

"I applied before you proposed. We girls like to play it safe."

This coming from Ambrosia sounded almost absurd. At least she didn't burst into another chorus of "I did it My Way". Nevertheless, for now, joy and Frank Sinatra prevailed in our penthouse.

News traveled fast. That same day came a phone call from Dean McGinnis. He sounded very apologetic for having disturbed me, us, but, if Miss Milos were available, could he possible have a word with her?

This was the first time I've even heard his voice. I thought he'd make a good politician. I held the receiver at arms length and shouted, "Miss Milos!"

After a few seconds Ambrosia answered from her lab, asking who was it. I shouted again, "McGinnis!"

She shouted back, "Busy!"

I am absolutely sure that the Dean heard the whole exchange. I smiled, and counted to ten.

"I'm most terribly sorry, sir. I regret to inform you that Miss Milos in not in at the moment. Perhaps at some other time?"

And not waiting for his reaction I hung up. "How did I do?" I asked.

She walked in through the interconnecting terrace and

held up both thumbs. "You're learning," she declared, smiling all over.

"So when are we jumping over to Milos?" I asked conversationally. I still had three weeks before my own season started.

"Do you have a death-wish?" she replied, smiling sweetly.

"I thought they paid you for…"

"…the theory. I'm a theoretical physicist. My lab is almost elementary by big lab standards. It so happens I think my theories work, but usually the confirmation of theories are left to the experimental physicists."

"That's a lower class of scientist all together?" I tried to make it sound like a question.

"No, Simon. It is not a lower class of anything, although… I must confess, I've met theoreticians who liked to think so. No. The point is that you can have a dozen or a hundred experimental physicists working on a single theory. More often than not, the theory itself matures under such communal effort."

"So you are selling immature theories?"

"Eat your breakfast, Simon."

"Yes, Ma'am."

I thought it was the right time to stop pulling her leg before I'd be on the receiving end of it under the table. That's another habit she had that I hoped she'd grow out of. I forget what the first habit was.

Later that night I decided to practice, again, my autohypnosis. This time Ambrosia was there, from the beginning, ready to do her part. She was to keep tabs on me to see if I could contribute anything new to the established history of the New Testament, which took place in Greece.

"Can you imagine what fun it would be for my mother?"

she asked.

That was settled then. We chose a number of locations, the seven churches named in the Apocalypse of John.

"Why don't you try Smyrna, Pergamum, Thyatira, Sardis, Philadelphia, Hierapolis, Laodicea or Ephesus," she recited them like a machinegun. "Anyone of them. They are all mentioned as having Paul visiting them. If you can visit any of them at the time that Paul was there, this could be truly fascinating."

"Pergamum, isn't that where Paul refers to Zeus's altar as Satan's seat? It would be interesting to see what was so very evil about the presence of Zeus's worshipers. He always struck me as a reasonable fellow. Now Hera..."

"Simon, you are misogynist. Any of the locations would be interesting if you could pinpoint the time when Paul was there."

We went about it in a very business like way. I've put myself under, Ambrosia deepened my trance, then she mentioned the various locations, the churches, to see if we could score a hit. The whole business took about half an hour to set it up. We also switched on the recording machine, to make sure that no word I utter would be lost to posterity.

As I said, we took the exercise very seriously. Then we were ready. According to indications on a yardstick I've reached a depth of twenty-nine. That's within seven points of the deepest there is. Ambrosia was ready to ask her questions.

Slowly, one by one, she spoke the names of various churches.

"Smyrna..." she said. Slowly and clearly. "Tell me what you have seen in Smyrna."

There was little danger I'd be willing to make up stories, for the simple reason that I've never been to Smyrna. I don't mean in Paul's days but, judging by my silence, ever.

When no response came from my hypnotized brain, or mind, or body, whatever gets really hypnotized, Ambrosia would move to the next location, repeat the name of the town a few times, before moving onto the next one.

An hour later we had a perfect score. Zero. It was apparent that either the whole system didn't work, or that I've never been to any of the places in Greece she mentioned.

She counted me back from five to one, and clicked her fingers. She waited a few moments for me to orient myself and then told me the bad news.

"But it worked with my ankle!" I insisted.

"Yes, darling," she agreed. "But with the ankle, by definition you must have been here. I didn't mention a place, I mentioned your ankle, with which you obviously had very strong emotional ties."

Half an hour later we agreed that we must completely rethink the program. The first thing was to find many more people. The more people took part, the greater would be the chance that one of them would connect with some historical period. Emotionally or otherwise. All we could do was to try.

It seemed that at least on that day, I wasn't going to do it my way. We'd have try and try again.

We did.

***

Chapter 26
More on Devolution

"Spirit descends into complex objects** that can be imbued with life, i.e. which can manifest change. Spirit and Life-Force are synonyms. Nothing dead appears to exhibit the presence of spirit. On the other hand, nothing is totally dead. Spirit is omnipresent."

It was Saturday. A slight drizzle kept us on our covered terrace. Usually we would be gallivanting on the forgotten trails of Mount Royal. Her threat to teach me tennis had to wait for a better day.

Ambrosia just leaned back, and listened to my convoluted ideas. I needed to bounce them of somebody before I'd venture into philosophical quagmire from which I might not be able to extricate myself.

"Quite true," she commented. "All elements have half-life. Half-life manifests change."

"Half life?" I asked.

"Originally used to describe unstable atoms, now half-life denotes half the time it takes a substance to decrease by half."

"Better half-life that no life at all," I murmured.

She smiled.

I wasn't trying to be funny. I decided to resume my diatribe against sacerdotal fraternity, which, in my opinion, was attempting to mystify just about everything.

"The Hindus managed to confuse their people with countless predictions, mostly to spread utter gloom and destruction, without ever mentioning that the original writings were dealing with spiritual more so than physical matters. The Buddhist joined them, mostly under the belated baton of Madam Helena Blavatsky, whose dissertation on *Esoteric Buddhism* managed to get even Einstein in its grip. Hence the proposed Big Crunch, which had to follow, inevitably, the Big Bang. In Blavatsky's otherwise fascinating harangue there are seven races, the last being the yellow race, which would come into dominance, rather as the white did till recently, before the dissolution of the universe could take place. Welcome China."

"So we don't have long to go, after all?" Ambrosia sounded amused.

"You can hardly look smug. Until the theoretical physicists got hold of the multi-universe concept, let alone the mega-universe proposal, you were all just as keen on the Big-Crunch!"

"Guilty as charged," she admitted, "but at least we didn't threaten anyone with hell if they didn't believe us. And... don't forget I chose the micro rather then macro."

I nodded.

"The last but not least are the Catholics. The Jesuits have inundated us, and I speak from personal experience, with mysteries. The mystery of the Holy Trinity, of the Virgin Birth, of the Incarnation, of Transubstantiation, of the Immaculate Conception, of Transfiguration, Ascension, Assumption, Resurrection, the mystery of the Original Sin, the mystery of Infallibility, the mystery of the Seven Sacraments, the... whatever-I-can't-understand mystery."

"Well, can you explain them?"

"I'm not sure it's my exclusive job, though if it stops us in our careering devolution, I'm willing to at least try. It shouldn't be too difficult. After all, both Mathew and Luke assure us in their gospels, repeatedly, that '...*there is nothing covered that shall not be revealed; and hid, that shall not be known.*' And '... *it is given unto you to know the mysteries...*'

What say you to that?"

"At least the Catholic ones are not cataclysmic." Ambrosia sounded on the defensive.

"You want cataclysmic, read the Apocalypse, and interpret it the way fundamentalists do."

We needed a break. It is not the first time we discussed the problem of devolution. Luckily, at least the scientists changed directions before the "dark matter" people could scare the living daylights out of most of us. Alas, I had to deal with Comparative Religion. Some of my authoritarians were also infallible, no matter how wrong they were. Just look at Galileo.

I was beginning to boil. Lately, both, the scientists and the religionists got me hot under the collar—and it wasn't even clerical. Dog collar?

Never mind.

After a while, I cooled down. The last thing I wanted was to have a fight with Ambrosia.

"Can we return to the beginning? To spirit descending into complex objects?" I asked.

"Be my guest. I prefer evolution to devolution."

Once again, I cleared my throat.

"At first there was little to enable the spirit to flex its muscles. I read somewhere that a young Buddhist meditated that he was a stone. A largish rock, I suppose. When asked of his impressions, he replied 'It's not a bad way to be'."

"I think that was the crux of the matter," Ambrosia took over. "It was not a bad way to *be*. Not a good way of *becoming*, though. It is a form of near-stasis. On the other hand, isn't this what happens in most minds of most politicians? Maintaining the status quo?"

She was probably thinking of McGinnis.

I didn't think she was in the mood for a serious discussion. On the other hand, perhaps it was just as well. What if I were wrong? What if all religions, and the scientists, before they escaped into the multi-universe theories, were right also? People like Einstein?

A little cloud passed over my pink horizon.

"Something tells me we must escape this reality, the reality we presently choose to live in, before it becomes too late," I murmured.

I was lucky she didn't appear to hear me. I pretended I got busy with my book. Yet even as I read a fascinating account about the life of a dog, my mind kept going back to devolution. Even if there was no cataclysmic destruction in the foreseeable future, who wants to live in a world which was devolving at an astonishing rate?

Two hours later I decided to give my new hobbies another chance. It was time to get serious about OBE, and autohypnosis, and quantum tunneling. Serious about all three. I could only hope that one of them would give us a way out.

The first thing to do was to call Mama Milos. It was becoming obvious that without her help we would tread water until one of us managed to drown in an ocean of consciousness, to which we continued to fail finding access. Frankly, I'd rather swim in the Aegean Sea.

We couldn't call her now. On Milos it was past midnight. We were on our own.

"Want to try?"

"What?"

"OBE. Only first I want us both to relax and attempt to put ourselves under."

"You want to combine hypnosis with astral travel?"

"I prefer to call it the Phase. At least the Phase refers to REM, which corresponds to specific brainwaves. At least I think it does. Hopefully those halfway between waken and sleeping states. As for your question, I'd jump up and down on the moon, if that would give me results," I replied. I was getting close to desperate.

"Phase in waves is the fraction of a wave cycle which has elapsed relative to an arbitrary point," she read it out from her portable computer. "Is this what you mean?"

"I haven't understood a word you've said," I murmured.

"All right, Simon. It's your call. Phase it is. As in OBE."

I was glad we got that straight. After all, it was her mother who was supposed to be an expert at it, not I.

"I'll try to reach a minimum depth of say, twenty-five to twenty-eight inches on the yardstick. Then you'll tell me to roll out, or levitate, or whatever... into the Phase. Once there I'll presumably be on my own. I don't believe the two realities can communicate. Anyway, we shall see."

Soon I was lying on my king-size bed, trying to forget all the problems that plagued me with devolution or mysteries. In no time at all I reached the stage of being sufficiently relaxed to attempt to go under. Once there, Ambrosia would take over.

Through a dense fog, I heard her giving me some instructions, which must have connected directly with my subconscious. Then...

...then I was floating about two feet above the bed. I was surprised how easy it was. It happened quite automatically. Spontaneously, perhaps, is a better word. I think I actually chuckled.

I looked around and decided to stand on the floor. Next to me a body, yes, my body, was lying on the bed. Next to it Ambrosia was sitting looking dreadfully serious if not a little worried. It made me smile. There was nothing strange about it. I was just standing there, perfectly relaxed.

I rubbed my hands together, then closed my eyes and dove, head first, through the penthouse window. I always wanted to do that, and never could; I mean in my dreams. I always thought how wonderful it would be to soar, like a kite, on the warm air rising along the surface of the facade. It was, only now I didn't need the air current. Wherever I directed my attention, there I flew. Floated. Effortlessly.

I took a couple of loops over the treetops of Mount Royal, touching the topmost branches. They were soft to the touch, much softer that down there, where we walked so often. I felt the need to share this wonderful experience with Ambrosia. The same instant I felt a slight electric shock, actually quite pleasant, and I looked up at Ambrosia's face bending over me.

I was back.

"I am back?"

"It worked?" she asked, peering into my eyes.

"How I wish we were there together..."

"Tell me every single detail. I want to know everything."

"There's not that much to tell. Remember, I'm very much a beginner."

"Everything!" she repeated threateningly.

I did. Word for word, as I remembered it. Every detail, including the softness of the leaves at the top of Mount Royal.

"It was as though they've been made of soft cloth. Like velvet..."

While I was describing my experience, she didn't say a word. She continued to study my face, as if having doubt if I was telling her the truth. I don't blame her. It was a glorious interlude.

"And the whole trip, if we can call it that, was accompanied by a wonderful feeling of freedom, of absolute carefreeness... oh, darling, it was wonderful."

She stretched out next to me on the bed. We remained quiet, perfectly still. Then she turned towards me.

"So this really happens? You have real memories, as though it were all real?"

I had to smile. "It was more real then you lying right here, besides me. It was more real than any dream I ever had.

Out there, the reality is more intense…"

"And you were never scared? Afraid that you might not be able to get back?"

"Of what? The moment I thought about you, I found myself back in my body. Instantly," I repeated. Then I thought about it. "In fact this is what we must look out for. Not how to get back into our physical bodies, but how to remain in the Phase longer. How to control the exit. I rather think that there is nothing one cannot do in it…"

"Mother told me it takes years of practice. Years." Suddenly Ambrosia's face clouded over. "And all this time you'd be apart from me. Quite apart."

"There is a way out, you know," I said.

She looked at me as though I'd just saved her life.

"If you also have an OBE, then you can conjure me to be with you all the time."

"That's what my mother told me. But I don't want to have a facsimile of you. I want you, the real you…"

"As I said, darling, I'm a beginner. But I strongly suspect that you can create with your consciousness a me much more real that the one speaking to you right now," I said with conviction.

"You talk as though, out there, you were god!"

"Out there, you are god. Nothing is impossible for you. For crying out loud, I flew over the Mount Royal! Whatever you can imagine or think of becomes your reality." Most of this I knew from reading.

"You talk as if you were quoting the Bible describing heaven," she said, her voice slightly shocked.

"I know. I'm sorry if that offends you. But ten minutes ago I couldn't fly. Now I did. And it was the easiest thing in the world. Any world?"

For a while we lay there examining our thoughts. There was a great deal to stew over. Then a new idea struck me, different than anything I realized before.

"You know, Ambrosia, I think I am beginning to

understand why I find this concept of devolution so repulsive. The more we advance technologically, the more we shall be tied to the prison of our physical body." I turned to face her. "The further we would be from the paradise which I'd visited minutes ago. A paradise where the word freedom has a completely new meaning. Where there are no prisons."

"No walls?" she asked.

"Where there are no walls to build, no walls to pull down, no walls to restrict our freedom."

"Yet freedom where we are always apart."

"No, darling. Freedom where two become one. It's like the man said: You within me, I within you. Isn't that what he'd said? Ask your mother."

The following day, allowing for the time differential of seven hours, we did ask her. It was late evening out there, on Milos. We telephoned just in time; Mama was ready to retire. Her face appeared on the Skype screen in less than a minute.

"I've been expecting you, children. I thought you are just about ready."

"We are not disturbing you?" Ambrosia asked.

"I am seldom disturbed, Ambrosia. I was about to go into the Phase." She seemed to have smiled at the thought.

"You do that often?" I asked.

"I spend my nights in the Phase. Instead of dreaming. Some hours I just sleep."

"You mean all your dreams are lucid dreams?" Such control sounded incredible.

"Usually. And you children, how are you doing with your OBEs?"

"That's why we are calling, Mama. I have a question to which, it seems, only you can provide an answer," I said, still not knowing how to formulate my question.

She neither asked nor urged me on. It felt as though for

her time was of little consequence. It is I who had to press on.

"Mama, is the Phase the true reality?"

"That's it? Yes, Simon, of course it is true. I think you already know that."

That didn't come out very well. "That's not what I meant. What I wanted to ask was if the Phase is the real life, and here, in the physical universe we only, well, we sort of imagine things…"

My voice trailed off. We were calling her too early. My questions were not yet formulated properly.

"What Simon is asking you, Mama, is whether we can retire from the physical world and continue our life in the Phase," Ambrosia stepped in, with her usual precise if slightly excessive definition of my problem.

Mrs. Milos started laughing. She then asked us to adjust our seating so that she could see both of us on the computer desktop simultaneously.

"Of course, you can. But it would be very foolish," she was still trying to stifle a giggle. "You'd be like cockroaches or turtles, which haven't changed over millions of years. They found some in Baltic amber that are forty-to-fifty million years old, which look like close cousins of our present day critters. At least, they now count up to 4500 different species. We, humans, have but a few. Turtles, on the other hand, are said to date back to the Jurassic age…"

"Mama, we really need your help," Ambrosia stepped in.

"But I am trying to help you. If you remain in the Phase, you'll enjoy every imaginable fragment of the past. You'll even be able to project the most likely futures for whatever you are, or whatever you are doing. But that is all."

"The future?"

"Of course. You told me once, that in quantum mechanics you work with probabilities. The same is true of the futures. There are an infinite number, but some are more probable than others."

"And what does this have to do with us moving over, or trying to move over…"

"To the Phase? Do so, my darling. Do it at night, when you dream. The Phase is heaven—at least the first level of heaven. There are many stages above it but you must start with OBE. Even in the first heaven there is no good or evil. There is no morality, no ethics. It is a free for all, where you are not punished for your mistakes."

For a while, there was silence. Then, very slowly, I felt as though I began emerging from a great depth, in which all things were possible yet only some were worthwhile. I was watching Mama's face, which continued to smile with growing, if enigmatic, understanding.

"Some time ago—perhaps a few thousand years—an advanced individualized consciousness decided that physical reality, where good and evil are inherent to every thought, every action, every event, is the fastest way to advance. In the Phase, you enjoy so much of what you have, that you have absolutely no incentive to advance. To go forward. To… evolve."

The last words she said very quietly. It was as though she knew that she was destroying our dreams of our version of heaven. Heaven right here, on Earth, right now.

"And the dangers were such that they had to put a time limit, on how long we can last in this… this… imaginary reality?" I picked up on the idea.

"Something like that," Mama smiled again. She looked pleased. Her children were beginning to get the point. "In the beginning, people on Earth lived a very long time. Close to a thousand years. As our physical consciousness grew, expanded, its power had to be diminished as it began to encroach on the freedom of others. Today, even empires have a limited time span—for the same reason. You can only evolve with a good dose of free will."

"How come, they lived so long, Mama?" Ambrosia's voice was anything but convinced.

"It's the Phase, dear. In the Phase there is no time. One doesn't age."

I kept staring at Mrs. Milos' face, suddenly understanding why she looked like Ambrosia's sister. There could be but ten or twelve years between them.

"You don't age in the Phase...?" Ambrosia repeated as though not hearing properly.

"As I told you, dear, there is no time there. The physical time ticks on, but it has no effect on you. You are where your attention is, in the Phase. Even in ordinary dreams time is hardly noticeable. Haven't you noticed?"

Things, concepts, were gradually falling into place.

So a great many of the religious prophets were right. You had to grin and bear it, and had to treat the physical consciousness, at worst, as a necessary evil. I remembered a statement I read recently in the gospel of Thomas, the Gnostic gospel bishop Irenaeus had not managed to destroy. Logion #42, states quite simply: "Jesus said: Become passers-by." How did Jesus know all that, some two thousand years ago?

It seems that at least one mystery was finally solved.

**

Chapter 27
The Carousel

"We dissolve into an ocean of love,"** I told them at one of my past lectures. They didn't like that much. It was an answer to the question, "What is death?" I also told them, later, that there is no death, that there is only erasure of your personality, your consciousness is indestructible.

Frankly, I'm not sure they liked that very much either. What people really want is to preserve that which makes them different from each other. Not that which unites them. Unfortunately, the myths I studied said otherwise.

Nevertheless, such attitude of mine dated back to before I've heard about the out of body projection; to before my OBE experiments. Now it seems that we dissolved into the reality of the Phase. But not completely. That which made us individual expressions of the Whole remained. Heaven took on a new, a very different, meaning. It was full of joy, of fun and games, but it was also static. It did not evolve. Ever.

People, it seemed, wanted to continue on the other side of the Great Divide, even though they had absolutely no idea what they might find there. Other than the Muslims, of course. If they played their cards right they would get seventy-two virgins. In spite of my extensive studies, I still wasn't sure what was in it for the virgins. Or for the gays and lesbians, for that matter. Their business, I suppose. I wished them luck. Anyway, I'll stick to my own theories.

The day was so sunny and beautiful, and almost warm, that we couldn't resist it. We were back on our terrace, this time wearing our anoraks, warm trousers, and the almost perennial glass of red in hand. I suggested something stronger but Ambrosia declined.

"It interferes with my thinking," she said. Actually, it wasn't the first time that she refused. She never touched anything stronger.

The mountain would soon turn to reds and golds, flaunting its beauty, haphazardly, with utter abandon, refusing to die until it became imbedded in our memories forever. Ah, yes. The beauty of becoming. You cannot have birth without death, nor death without birth. You cannot have change without either.

"To return, to reconstruct our personalities, here, on Earth, in our successive reincarnations, we must make it worthwhile for the consciousness frolicking in the Phase; to imprison a new indivisible part of itself, once again, in the reality of becoming. Most of this is set on automatic. To partake in the process at a conscious level takes a lot more than just willingness."

Ambrosia nodded, though most of the time her eyes were busy feasting on the mountain.

"Various fragments of our personality, of that that makes us different from one another, hangs suspended in the matrix of the universe. In the ethereal Phase. If and when required, it is recycled. If and when we want to advance."

I wasn't sure if this didn't contradict my previous thesis. I was about to continue my rambling, when Ambrosia turned her head.

"To where?" she asked. "Towards infinity? That's quite a long trip. No wonder we have to be immortal to get there. I'm so glad we, the scientists, have finally decided that the universe is well... as good as infinite."

"About time," I put in with a metaphysical smirk. "On the other hand, if it hadn't been invented yet, you'd invent one any time now."

"Aren't we smart?" There was just a little less humour in Ambrosia's eyes than usual. I thought she was just a mite embarrassed. And then she turned on me with both fists. Well, one fist and one glass of wine.

"We just did, I told you." She demanded recognition.

"Sorry, darling, I forgot. That's right. You just did."

We sipped wine for a little while, before I resumed my musing.

"You must make it worthwhile for the Whole, the Source of all consciousness, so to speak, to restore Its individualizations, on which to build a consciousness of becoming. I still think that out there, within the Phase, every individuality is a complete universe. Each one of us is within all others—all others are within each one of us. We discussed it before but it warrants repeating. You cannot have a part of god. God is indivisible. Zen Buddhists first discovered that the totality of divinity is present in the most insignificant of its parts."

I was surprised hearing my own voice. It sounded very profound. I tried to lighten the mood. "Mama said that out there you can be an elephant, or a bird, or a beauty queen, and then..."

I realized I was rambling, again. The splendor of the mountain was almost intimidating. Did we, pilgrims on our eternal journey to nowhere, deserve to witness such moments of exhilarating beauty?

I looked down at my work.

"...sometimes there is so little worth preserving from previous reincarnation that one would never recognize it as following the previous personality, or that which made it different from other forms in the same species."

"Round and round we go. A carousel." Ambrosia sounded sad. Or was she resigned? "I thought that one day, when we've done a decent job of our stint down here, we wouldn't have to go out any more."

This took be back. That was almost exactly what John implied in his Apocalypse. *"Him that overcometh will I make a pillar in the temple of my God, and he shall go no more out."* I remembered that phrase because I couldn't understand it. Not sure I understood it now.

"I suppose there is a way…" I said quietly.

"Tell me?"

"You'd have to stop to be you."

"Is that supposed to make sense?"

"I'm afraid so. If you merge into the Whole, if you become completely One with the Whole, then there is nothing left of you on which to build a new personality. You'd no longer be you."

"…sort of 'become one with the Father?'"

"Sort of."

"I'm not sure I like that. I'd miss being me. I'd also miss being with you. Perhaps even more so."

"Perhaps that is why we are both here. But, don't forget, we have access to the Phase. All we need is faith and practice. St. Paul called it faith and good works, I suppose? Or maybe they meant prayer?"

The Phase was becoming an enigma. What if it was heaven? What if we only chose to get reincarnated here, in the reality of becoming, to gather more impressions, more deeds or achievement, to learn more, perhaps to disseminate more love and friendship, with which we could enrich our individual realities of heaven. Our personal, individual Kingdoms?

My convoluting thoughts were interrupted by the jingle of my telephone. I clicked it open and… couldn't believe my ears.

"It's Bob, Sir. You remember, Robert?"

It all came back in a rush. Mount Royal, the spies, CIA, McGinnis, we seemed to have moved so very far away from all those events.

"How are you, Bob. Good to hear from you."

"I will not be taking up of your time, Sir. I just wondered if you've seen the TV lately. The News will be on in five minutes. The CBC. My regards to Miss Milos, Sir."

And without another word, the man hung up, or whatever one did with the telephones in those days. I hated making phone calls. Except to Mama, of course. Funny how we always seem to call our mothers rather than fathers?

CBC would be the Canadian Broadcasting Corporation, I supposed. We really should have looked at the TV more often. There was a whole world, out there, a world we knew nothing about.

I called Ambrosia to come in. It was Bob that called, so it must have had something to do with her.

I clicked on the TV and searched for the CBC. Surprise! The ever-present commercials were still on. I cut the sound and told Ambrosia about Bob's call. She didn't look surprised. Then the CBC logo appeared on the screen. After the usual introductions, the speaker got down to business.

The CBC has learned that Dr. Herman McGinnis, the Dean of McGill University, has resigned amid accusations of *sub rosa* activities. Allegedly Dr. McGinnis has been appropriating part of the funds he has received, also *sub rosa*, from the unidentified secret agents. The alleged funds have been deposited in his American Account at the Royal Bank, which due to their alleged magnitude drew the attention of the auditors.

"That's an awful lot of alleged allegations," Ambrosia put in.

This just in...

The speaker has interrupted herself, this time without Ambrosia's assistance.

Canadian Minister of foreign affairs, the Right Honorable Bartholomew Rushbass, asked his counterpart at the White House to withdraw all CIA agents from Canada. The President of the United States, Laura Georgina Bush, has already contacted our Prime Minister to say that she agreed unconditionally. She apologized for the allegations, which precipitated this turn of events, and assured the Prime Minister that the officials responsible will be prosecuted to the full extend of the law.

Someone handed over a sheet of paper to the speaker. She read it, smiled, and looked up, doing her best to hide her smile. Funny, I thought. Don't they feed latest updates to the speaker directly on her computer screen?

As a follow up on the above story, the CBC had just learned that allegedly Dean McGinnis has also been taking additional bribes from the CIA. We shall keep you informed as the story develops.

I switched off the TV. It was hard to believe how far Ambrosia and I have drifted from the "real world". Not just our own private or, for that matter, professional lives were as far apart as Montreal is from Milos. I began to miss my two-week holidays already. There, on the island, people seemed to live as though on a different planet, in a different reality. On the other hand they had Papa to protect them.

I doubted that McGinnis's resignation would make much difference to us, though they would probably attempt to reinstate Ambrosia to her old post. I had no idea if she would be interested, but I did recall that, before the troubles had started she did love her work there. Technically, she could probably do the same work at home, but there was something about a collegiate camaraderie, which she must have missed at home.

A thought crossed my mind that McGinnis might have been behind the hacking of the McGill computers. He could have sold the goodies to the highest bidder. On the other hand, I could just be getting a little paranoid. Right now, I had work to do.

My autumn semester was approaching and I still had to finish writing my introductions. I wondered if I could give them my version of creativity. I let my fingers do the talking on the keyboard.

"One starts with an idea," I wrote, "builds a pattern, ignites it with emotions, and lets it happen. That is the creative process taken directly from the first chapter of the Pentateuch. Process derived from the triumvirate of the spirit, mind and emotions. In that order. Omit any one of them and you get nowhere. At least, so the Bible says."

It's a pity no one treats the scriptural writings as ancient knowledge, instead of myths to be enjoyed on Sundays and ignored the rest of the time. On the other hand, not everybody can study Comparative Religion. Not everybody gets lucky, I guess.

I should continue writing, but my heart wasn't in it. Ambrosia put a spanner in my works by asking me about raising the dead. She was referring to Lazarus, of course. I had no idea why she came up with such philosophical problems. Or were they biological? You can freeze a frog and restore it to life. Why not a human being. What of cryogenics? To my knowledge, her question had little if anything to do with theoretical physics.

Anyway, I looked it up.

According to some sources, The *Bible* records that Elijah, Elisha, Peter, and Paul raised the dead, as well as Yeshûa. Should we *raise the dead*? For some reason I was convinced that the Bible intended us to believe that it was the presence of consciousness that defined life. Yeshûa referred to some of his contemporaries as "the dead". Those *not yet* alive? It was always that fourth man, or the white horse that mattered. The rest was dispensable. The rest could be picked up from the matrix of the universe on the way to another reincarnation.

And then it hit me. It seemed that if Ambrosia were thinking of quantum tunneling a living organism, then, most probably, such a critter would die and then be "resurrected" on the other side of the "wall". The "wall" could, in time, be extended to miles, hopefully, great many miles. There shouldn't be even theoretical limits to the range of human thought. I wondered how close she was to an actual experiment. For some reason, the idea made me vaguely nervous. I didn't like the idea of playing a messiah.

My mind drifted back to the various modes of travel. OBE, self-hypnosis, and of course, Ambrosia's tunneling. For some reason, I was becoming more preoccupied not with the travel itself, but what you would do when you got there. What if you traveled by one of those strange means and ended up in heaven? It could happen, couldn't it? I recalled great artists recording moments of ecstasy on the faces of saints as they witnessed... what, heaven?

Perhaps we approached it all from the wrong angle. Yes, I was becoming more and more convinced that it all had to do not so much with travel, but what we could and would do when we got there.

"Darling," I called out. Actually she was sitting right next to me. It was I who had been far away. "And what of those moments of ecstasy we witness, sometimes on the faces of saints?"

She looked up with a distant look on her face.

"I spoke to my mother about that. She said those must be the moments when they experience Oneness. When their consciousness experiences the Whole. It must be all the joys, all the beauty, all the freedoms, all the experiences that consciousness accumulated in the Phase— only all at once. Simultaneously. Beyond and outside the limits of time."

She smiled wistfully.

"God! That must be incredible!" I couldn't help exclaiming.

"Yes," the distant look returned to her face. "Yes, I imagine God is."

But her face still showed a mixture of wonder and concern.

"What is it, darling?" I prodded gently.

She sighed deeply and managed a weak smile.

"It's probably nothing, Simon. But, well, I'm pretty sure I've been hacked, again. I installed every possible firewall, every imaginable barrier. I also changed my password almost weekly. It must have been done very professionally. There is hardly any evidence…"

There goes my theory about McGinnis, I thought.

"But who would want to have your…" And in this moment I remembered. "It's the tunneling, isn't it?"

"Theoretically, there's practically an infinite potential in the application of tunneling, Simon. If my theories are right…" She looked at me as though hoping that I would contradict her.

I couldn't. From what little I knew, I thought she was right. And then there were the boys from the CIA who couldn't have been too happy about her moving out of McGill University. They lost McGinnis and control.

This was way bigger than I've first suspected.

***

244 Stan I.S. Law

Chapter 28
More about Mama

Since Mama had Skype installed on her brand new 24"
computer, she could talk to us while watching both our
faces in greater detail. As Mama's computer also had a
built-in high-resolutions camera, when discussing the
intangibles we could observe her minute facial expressions,
subtle nuances, almost thoughts behind her words. And we
wanted to learn more about the practical side of OBE. A lot
more. We wanted to go in and out of the Phase at will. The
way she, Mama, apparently could. We already read up a lot
about the techniques of entering the Phase, also about
deepening it and even sustaining it, but we still weren't sure
about the real nature of the "out of body" experience. My
own successes were few and far between.

Were we really going *out* of our bodies? Or did it all
happen just in our minds. And talking of minds, were they
the byproducts of our brains, or the other way round? If idea
preceded its fulfillment, then mind had to come first. Did the
mind, then, reside in the Phase?

The Internet was so full of most incredible claims that
we were gradually losing faith that the whole affair was
worthwhile. Yet the potential attraction was undeniable. Was
it available only to the few?

Many are called, few are chosen...

No, I didn't like that at all. I much preferred that bit
about *asking in my name*. Or *knock, and it shall be open unto
you...* I suppose the name is the nature, which manifests in

the Phase. What else could it be?

Ambrosia was much more successful in this "mode of travel" as she called it, than I. It was strange, considering that her mind was scientifically trained, while mine dealt, most of my life, with metaphysics.

"Perhaps," she told me repeatedly, "your expectations are too high. Just relax and let it happen."

I did, repeatedly. It didn't happen; at least, not for quite a while, and then only for a few seconds at a time. Half a minute at most. Except for those very first few times. Beginner's luck?

I needed Mama's help.

Later that week neither of us could sleep. Without a word, we both got up and moved to my study. I clicked on my desktop, just in time to hear Skype announcing a call.

Mama came on the screen with a ray of sunshine cutting diagonally across the screen. Greek sunshine, or at least, sunshine from Greece. It had to be. We were still in the night. She forgot the time change.

The first five minutes we just talked about everyday things, unimportant but dear to us who knew each other. Papa was in the office, where he'd spent most of his time. Apparently his work reached out far, far beyond Milos, as I have had occasion to discover when I moved into our new penthouse. Essentially, he was an incurable workaholic. When Ambrosia and I visited Milos this summer to get married, it was, according to Mama, the first holiday he'd taken in years.

And then we talked about OBE.

"You can treat it as entertainment, Simon, or as something that will develop your psyche, but there are other fields which make me grateful that the gods gave us this elusive gift."

I think Ambrosia already heard this story. I remained glued to my computer screen.

"Do you remember, Simon—of course you do—the parables about the crippled walking, the blind seeing, and the deaf being able to hear?"

"Of course I do, Mama. What are you leading up to?" Mrs. Milos had me at a disadvantage.

"Well, there was another statement you'll recall. The same man who brought about the healing also said, 'my kingdom is not of this world.' Remember?"

I nodded.

"Well, Simon, as I'm sure Ambrosia will back me up, these acts and statements don't make much sense to a practical person of this day and age."

I had to nod again. I still had no idea where she was leading me with all this. I was conversant with the scriptures as well as any man—better than most.

"Years ago I was attempting to make some sense of all these things, when I stumbled into an out of body experience. Now don't get me wrong. At the time, I had no idea what it was. It could have been some sort of fantasy, or aberration of my fertile mind. But, after some tentative attempts, or experiments, with a few of my friends, I drew a number of quite stunning conclusions."

I held her eyes staring at me across the Atlantic and most of Europe. I was beginning to fall under her spell. She had a manner of talking that was both relaxing and commanding attention. She would have made a marvelous hypnotist.

"Well, Simon, whatever OBE is, however it is defined, it is a state of mind in which the lame can walk. They can walk better than they've ever walked on Earth. They can also swim, and they can fly. Now that's quite an experience for men and women who were born crippled."

For a while there was silence. My mind was working overtime to try and come up with some sort of intelligent comment that wouldn't sound absurd.

"Whether the soul leaves the body, or whether mind plays tricks on us, the lame don't care. They enjoy all manner of physical activity that was forbidden them in physical life. What do you think of that, Simon?"

The next moment the screen went blank. Without a word Mama had signed off. Perhaps she thought that I should give it some private thought, before sharing it with anyone, even with Mama.

Ambrosia was looking at my computer desktop over my shoulder. Her face wouldn't have been seen on her mother's screen, yet I felt sure Mama was well aware of her presence. Now that I switched off the Skype, she sat down next to me, her hand over my shoulder.

"Don't worry, darling. Mama had the same effect on me the first few times she talked to me about it. I also witnessed her talking to others, some of them… crippled. She has that effect on people."

We moved to the settee. The sun was just rising. The trees on the east side were undercut with countless sparks dancing from one trunk to another. Mother must have called about noon, her time, knowing that it would be 5 am in Montreal. I only learned some days later why she'd chosen such a strange time.

The easiest way to enter the Phase is when one is already rested, then returns to bed and enters the in-between state. Ambrosia called it the indirect technique. The stage when one is halfway between being asleep, and being awake, still motionless, before you open your eyes and your mind, or is it your brain, is still not very active. Ambrosia knew those things—she was her mother's daughter. She probably watched her mother entering the Phase when she was a little girl.

Now she took me by the arm and led me back to bed. She switched off the lights. With the curtains drawn, in the bedroom it was still night. Soon I relaxed; then, just for fun, I did some Phase entry exercises. The next thing I was floating above my bed. For a brief moment I was afraid that I might fall. The next moment I was standing, looking down at Ambrosia's and my own body lying side by side. I closed my eyes and imagined Mrs. Milos.

I was now standing in front of her, on her terrace, watching the distant birds looking for something to eat. I greeted her as though I were really there. She smiled and asked me to sit next to her.

"...and the blind shall see," she said, "with colour more beautiful than they could ever imagine. And the deaf shall hear most glorious music. And none shall suffer here ever again..."

And then, down below us, on the pristine beach I saw people filled with joy, dancing.

The next moment I was lying next to Ambrosia. She was breathing regularly, a small smile playing about her lips. I wondered where she'd been. Perhaps she was still there. Still in the Kingdom?

I was looking at the blissful expression on her face when she opened her eyes.

"Do you believe her now?" she asked.

"Do you know where I've been?" I asked in return.

"Tell me."

I spend the rest of the night, morning by now, telling her of her mother, of the blind and the deaf, and the lame that danced. I could have been in the Phase hardly longer than a few seconds, minutes at most, yet I recalled watching those people sing and dance, seemingly, for a long time. Could it be that the scriptures were describing the state of mental projection? Or whatever the Phase was... a spiritual experience?

"Where does mental end and spiritual begin..." I mused aloud, my skin still feeling the breeze of the Aegean Sea. Funny that, I thought, surely, my skin wasn't there. Not my physical skin.

"That is your field, darling. But does it really matter? Aren't they all just different aspects of the same thing?"

I didn't quite understand her words, but I sensed truth imbedded in them.

"All is One," I said, "and aren't we all indivisible parts of the Whole? Also, aren't these all just words, symbols, that our mind is creating in an attempt to make sense of something which is, as yet, beyond our understanding?"

Yet, I thought, Mrs. Milos understands them.

Ambrosia has been raised in the traditions of the Easter Orthodox Church. They took the Bible very literally. Frankly, the Church of England wasn't far from that same teaching, as were the Catholics. But there was still something missing, something I couldn't put my finger on.

"But surely, some of those healings must have been real. I mean physical healings of physical bodies?"

I had to smile at that. "Like my ankle, you mean?"

"I hadn't thought of that," she admitted.

"I would have thought that a great many healings that originate in the murky past, and are passed on either through some genetic process, or by subconscious inheritance, can be healed physically, employing non-physical means. Even as my ankle was. It's been months now, and I haven't had a single sign of my previous discomfort."

"Providing the healer had, perhaps, hypnotic power? Providing he was able to influence the delinquent mind, in some way. I'm told professional hypnotists can do it with ease."

We lay, side by side, attempting to solve mysteries that baffled mankind for thousands and thousands of years. For some, they would remain mysteries forever. Well, a good chunk of "ever". For us...? I strongly suspected that together, perhaps with Mama's help, we would keep digging until the keys to the Kingdom would be in our hands. Or minds.

We practiced on our own for a couple of weeks. Then Mama called. She wanted to know if we had any success following our previous discussion. I strongly suspect that she already knew the answer—by some magical ways known only to herself. Probably she was really good at reading facial expressions. A computer virtual desktop refuses to hide anything.

Mrs. Milos didn't wait for our report, but instead told us two things that, at least for me, were of considerable interest. The first was a quotation from one of the gospels, John, I think. She said that, according the Yeshûa, "whatsoever you ask in my name, that I will do, that the Father may be glorified in the Son."

She asked me to work out what is "my name"; who is "I"; who is the "father"; and finally who is the "son".

"You have to go back some two-thousand years to draw your conclusions, Simon. Remember, Yeshûa didn't have our modern terminology to pass on to the people."

If you chose to ignore the theological teaching of the Church, which didn't exist in Yeshûa's time, or the mumbo-jumbo, which ensued from it, that was quite an order.

And then she said something that really set me back on my heels. In addition to rectifying the inaccuracies of history in various scriptures, my only other desire, as far as hypnosis and/or out of body travel were concerned, was to be able to share my experiences with Ambrosia. I don't mean that I wanted to discuss them later; I wanted to share the actual trip.

It seems that Mama put some sand into my gears. She said that in order to succeed in my endeavour, "the two must be one."

"You and Ambrosia are two entities. In order for you to share an out of body experience, the two of you must become one. There is no other way. Duality is a characteristic only of dualistic or materialistic reality."

Two must become one. Could we synchronize our brainwaves and employ psychokinesis in some way? Then, while in transit leave our bodies when in quantum state?

Wouldn't Black Magic be simpler?

Never mind Black Magic—I think I was venturing into science fiction. If we can become one, we shall do so, now that we have Mama on our side. Though at this stage, I had no idea how.

On the other hand why couldn't we do it in transit? If our bodies were to convert to neutrinos... our states of consciousness should remain intact. No... it was our consciousness that had to be unified, not our bodies.

Yet, I felt in my bones that there had to be a way. Unfortunately, my bones had to stay behind. Dualistic mentality thinks in a dualistic way.

When Mama called again, Ambrosia was in her lab. There was one other statement from the Bible that Mama wanted to question. This time, she asked for my comments. She repeated the phrase we've discussed before.

"And whatsoever ye shall ask in my name, that will I do, that the Father may be glorified in the Son," she quoted from memory.

I've been studying this quotation already, without much success. But Mama had a different way of looking at it.

"If we disregard religious interpretations, I'd like you to tell me who is the Father, who is the Son, and how come we can get everything we want, if no one, to my knowledge, ever got everything they wanted. Not in this world, anyhow."

She looked up from the Skype image as though to seek inspiration. Then she added a statement that is still stuck in my ears.

"To my knowledge we can only get *everything* we want when we are soul travelling. When we are having an OBE. Is this what Yeshûa was talking about?"

I found it vaguely amusing that a Greek woman would use, repeatedly, Hebrew name for Jesus. After all, it was the Greeks who had changed Christ's name from Hebrew to

Greek. On the other hand, maybe that was exactly why she did it. To put things right? Etymologically, Jesus is meaningless in most languages. Yeshûa, or his full name Yehoshûa, means "Jah is salvation," wherein Jah, or Yah, was a poetic form of Jehovah, or Yahweh, which in turn meant "the Existing One."

Now, that's quite a name to carry.

The Existing One is a state of being, as in OBE. The son, Yeshûa, once said, "I am life." I am the state of becoming? Whatsoever you accomplish in your becoming will be yours in your state of being. By becoming you enrich the Phase. Your Phase. Your kingdom?

I thought about it for a long time. Unless Yeshûa's natural habitat was the out of body state, and he visited our reality only sporadically, the reverse of what we might do, then his statement was impossible to accept. Logically, that is. Theologians would say that there is no reason why god should be logical. On the other hand, if he *is* the Creator, then the universe would be in a very sorry state if he wasn't.

If, however, OBE were to be a sustainable condition of being, then it would completely change our image of heaven. Especially if we could go in and out, at will.

As I looked up, the screen was already blank. Mama had signed off.

I wondered what Ambrosia would say.

***

Chapter 29
More Tunneling

Ambrosia looked very serious. Her forehead, usually as smooth as her cheeks, now bore furrows of concentration that bespoke of the complexity of the subject we were discussing. She was attempting to translate intricate concepts of physics into a language I would understand.

"Originally we thought," she began, "that there was a probability that under certain conditions—"solids" being what they are, i.e. mostly empty space—a small bunch of electrons could weave their way through a solid barrier, and emerge unscathed on the other side. This is called quantum tunneling. Now we know better."

I nodded my understanding. It's just as I expected. The moment I begin to understand anything in physics, they come up with a new theory.

"Under the influence of psychokinesis, however," she continued, "as close as we can gather, quantum tunneling converts atomic particles to neutrinos, then reconstitutes them, when slowed down, to their previous characteristics. It seems equivalent to our genetic memory, wherein the genes, or better still the sperm and the egg carry all the latent characteristics of a human being. Well, a baby, anyway."

She checked my expression. I nodded.

"There is a problem," she continued, evidently satisfied that I didn't look like a complete idiot. "To date, we have no idea how to slow them down. Very small quantities appear to revert to their previous nature automatically. Larger volumes, or quanta, and larger would be something as small as a pin or the stub of a pencil, seem to disappear from our reality. It's probably hovering somewhere in space-time, waiting to rejoin our world. Their return to us might be conditional to a number of factors, such as passing through or near a great mass, enormous densities, equally horrendous gravitational fields, or any effect not yet known to science."

She looked frustrated. Having sighed deeply, she continued, her eyes seemingly looking for help. I took over trying to define my understanding of the problem.

"So theoretically," I said slowly, "I could face a wall in Montréal, and emerge on the other side of the sun. Hopefully I'd be still alive and breathing in the outer space."

She nodded. "Although *hopefully* would hardly be the word I'd choose."

Nevertheless, I was hoping Ambrosia would eventually gain control over distance and destination. Not to mention the aspect of reversal to original form. But I saw from her expression that that might take time. She spent the rest of the afternoon trying to enlighten me on the intricacies of quantum mechanics.

"If I could only freeze the pattern…"

"Pattern? The essence of pure mathematics? As in fractals?" Not that I knew anything about fractals.

After another long while, she smiled, shrugged, and went on the terrace, just to breathe normal reality. There was still real world out there. Meanwhile, I continued trying to decipher her theories.

Apparently, this was not the only manner in which quantum tunneling worked, but it was a theory, which under laboratory conditions, when applied under psychokinetic wave propagation, gave best results. At least that's what Ambrosia told me, and I had no expertise to approve or deny her conclusions.

It was my turn to feel frustrated. When I turned to ask her about it, she'd already disappeared into her lab. She had a habit of doing that. She couldn't do better with tunneling.

One moment she was on the terrace, the next, presto, she was gone. And I thought she was on the verge of "Beam me up, Scotty," scenario. Better still, "Beam me up, Simon." Only not up but, well, sort of laterally.

I was thinking of facing our bedroom wall and finding myself on Milos, on the terrace in my parents-in-law's villa.

And then I had it. In my lectures I taught that man, speaking generically, is a four-in-one proposition. We have spirit, mind, emotions and physical body. Spirit would correspond to consciousness or ideas. The mind would be the pattern, such as brainwaves. Emotions would correspond to imagination, which would act as a guide to the way the patterns would or could become manifest. Our physical bodies were merely the result.

No computer had ever been invented that could compete with the human brain. Computers were the most magnificent calculators, but this function was but peripheral to our neurons. I clicked on my Wikipedia.

I was amazed.

Briefly, the human brain contains between 80 and 90 billion non-neuron cells, and an equal number of neurons, of which about 10 billion are cortical pyramidal cells.

Whatever those might be... Aha!

These cells pass signals to each other via some 1000 trillion synaptic connections.

That's one quadrillion connections!

God only knows how many electrochemical discharges take place every second with such hardware. I had to sit back and stop thinking for a while. It's a wonder our heads didn't boil. Did you ever try to stop thinking? It's not easy. You have to stop one quadrillion synaptic connections from firing.

No wonder it takes yogis, in the Far East, years...

Never mind.

Actually, it's not so bad. Many of those discharges probably deal with just keeping our physical body going. With keeping us biologically alive.

If I understood Ambrosia correctly, the psychokinetic brainwaves did the neutrino conversions. But it would be the emotional input—you might call it your imagination—that would take care of the location and the reconstitution. You must imagine yourself in a certain place, presumably in a certain condition, before you initiated the neutrino transfer. Due to the complexity of the subject mater, your imagination would have to engage your subconscious.

Enter hypnosis!

There was only one problem.

Unless I developed a whole team who'd work with me on regression, then the only way I could prove her theory would be to do it myself. If I were wrong, it would be... goodbye Simon. Also, I obviously needed Ambrosia's help. I could magnify my imagination—or my ability to apply my imagination—exponentially with posthypnotic suggestion. What I couldn't do would be to operate her super-duper souped-up, fangle-dangle computers, Ambrosia and Papa had installed in our penthouse, to get the right brainwave equivalents. That was her department. It wasn't just a question of software, but also of some, incomprehensible to me, cooling systems.

Who knows, I mused, perhaps we were meant to be together. Only together we might be able to conquer the mysteries of both, time and space. As some mystics reputedly did in the past, only this would be much closer to science.

Didn't someone say that magic was the science of tomorrow?

The next moment I was lying back on my settee, imagining myself turning brown on the Milos' terrace. I wondered if I should also imagine myself being covered, head-to-toe, with sunbathing cream, before I got burned to a crisp. Ah... the wonders of imagination.

About then Ambrosia returned. I suspected she'd go directly from the terrace to her lab on the other side of our penthouse floor. There she'd continue doing her incomprehensible, at least to me, tricks with her computers and theories. I got up and greeted her as though she'd just retuned from McGill. It was a little game we played. Apparently I have been smiling so much my face almost cracked.

"All right, Simon darling, what is it?"

I could get nothing past her. Not that I really wanted to. After all, I needed her help. I waited until she sat down and asked her how was work.

"Simon, I appreciate you being polite," she said, "but your idea or ideas are bursting out of your ears. Now out with them."

I sighed.

"Ah well, if you insist," I started, which made her laugh outright. With no other reaction, I began.

I started at the beginning.

I reminded her about the lecture at which we met, actually for the second time, but first time face to face. That produced another outburst of laughter, which didn't do much for my ego. Then, I reminded her about the three sons of Noah, about the Babylonian fire pit, about the four horses of the apocalypse, even about the Egyptian Sphinx. Then I translated those ancient sentiments, once more, into modern language, using terms like subconscious instead of animal soul, consciousness in lieu of spirit, and so forth. To my delight she listened attentively, without even urging me on.

"What struck me was that even by the law of averages, all the ancients couldn't be all wrong, all the time. So, I wondered, how could we apply all of the above to our modern way of thinking."

This time she was ripe.

"Cut the spiel and lets have your ideas, Simon."

I told her. Then I retold her. Then she asked me

questions, then more questions. Then only one question remained.

"So who is going first?"

I was hoping she wouldn't be difficult about it.

"Well," said I, assuming my best pontifical tone, "only one of us has the experience in hypnosis, right?" It was a hypothetical question.

"I won't allow it," was her curt reply. Then she looked up at me, a slightly voracious look in her eyes. "I was thinking of someone who wouldn't mind taking a risk for a reasonably large sum of money."

I knew she was thinking of Papa. Not to send him to the never-never, of course, but to supply the bait. I also wondered if she was thinking of kidnapping Dean McGinnis. Wouldn't that be fun? Believe it or not, I wouldn't dare to propose it to her, though I felt sure that her Papa would find a way.

For a while we sat in silence. By that time I knew Ambrosia well enough to know that if my mental perambulations were little more than nonsense, she would have told me already. So, there was a chance; perhaps hidden, veiled as yet, but with her brain and my willingness, we had a chance to find a way out of this valley of tears, while still alive. I knew it sounded crazy, but isn't that what they said about most great men of the past?

Well, some of them. And some not so great.

But I felt that without new ideas there was no progress, and at the moment we were in an accelerated curve of descent. I never forgot that regardless of what the rest of the world did, of all the fauna and flora it was the human race that was devolving. I simply refused to take part in this farce.

After a good ten minutes of silence, Ambrosia opened her eyes. She had that unnerving habit of closing her eyes when she was thinking.

"I'll have to think about it," she said.

"I thought you just did?" I asked.

"Well... yes and no. Actually I was musing about some people I wouldn't mind sending into outer space; or into the centre of the sun. Or... There are so many places..."

"Let's be serious for a moment. Is there a chance that my ideas might work?"

"Is there a chance that things heavier than air could fly? We won't know till we try it. Or them. But... it's finding a guinea pig that is a problem. And the second, bigger problem is that we wouldn't know if we'd succeeded."

"Unless we used the translocation technique right here, on Earth. We have walls right here?"

"Of course, I was thinking about mega gravitational pulls and suchlike. That's the problem of being too close to it. You lose the perspective." She smiled her best smile, hiding her embarrassment. "I suppose that would have to be the way." Then she turned those exquisite eyes at me. "You know, my husband, you are an exceptionally cleaver man. A pity you're not a scientist."

Her genius notwithstanding, she omitted to note that had I been one, I would never have thought of the four metaphysical aspects of man, and we wouldn't have had a working hypothesis. I loved her anyway. Still do. I guess, I always will. She really did feel like an integral, inseparable part of me. Like soul—the spiritual aspect of man? Not the animal soul, but the immortal, integral, inseparable part of God. The omnipresent One. Not the one with the long beard on the ceiling of the Sistine Chapel. It was as if she and I were one.

Who could tell? Perhaps, in the fullness of time, we'll discover that we really are one. I think I'd like that.

We scheduled our first experiment for Thursday. It was to be conducted under conditions of absolute secrecy. We already knew that should the CIA, or any other combination of alphabetically arranged capital letters hear of our efforts, we would be whisked off to Washington, Beijing, New Delhi, Bombay or some other growing or fading potentiate, without the aid of our computers or any other brainwave producing devices.

They wanted Ambrosias brains for their own nefarious ends.

For our part, we decided to revert to sanity. As we both loved animals, our decision wasn't easy. Finally we ended up applying to the Montreal SPCA to take a dog, or a cat, off their hands; an animal that had already been scheduled for being put to sleep. Permanently. It seemed the best of the best jobs, and for some reason, I had a bee in my bonnet that the results might be surprising.

Part of the problem was that we couldn't tell the good people at the SPCA why we both wanted a dying animal.

"If he's not suffering, we could make his last days more pleasant?" This was Ambrosia's idea.

They nodded their understanding.

The staff at SPCA selected a cat, a black and white, middle-aged cuddly bundle of fur, which while being very sick, in fact incurable, was not suffering. Also, if need be, we had been given drugs, and we had absolutely no objections of keeping it drugged exactly as per instruction of the veterinary doctor. All the same, we refused to learn his name. It would make it all too personal.

"We'll decide what to call him," Ambrosia said, her tone losing some of its previous assurance. I think I saw a tear swirling in her eye.

The nameless feline was about to have a surprise of his life.

We were both nervous. While the whole affair was fairly close to a scientific experiment, only my imagination complementing the computer generated psychokinetic brainwaves could define where and in what condition the cat could arrive on the other side. For our purposes, the other side was the wall of our bedroom. A wall the cat had to cross and stay alive.

We went to Ambrosia's lab. The cat seemed curious what was going on. He didn't strike us as a very sick animal, but the vet said it had something to do with a malignant growth on his liver. It was, he said, inoperable. Poor thing.

We left the cat in his cage and went back to our bedroom. I lay down, relaxed, and counted myself into a relaxed state of hypnosis. Ambrosia checked on the depth I reached, and then programmed me to imagine the cat arriving in perfect condition on the other side of the wall.

"You will continue to imagine the cat on the bed with you, until he arrives" she said slowly. Then repeated her suggestion imbedding it in my subconscious.

I confirmed her instructions, and Ambrosia returned to her lab. In spite of being under hypnosis, for an instant I was hit by a wave of panic, thinking that the moment the cat arrived a mass of wires would strangle me. I was sure electrodes, which in turn were connected to Ambrosia's infernal machines, surrounded the cat. On the other hand, I had no idea what Ambrosia was doing with the poor creature.

I took a few more deep breaths, and repeated Ambrosia's suggestion twice more. I felt myself drifting far, far away.

I was hoping that by the fickle fate or a scientific quirk of nature, on transfer, the electrodes would stay behind. I also suspected that Ambrosia managed to tune her psychokinetic waves to affect organic matter only.

I continued breathing deeply, yet again reaffirming the suggestion Ambrosia implanted in my subconscious. I concentrated on seeing the cat with me, right there, touching me, and... being very much alive.

Renewed self-induction procedure followed.

When in a hypnotic state, you lose the sensation of time. Evidently time, as we know it, is an integral part of our physical reality. It does not affect other realities, or at least, not in the same way. I have no idea for how long I lay there, but at a certain moment I felt something soft pressing gently on my chest. I was still under, but the best I could discern was that the slight weight was not dangerous.

Then I heard Ambrosia's voice, telling me to wake up.

"How did it go?" I asked.

Then I saw a ball of furry softness purring on my chest. Ambrosia had tears in her eyes.

"We must keep him. He looks so happy there. Can you hear him purr?"

There was a good reason for his purring. The next day the veterinary doctor X-rayed our cat, later examined him from head to tail. Literally. There was no sign of any malignant growth. The vet suspected that we swapped him with another cat.

"Things like that just don't happen," he tried to convince us. "They just don't happen," he repeated, chewing on this stethoscope. "Look, here is the old X-ray, see?"

I didn't see, and if I saw I wouldn't care. I deal in metaphysics. Miracles are bread and butter in my trade.

"No, doctor, I suppose they don't," Ambrosia agreed. We were anxious to go home to play with our black and white ball of softness. We still haven't named him.

The addition to our family was as fit as a fiddle. Or, as a cat who defied the laws of physical universe.

And... you should hear him purrrrrrr...

We called our cat Lazarus. After all, he left this world and came back again, right on my stomach. For fairly obvious reasons, his name quickly degenerated to Lazy, though he's officially registered at SPCA as Lazarus. They still don't believe it's the same cat.

***

Chapter 30
Lazy

The rest is history. At Ambrosia's request, Papa, who refused to admit that there is anything in the world that he wouldn't do for his *mikro koritsi,* reconstructed all of Ambrosia's equipment in the attic of his villa on Milos. The lab was smaller, but fully air-conditioned, and fully functional in every other respect. And yes, he played safe. He also installed a generator.

"No one will take half of my daughter away," he declared. Luckily, Mama Milos had no idea of what he was talking about.

Actually it took more than six months, a dozen cats, and three large dogs to go through our quantum mechanical transfer, before Ambrosia, by then a complete nervous wreck, would let me be the first human, as well as the next guinea, pig. I know, this sounds like an oxymoron. Too bad, you know what I mean.

I should mention that the three dogs, a Rottweiler, a Beauceron, and an extra-large Old English Mastiff, who had all been scheduled for permanent retirement at the Montreal SPCA, have travelled two hundred kilometers each, a little less as the crow flies. Their incurable ailments disappeared in transit. To keep our operation secret, we had arranged to give them up for adoption to people far away from Montreal. At the time of the experiment, I had to travel to Ottawa, to be on the receiving end of the transfer. My good friend from my student days, with whom I continue to experiment with hypnotic regression, was kind enough to let us use his house. While Ambrosia operated the computer and her black magic in Montreal, at the precisely coordinated time, I counted myself into as deep trance as I could, implanting a suggestion to see the dog by my side. Evidently, it was sufficient.

Back to the guinea pig. *Moi*. My own transfer.

To my surprise I wasn't nervous at all. The fact that I was in a deep hypnotic trance while in transfer may have had something to do with it. Ambrosia had preset all her electrodes and other mumbo-jumbo, and acted as my guide. Her post-hypnotic suggestions were as efficacious as my own. She was a very fast learner.

My first travel, from Ambrosia's lab to our bedroom, after making sure that Lazy was nowhere near my bed, went amazingly well. My wife was waiting for me on our bed. We, well, we celebrated in our usual way. After all, according to previous experience with cats and dogs, I have been renewed to a perfect condition of health.

"Darling! You were fantastic!" was her deeply scientific comment. "I think I'll pass you through a wall at least once a week…"

I managed to avoid this threat.

By then, Ambrosia was also competent at undergoing self-hypnosis. I was beginning to wonder if there was anything she couldn't do. However, experimenting with inanimate objects we discovered that in this mode of travel, two heads are not better than one. Even a minute deviation in the subconscious designation of the arrival point of the object produced frightening results. A pencil stub arrived in seven parts, each connected to the other by a hardly visible to the naked eye connections. We threw the aberrant pencil away. As I said, associations of what might have happened to a live object were too dire to contemplate. This was yet another proof that we are only gods as individuals, not as a group, no matter how well intentioned. Unless… we become one, of course. But for us, this unity acquired a completely new meaning.

We both needed a break. On the top of that, my family was weighing heavily on my conscience. Although I did fly to London since Milos, Ambrosia was too tied up with her experiments to come with me. Since then, she was continuously nagging me to visit them.

"Even for a weekend, Simon, I really want to meet them," she repeated almost daily.

We left the day after the unsuccessful pencil transfer. No, we didn't tunnel to London. We took a 747 to Heathrow. Economy this time. I hated it. Perhaps I'm becoming claustrophobic? Or perhaps I just like to breathe air. Nevertheless, my parents were overjoyed and, not surprisingly, my father kept shaking his head at my wife's beauty.

"They don't make them like that, anymore," he kept repeating. "What a pity... what a pity. They didn't even make them like that in my time..."

In the end my mother told him to go and take a cold shower. "You're old enough to be her grandfather," she said.

"I very nearly am," he replied, surprised. "I very nearly am!" he repeated proud as peacock. "Do you think she gets her beauty from me?"

After of week of dad's salivating, and repeating the story again when my sister came with two beautiful and very noisy children, we were ready to return to our penthouse solitude.

Still in London, I read in the *Daily Telegraph* a story that stuck me as peculiar. Under an enigmatic heading *US ESCAPES*, the article carried a long if cryptic subtitle:

Authorities baffled by record numbers of prisoners escaping from Federal prisons.

The newspaper reported that, in various part of the United States, there had been repeated and unprecedented escapes from high security prisons. The strange thing was, that only escapees serving long-year sentences seemed to disappear. Most were lifers. Perhaps the short-term jailbirds didn't want to take a risk?

The problem had apparently began in the infamous Guantanamo Bay, in Cuba, where within a single week, 27 suspected terrorists disappeared. During the following months, this new security malfunction has spread to federal prisons in the United States. By the time the breach was reported to the press, some 37,000 prisoners have found freedom. This accounts for federal prisons only. There was no word about local, municipal, or county jails.

Equally as surprising was the fact that not a single escapee has been caught and returned to custody.

No wonder this news flash was now circling the media.

As the USA have long sported the highest *per capita* number of prisoners in the world, it was to be expected that, sooner or later, the lifers and/or others serving long-term sentences would find a way out. You cannot keep more than 2,500,000 people behind overcrowded bars and not expect something peculiar to happen. I suppose it would have become increasingly difficult to maintain the necessary security by the underpaid guards.

Those items were of interest to me because, before leaving for London, I have been writing a lecture on our self-imposed imprisonments.

About a week after our return from London, I mentioned the article to Ambrosia. To my surprise, her face froze.

"So they got it, the bastards!" she said, her face a mixture of surprise and anger.

"Who got what, darling, and why…"

"They got my software."

I was beginning to smell a rat.

"You mean…?"

"Of course. The hackers duplicated my software and are sending their crooks and murderers, god knows where! At least now we know who the hackers were. They needed the money."

"They were paid for hacking…"

"No, silly. The US needs the money they're spending on federal prisons. It must go into billions…"

I was beginning to catch up. Various events of our immediate past began to fall into place. The CIA shenanigans had nothing to do with Papa Milo's real or imagined idiosyncrasies. The secret agents, while being helpless to act in the interests of their countries inside the US borders, did their job by trying to help, as best they could, from without.

It seemed that the US computer experts must have been very close to Ambrosia's solution themselves, and they, the CIA guys, suspected, quite correctly, that she, being a theoretical physicist, might add a different slant to the possibility of biological tunneling. Adding her research to their own, they put the results to good use. The total absence of any CIA follow-up on their previous invasions of Ambrosia's privacy confirmed my suspicions.

Yes, it was all beginning to fall into place.

The governors and wardens of the US prison system were repairing their budgets. While, in the past, occasional escapes, even from the highest security prisons, had been reported, in recent years, the new technology made such attrition virtually impossible.

What could be cheaper than reducing the number of prisoners without endangering the public? The stupid thing was that we could neither prove nor prevent it. What the hackers didn't seem to have stolen, however, was the need for the destination guidance under hypnosis. God only knows where they were sending the poor bastards. Somehow, the fact that the disappearing "lifers" were mostly murderers—

gross repeat offenders, at best—didn't make it much better. Of course, by definition, there was not a smidgen of evidence left behind to prove my speculation. For now, we were helpless.

Either way, there was nothing we could do about it. Should we attempt to leak our suspicions to the press, all hell would bread loose, and we'd risk having Ambrosia spending the next ten years in international litigation. That's if anyone would believe us. In the mean time, the disappearances would continue.

It seemed that the CIA agents weren't dumb after all. Without judging their motivation, they were the first to recognize Ambrosia's genius.

Still, right now, Ambrosia looked worried.

"Darling," I told her, "we can hardly blame Einstein for Hiroshima and Nagasaki."

She took a deep breath. "I know," she said softly, "but it still hurts."

Nevertheless, the rest of the world continued to unfold, as it should. I didn't stop giving lectures at McGill, and Ambrosia continued to do her research into tunneling. She now wants to find a way to visit nearby planets. The problem that stumps her is, how to get back. One could hardly transport her brainwave generating equipment to various locations in the Solar System, just for the fun of it. There was also the problem of supporting physical life in inhospitable conditions.

"No problem," replied Mama, at our next Skype discussion. "You can visit them all in your inner body. In your mind. Don't forget, that in your real Kingdom there are no limitations of time or space."

Mama Milos was like that. For her, the two realities were as accessible as we hoped they would become, one day, for us.

She was right, of course, but Ambrosia was still a scientist. She'd probably remain one for a little while. On the other hand, our Milky Way is said to contain between 100 and 400 billion stars. I'm sure some of them have planets capable of supporting human life. If they exist, Ambrosia will find them. Perhaps through OBE? She's that sort of a girl.

My group of men and women who wanted to participate in the regression experiments has grown to twenty-one. We began publishing some of our results. Various churches were the first to object.

"That's not what the Bible says. Bible is the Word of God!" they stormed.

"Infallible? You sure the sun is still spinning around the Earth?" I asked.

Then I just shut up. I was not in the business of making enemies. On the other hand, by their interpretation, that would at least give me someone to love. I quote my official reply from one of my lectures at McGill.

"The word of God notwithstanding, the Bible or at least the Old Testament, had been written in capital letters only, in continuous lines without any breaks for paragraphs or punctuation. No proper names of either people or places had been identified in any way. All we have is a flood of words, flowing like a beautiful stream, perhaps a mighty river..."

My students have learned to trust me, which cannot be said for all sorts of sects claiming to be infallible.

"For centuries" I continued, "self-proclaimed experts imposed their opinion on what those words mean. In extreme cases, those who disagreed with the scholars approved by the Orthodoxy had been burned at the stake. You needn't worry. In most countries murder and torture for religious beliefs is now illegal."

There were vague, uncertain giggles and throat clearings.

"The Bible has been written essentially in two languages; the Old Testament in Hebrew, and the New Testament in ancient or classical Greek. Greek is a relatively easy puzzle to resolve, but Hebrew? To find the meaning of the Hebrew words the scholars had to reach back to etymological roots of more than a dozen ancient languages. In my studies I came across references to: Akkadian, Arabic, Aramaic, Assyrian, Avestan, Babylonian, Egyptian, Ethiopic, Greek, Hebrew, Masoteric Text, Old Persian, Sanskrit, Syriac, Ugaritic..."

I looked up at my audience that has grown from some 150 people to twice that number.

"I am sure the list goes on," I concluded.

No one moved.

After a few seconds of silence, first slowly, then with increasing animus, they began a slow handclap. Then the first row, followed the others, got to their feet, and created an avalanche of applause. For a moment I was pleased, but soon reality caught up with me.

My audience has found a new idol. It was time to retire from my professorship.

Of course, there were other alternatives. I could, with a little effort, blow on the embers that I appear to have lit in my last lecture. I'm sure that, in no time at all, I could declare myself a head honcho of a new church. How about the church of the "Unveiled Mystery"? Or, "Church of Gnosis"? Or "Popes Unlimited", where everybody knows what's good for them, and everybody is infallible? In the matters of their own, personal faith, of course.

Or I could write a book declaring myself an expert, like all the other experts on TV.

Fun?

It doesn't sound like much, and the tax exemption advantages were all but gone, but there was still the TV audience who liked to send in donations in exchange for a certificate guaranteeing them access to heaven, on a first come first get in basis.

On second thought, I think I'd rather resign.

Ambrosia and I were free. Free in the definition of the word never before imagined by the human race. There was one problem. Theoretically, within the confines of Mother Earth, we could travel virtually anywhere, with or without our physical bodies. But the challenge lay not in the destination, only in what we might do when we got there. Consciousness needs to expand, to increase, in whatever location or realm it inhabits. Consciousness is life and life is change.

It wasn't always easy.

Our out of body travel was by far the most enjoyable. It really was a free ticket to paradise, at any time, to any place. Yes, we did learn to travel together, but once again, not in the strictest sense of the word. Throughout my OBE Ambrosia was with me. She had to be—she was within me. The same was true of her travels. On our respective returns, our memories would be similar but not identical. On the other hand, had we traveled in our physical bodies, our memories or impressions would also vary. Perhaps more so than after an OBE. One can plan one's OBE, one can program it to the last detail. No that it always works out. But it's always worth trying.

That is the beauty of individualization. It is reminiscent of the phrase the Americans adopted for their motto: *In Pluribus Unum*. That is what we became, One in Many, or in our case, in Two.

What made our Phase experiences similar was the proximity that our souls, our subconscious, have achieved over the period that we lived together; and as we later discovered, a number of previous reincarnations that we shared in the temporal realm.

Here again, Mama Milos was right. In order to travel together we'd have to become one. We are still trying. As with all other aspects of consciousness, we are concerned with oneness of our minds, or souls, not of physical oneness of bodies. That last, well... that would be very painful to achieve. I wouldn't dream of suggesting it to Ambrosia. With her imagination and genius for theoretical physics, she just might make it possible...

Ouch!

The installation of computers capable of supporting Ambrosia's software on Milos enabled us to travel to and from Montreal, without the knowledge of the authorities. Together they were comparative to the IBM's Blue Gene, which is said to have been used to simulate approximately one percent of human cerebral cortex, some 1.6 billion neurons, with some 9 trillion connections.

Not that it mattered, there were no more CIA problems, but Ambrosia didn't like to be manhandled by the airport staff, or to be photographed virtually naked. Years have passed since the last attempt at blowing up an airplane, but, apparently, the authorities never lose hope. They continued hoping to find a bomb in someone's underwear. They continued to terrorize their own people.

Regardless of what our friends did south of the border, for now, we continued to maintain secrecy of our experiments. In time, this method of travel could eliminate about 95% of pollution. On the other hand, people would have to learn self-hypnosis first. Most people are much, much too lazy. Mentally lazy. (No offense to our cat). Also, the computer equipment wasn't cheap, either, though much, much cheaper than the cost of an automobile, let alone an airplane.

It seems that thought-waves, as generated in a hypnotic trance, were not affected by distance. All we needed was to synchronize our watches and hey, presto, we crossed a few thousand kilometers in seconds. Thought-waves were generated within the confines of the speed of light, but not limited by its velocity once released. You can think of the moon and Andromeda in the same breath.

Lazy traveled with us. Not simultaneously, but in tandem. He didn't seem to mind the changes in climate. And by the way, at the request of the Montreal SPCA, Lazarus became a father. They wanted to know if his "miraculous" healing would show up genetically. It did. His children are all healthy.

Ambrosia and I are still waiting for our first.

But the real joy we both derived was from working with Mama Milos. Under her tutelage, we learned to extend the duration of our OBE to many minutes "earth-time". My own record was twenty-seven minutes. In that time I traveled half the galaxy, visited three distinct historical eras, listened to four Old Masters giving lectures, and...

"I spend most of my nights there, especially when Papa is not here..." Mama confessed. She was referring to most of her REM sleep.

There was a dreamy expression on her face, as though on one who was looking for someone with whom she could share her exploits. Perhaps, in time, Ambrosia and I would fulfill her needs. We owed her so much. It was not easy to discuss heaven with someone who's hardly entered the antechamber. It was even harder to discuss it, when one could make heaven anything one wanted.

One day, with just the three of us on the terrace, Mama smiled her usual, kind smile, only this time it also was imbued with a strange expression that spoke of, what I can only describe as, the wisdom of the ages.

"Gods have a great onus imposed on them," she said. "They are immortal. You, like they, must live as though you were immortal. Likewise, whatever you think, or feel, or do, or fail to do, will carry its echoes, its vibrations, for the rest of eternity. That's an awesome responsibility. Heaven is neither good nor evil. Whatever you do on Earth, in your becoming, with that you will characterize your heaven. It is *your* Kingdom. And… there is no escape, my children. There are brief moments of respite, short holidays on a Greek Island, perhaps, but there is no escape. You really are immortal."

We looked at Mama with a love and admiration. There was one problem with being immortal. There is never any hurry. No rush. It can very easily make you lazy. Perhaps our cat knew something we didn't. Yet.

"But most of all, my children," she continued, her whimsical smile gracing her ageless features, "never forget that this world we all live in is not real."

I remember Ambrosia telling me that what we in fact see is light reflected from various objects. What Mama was telling us was that by the time the reflected light reached our retina, the object has already changed. We saw what was, not what is. Like a micro-universe of the light from a distant star.

She confirmed my suspicions.

"Every single second, every fraction of a second," she said, "the whole universe changes—every cell in your body, every star, every galaxy… What you register with your senses is already gone. Here, on Earth, you, yourself, are the process. You are the expression of change. Of life. You are life itself."

***

The Epilogue

"Only two things are infinite, the universe and human stupidity, and I'm not sure about the former."

Albert Einstein

Some years later

In March 2017 Ambrosia registered a copyright for her software, which enabled the transport of goods to and from any place on Earth to any other, for a tiny fraction of the cost of any other form of transportation. This was as revolutionary as the airplane has been its time. She managed to do so before the hackers managed to do it. Perhaps they couldn't take the risk of revealing who they were for the fear of prosecution, or... international scandal. We shall probably never know.

As for Ambrosia, within one year, she became a multi-millionaire. Billions were in the offing. She said that without me she'd never have made it. Ha, ha, said I. Ha, bloody, ha, my father repeated, when I told him. But she insisted. The copyright was registered in both our names. The funny thing was, she had no use for money. Frankly, nor had I.

An obvious benefit of her discovery was that her method did not require any roads, rails, airplanes or ships. Other than a nominal cost of electric current, it also produced zero pollution.

This was the first break Mother Earth got since the beginning of the Industrial Revolution.

"You know, darling, we might not be too late to reverse

the adverse effects of global warming," she said. This was the first time I detected a smidgen of pride in her voice.

Just as well, I thought. Mother Nature was a patient lady, but she was getting upset. Hurricanes, tornadoes, vast forest fires, earthquakes and the resulting tsunamis, have, in recent years, doubled in size, scope and frequency.

As for the technique, there was no longer any need for psychokinetic guidance by hypnosis. I don't understand all the details but it had something to do with transmitting the molecular pattern of the goods to the receiving address ahead of time. Apparently two identical things cannot exist in the same reality simultaneously. When the pattern was "switched on", it acted as guide, or a sort of psychomagnetic pull, for the goods intended for transfer. You had to have facilities, of course, capable of receiving such transfers.

I also had a measure of success. After somewhat shaky beginnings, my regular team of researches now consisted of seven groups, each of some twenty people, who met once a week to regress, under deep hypnosis, to ancient times in search of truth. We now regularly publish our proven findings, often raising great cries from the established scholars, who based their supposed facts on traditions, or reputed misstatements, of countless generations of people groping in the dark. My work is now firmly established as an accepted scientific method of procuring facts as they really happened.

Oh, yes. They also offered me tenure at McGill. The job I hardly needed but, well, it made me feel very important. Ambrosia began addressing me as "Professor." Actually, she took active part in my work.

The first commercial transporters went into operation by 2020. After some teething problems, they've proven an unprecedented success. By the end of the year, 42 countries have built, or were in the process of building, transfer facilities. It was a good start.

Down South, the prisons have cut their population in half. The Justice Department of the USA still claimed complete ignorance how all this could have happened.

"It's the Chinese, trying to pollute our populations with undesirable elements," some officious looking, not very civil, public servant proclaimed on TV.

The Chinese ignored him.

Others didn't believe that anyone escaped from the prisons at all. That it was all a subterfuge to reduce financing for the penitentiaries. We, Ambrosia and I, only hoped that they'd sent the poor blighters into our own past, and not into outer space. Either way, although Dr. Kevorkin was no longer with us, the Department of Justice seems to have found a way around euthanasia.

Later, things got even more serious. It seems that some inconvenient members of the opposition began disappearing. We couldn't keep our secret of biological transfer any longer. If they believed us, then borders between counties would collapse. It would be the end of nationalism, political posturing, and bureaucratic oligarchy. The world would finally become one.

We had other problems. Our son, Amadeus, was five, our daughter, Athena, four. The claimed a goodly portion of our time. By the time Amadeus was four, he could enter an OBE. He told us the most incredible things that we never thought existed. A young mind, perhaps under the watchful eye of his grandmother, had a different outlook on the universe. A year later, Athena joined us in our excursions.

Ambrosia and I have retired from active life. Fulltime work, perhaps, is a better word. We spend a lot of our time on Milos, but we maintain our penthouse, mostly for our children, who attend the school in Montreal. Amadeus and Athena like the Montreal climate. They like skiing, skating, and even watching hockey. They are true Montrealers. With just seconds separating Milos from Montreal, we can alternate at will, and still be there for the children.

From the professional point of view, we are both visiting professors at a number of universities of northern North America. As long as we move around, there is no danger of idol worship developing around either one of us, although I continue to worship Ambrosia. Also, we like to keep our options open. Who knows what future might bring?

Theoretical scientists are not yet confirming that the Multiuniverse consists of an infinite number of universes, and that it is in a state of flux, oscillating between infinities, for which equations have not yet been developed. But their equations do suggest that it might be so. That it is a strong probability. As no one seems able to find the beginning or the end, of either time or space, of the Multiuniverse, there is a good chance, they declared, that the Multiuniverse might prove to be infinite. If this hypothesis is declared valid, the scientists intend to declare God obsolete. A number of theoretical physicists declared that the probabilities were infinite.

PS. Ambrosia told me that while this thesis would seem to confirm Albert Einstein's suspicions about the universe, the spokesman for the International Society of Theoretical Physicists—who insisted on remaining anonymous—reserved his judgment on Einstein's parallel assertion regarding human stupidity.

***

If you enjoyed this story,
please write a brief review.
Your thoughts are important to me.

Acknowledgments

I would be remiss were I not to thank my many friends who read the galley proofs, none more so than Ronald Piecuch, whose diligent editing/proofreading efforts helped to make this book a success. As usual, my gratitude to my wife, Bozena Happach, who put up with being a grass widow for weeks on end and then allowed me to benefit from her insights.

Some of the subjects mentioned in this novel are discussed in greater details in following sources:
Stanislaw Kapuscinski's *Beyond Religion Vol. II* Chapter 15, Mystery, Inhousepress, Montreal, Canada;
Stanislaw Kapuscinski's *Dictionary of Biblical Symbolism,* Introduction, Inhousepress, Montreal, Canada;
The Nag Hammadi Library, James M. Robinson General Editor, *First Apocalypse of James,* Harper SanFrancisco.

Sincerely,
Stan I.S. Law

A Word about the Author

Stan I.S. Law (aka **Stanislaw Kapuscinski**), architect, sculptor, and prolific writer, was educated in Poland and England. Since 1965 he has resided in Canada. His special interests cover a broad spectrum of arts, sciences and philosophy. His fiction and non-fiction attest to his particular passion for the scope and the development of Human Potential. He authored more than thirty books, most of them fiction.

Under his real name he published seven non-fiction books sharing his vision of reality. He also composed two collections of poems in his original native tongue in which he satirizes his view of the world while paying homage to Bozena Happach's sculptures.

***

The story continues in
Pluto Effect
and
Olympus—of Gods and Men

INHOUSEPRESS, MONTREAL, CANADA
http://inhousepress.ca